WHAT PEOPLE ARE SAYING ABOUT

BALD NEW WORLD

After my heart gives out and I'm on the operating table for emergency surgery, I will have told my physicians and surgeons to replace my heart with Peter Tieryas Liu's *Bald New World*, or any of his books really, because that's what I think of when I think of his writing—heart. Similar to the work of Philip K. Dick, this parodic dystopia is steeped in futuristic technology that further bridges the gap between man and machine. Still, whether watching the latest episode of the immensely popular reality show *Jesus the General* or sparring against an opponent in the blood-sport known as cricket fighting, the humanity of our narrator shines through. Although we humans are capable of doing and creating sad, funny, glorious, devious things, we also persevere and adapt, survive. I wonder what Huxley would think of this, but he's dead. You're not, so read this book, feel alive.

Jason Jordan, author of *Pestilence*, editor of *decomP*

The boldly imaginative *Bald New World* follows Nicholas Guan, a military type tasked to digitally touch up scenes of carnage, in his misadventures from Korea to a futuristic California and in his frenzied dash from Gamble Town to China. The novel tells of beautifully flawed characters, the blurring distinction between reality and virtual environments, the comical yet chilling wave of religious fanaticism, and a world battling a strange malady called the Great Baldification, an ingenious symbol of human vanity. Peter Tieryas Liu's *Bald New World* is vivid, exhilarating, and wildly entertaining.

Kristine Ong Muslim, author of *We Bury the Landscape* and *Grim Series*

Bald New World is a hypnotic, surreal, and insightful novel, blending *Blade Runner* and *The Wind-Up Bird Chronicle* to create a dark, funny, and captivating story. One of the best books I've read this year.

Richard Thomas, *Staring Into the Abyss*

Bald New World

Peter Tieryas Liu

Bald New World

Peter Tieryas Liu

PERFECT
EDGE
BOOKS

Winchester, UK
Washington, USA

First published by Perfect Edge Books, 2014
Perfect Edge Books is an imprint of John Hunt Publishing Ltd., Laurel House, Station Approach,
Alresford, Hants, SO24 9JH, UK
office1@jhpbooks.net
www.johnhuntpublishing.com
www.perfectedgebooks.com

For distributor details and how to order please visit the 'Ordering' section on our website.

Text copyright: Peter Tieryas Liu 2013

ISBN: 978 1 78279 508 7

A CIP catalogue record for this book is available from the British Library.

Design: Lee Nash

Printed in the USA by Edwards Brothers   alloy

We operate a distinctive and ethical publishing philosophy in all
areas of our business, from our global network of authors to
production and worldwide distribution.

CONTENTS

Dedicated to my Father-in-Law and Mother-in-Law
For teaching me what family is

Prologue

I was eleven when everyone in the world lost their hair. I got up from bed, terrified to see that all my hair had fallen out. In the mirror, the uneven bumps on my head formed an alien tapestry that made me feel like I was staring at a stranger. I spotted a thick black mole above my ear that I'd never seen before and scratched it, only to find it wasn't going away. Both of my parents were away on a business trip so I ran to my older sister, Kelly, hoping she knew what was wrong with me. I found her crying on the bathroom floor, clutching her own fallen hair. My eyes went to her scalp, an oddly shaped oval with protrusions jutting out. "What are you looking at?!" she demanded.

"Your head," I replied. "What happened?"

She got up, pushed me angrily, then ran out of our apartment. I chased her, not wanting to be left behind. When I exited our building, she was nowhere in sight. Instead, a sea of bald people confronted me—everyone on the street had lost their hair. There was a frenzied madness in their eyes, confusion causing many of them to walk in a daze. I trembled as strangers accosted me and yelled that, "The whole world is doomed," and, "We're being punished for our vanities!" The Los Angeles Police blocked most of the major roads because riots were breaking out and I went from barricade to barricade in a daze. Trash littered the streets, stores were burning, and looters stole everything they could. I wanted to get to a 24-hour restaurant where Kelly's friend worked when I noticed a man lying on his back on the sidewalk, motionless. His eyes had an apathetic gleam and his hands were covered in blood. Motorcycles honked and periodic echoes from bullets triggered car alarms. He was impervious to noise. "Sir?" I called. "Sir?" He didn't answer and when I stepped closer, I saw that he wasn't breathing. I stumbled back, shocked by the sight. It was the first dead man I'd ever seen.

and bio-terror as well as solar spikes. Some had feared it was a disease similar to alopecia universalis that would worsen with time, but no further symptoms materialized. The follicles had sealed at a cuticle level and a chemical reaction in our bodies had inexplicably caused the permanent termination of hair growth. Baldness became a fact of life.

I don't want to blame everything bad that happened on the *Great Baldification* as it came to be known. But it was the beginning of a lot of social change in the world. Marriages broke up at ten times the normal rate and my parents ended up getting divorced two months after the Baldification. Maybe it was the strain from endless fights or that they never liked each other much to begin with. I never heard from my biological father after the divorce. My biological mother dropped me off permanently with Cousin Baochai so that she could pursue her dream of being a travel blogger. My sister, Kelly, going against the trend, married her rap star wanna-be boyfriend and I rarely saw her again after that.

Our economy regressed from disastrous to beyond redemption. Accelerated resource depletion forced countries into a war over Africa even though we were technically all part of the United Nations Peacekeeping Force. Unemployment rates were at 56% in the States (though official reports had it at 5.5%), so soldiering was the only chance for a career most of our generation had. I signed up for the army and was assigned to the media department because of my passions for cameras despite all the combat training they gave me.

My job was sanitizing war for the public. Did one of the scout ships record a scene that was too bloody? I brought out my digital brushstrokes so that limbs could be replaced real-time, scars mended, and disasters contained. Constant warfare made the fickle weather even moodier, especially with all those atomic bombs going off. Gasoline got replaced by electricity, everyone forgot about the Middle East, and flight technology advanced to

I got out my phone to call my parents but accidentally pushed the button for the camera. On the digital screen, the corpse didn't look as horrifying and in some ways, looked fake, especially as I could alter the angle of my view. That sense of control calmed me until I heard a spray of bullets from behind. I turned the camera in the direction of the rioters and saw they were charging the police barricade. The police responded with smoke bombs and guns. I turned around and ran home as fast as I could, dodging rioters and masked thieves who targeted stragglers.

It was a miracle I got through alive. I called my parents several times though none of my calls connected. My sister's phone was off as was my cousin's, Baochai, who wasn't home even though she was supposed to take care of us while my parents were away (probably partying in downtown like she did every night). My legs wouldn't stop trembling and I accidentally knocked over a stack of bills on our apartment floor. I cleaned up the mess, only to stumble into the buckets that were substitutes for toilets to save on our water fees. A string of explosions lit up the sky outside and I heard people screaming in pain. Their cries scared me and I hid in the closet, covering myself with blankets just in case anyone broke into our unit. Our building was shaking and I wished someone, anyone, was home. Unfortunately, my only companions were the roaches swarming my feet and I was stuck imagining a thousand horrible deaths. Every noise made me want to break into tears and whenever I heard running outside the walls, I wondered if people were coming to break the door down. I tried watching the video I'd captured earlier only to realize I hadn't hit the record button. Sleep was impossible and not just because of the stream of gunfire outside. I counted the minutes like they were hours.

I never found out who the dead man was and in the same way, almost twenty-five years later, the best explanation for the hair loss researchers had were still just theories. Speculation ran rampant as the accused ranged from pollution to global warming the point where flights from Los Angeles to Beijing took two hours minus the three-hour security checks.

After the African Wars ended, many of us wondered what we should do next. I took to making films with a fellow grunt, Larry Chao. He nearly got discharged from the army twenty times because he was always running off "in love" with some new girl he swore was "the One." He wasn't especially handsome, but had a jovial grin that made everyone feel welcome in his presence. Between his indefatigable exuberance and his easy-going nature inspired by an early bout of mutated typhoid that nearly killed him, his charm more than made up for his plump nose, small eyes, and fat lips. He had a suite of women who worshipped him. For my part, I never thought our lives would become so intertwined, our names would be synonymous with each other.

As only humans were affected by the malaise (animals still grew fur and hair), wig factories were booming. Larry inherited a wig factory from his father who died of stomach cancer after eating too many Sichuan spices. The factory (or factories, as there were about thirty located throughout China) were raking in the dough. Larry was super rich and after I found out, I asked him why he joined the army when he didn't need to.

"I got bored and wanted to try something different," he said, and that was the only explanation he offered.

Instead of reinvesting his fortunes, Larry wasted it making pointless movies throughout China about tragically dumb characters. I, Nicholas Guan, became the cinematographer for many of his films, a bald 36-year-old half-Korean half-Chinese guy born and raised in America whose job was photographing— or beautifying—baldness.

My latest film with Larry was about a crazy filmmaker who wanted to save the rats of his city from extinction. He called it *Rodenticide* and it was full of pathos and pathetic soliloquies masquerading as drama. There was more than his usual spew of nonsense about age and life which the Beijing actors loved. Larry was 39 and I realized his age was bugging him. Maybe he'd hoped for more success with his films by now. I probably should have paid more attention, but you know how it is with anyone close to you—you never notice until it's too late.

I passed off his doubts as Larry being his usual idiot self, especially when it came to women. You can't blame a guy for chasing a girl he loves. Fortunately, the two of us had completely different tastes. He liked tall, lanky women with gazelle legs and I liked chubbier girls with cute faces and puffy cheeks. It was easy for us to become good friends. Or at least wingmen for each other.

When he invited me out for another night on the town at his favorite Korean restaurant in Beijing, I heartily agreed. I felt like a good BBQ, even though I'd been gaining way too much weight of late (I promised myself not to check my weight every morning even though it was the same as the day before).

"Nick!" Larry had yelled into the phone when he called me. "I need you. I've been dating this girl for two weeks and she has a co-worker she insists on taking out so I need your help. Oh, and don't tell anyone this yet, but I think I'm in love. I kid you not, I think she's the One."

Of course.

1. From Pyongyang with Love

She was too skinny. Yes, she was tall with lean legs and a pretty face, but her nose had that elongated stoop that made it resemble a horse's nose at certain angles. Plus, she wore way too much perfume. There was a disdainful look about her, dismissing me with a glance. She was one of our waitresses and her name was Shinjee. She wore a short black wig that she'd tied up in two buns above her head to resemble pictures in Korean history books of what women looked like. I thought it was antiquated and quaint. Larry thought it was "classic."

He was in a festive mood and ordered all kinds of meat; pork, beef, chicken. He asked if I wanted lamb but I told him my conscience wouldn't allow it, thinking of a neighbor's sheep I used to play with when I was a kid. The restaurant was spacious with three floors, bedecked in Korean architecture and cooking grills where we could cook our food. A central courtyard hosted hourly performances on weekend evenings. The place was bustling with activity, the crackle of burning beef and drunk customers making it hard to hear myself. Our black marble table was replete with small *banchan*, side dishes that were Korean versions of tapas. The meat and garlic mushrooms smelled incredible, steam from both mixing in with the pungent scent of the spicy soups.

Larry had on his nicest fedora. He always wore fedoras. Not the kind from old noir films, but glowing ones that were red, dapper, and scintillating in colors. If those mystery flicks made icons out of trench-coated detectives, Larry represented the iridescent director solving the conundrum of life through bizarre fashion statements.

"Have you heard of live monkeys with their scalps cut off so their brains can be eaten fresh in the Sichuan area?" he asked.

"I think I saw something like that in *Faces of Death*," I muttered back.

Larry was right. The waitresses were stunningly beautiful in their traditional Korean costumes and they were friendly too, pouring us drinks and making sure our meat was well-cooked while laughing at our dumb jokes. We downed several beers and Larry whispered to me, "Be careful what you say. These girls are North Korean spies."

"What?"

He nodded and gave me a knowing nudge. "Everything we talk about could be reported to the North Korean high command."

"You're joking right?"

Larry's face was red from drink and he shook his head. "Haven't you heard of the Asian beauty trap? Don't be surprised if our whole conversation is recorded."

I couldn't tell if he was serious or pushing my buttons. North Korea had been the most isolated country in the world for over a hundred years and it seemed that would continue another century. There had been rumors of ex-soldiers in China being kidnapped by the North Koreans to be indentured into a life of servitude. The kimchee and the garlic broccoli stuck in my throat. The demure gestures from the waitresses seemed sinister and furtive glances in the direction of their management felt ominous. Larry and I had served in the UN Peacekeeping forces, but that'd been almost a decade ago and we didn't have any information now. The food didn't taste quite as good and I checked if the alcohol had been tampered with. One of the waitresses said to me, "You should visit North Korea. It's very beautiful there."

When I hesitated with an answer, Larry replied, "We would love to."

After they stepped away to perform a cultural dance for the patrons, I asked, "Are they really spies?"

Larry chugged down his beer. "Don't worry about it."

"I don't want them to report me."

He laughed and said, "I forgot to mention that in Sichuan, they're only interested in the big monkeys."

"The girl you like—"

"Love," he corrected me.

"Is she—?"

He nodded. "Our job is to convince her to leave."

"To leave North Korea?"

"Yeah. We can swing it, can't we?"

"They're indoctrinated with super-advanced machinery so that normal persuasion techniques don't work. More likely, she'll convince us to join them."

"I did promise to help her make an ad for her restaurant," Larry answered. "We're going to talk about it with her later tonight."

"What?"

"It'll be fun. Don't worry about it, man."

"Where are we meeting them?"

"Here. We'll head over together to this super swank arcade near Houhai." Every instinct in me blared caution. But Larry, knowing my soft spot, said, "Her friend has a thing for photographers and I swear to you, she's your type. She kind of looks like Linda too. I think you'll like her."

Damn me for caring.

II.

I blamed Linda Yu, my ex-wife, for all my woes with women. Next to her, all the women I met were like baby frogs croaking next to a falcon gleaming through the cold blue moonlight (I mention that specific image because she painted a portrait exactly like that). Linda Yu lived in Los Angeles when I first made my home in Beijing. She flew out to help Larry do makeup. Linda was a makeup artist who liked coloring people in ways they hadn't imagined. Often, the results were ugly, but always startling. She begged people to resist looking like a magazine cover, the anorexic's dream of a heaven without calories. It was ironic because Linda looked like she belonged on a magazine cover. But she disdained her beauty and often made her wigs resemble roosters. She told me later she was initially attracted to me because I looked so strange.

"Thanks?" I remembered saying to her.

Larry and her clashed because she refused to do makeup the way Larry wanted. She made the actors resemble zombies and the actresses look like blue meat faces, which was the only way I could describe them. In between disagreements—Larry having run off to deal with some other issue on set—she would tell me little tidbits about herself, like the fact that she was named after a mythical crying flower called the Vermilion Pearl that wept to pay back the nourishing water it received throughout her life. Right after she was fired by Larry, she told me I should visit her in Los Angeles.

I hated going to L.A. and not just because I grew up in the city, but I didn't like having to wear a bulletproof vest all the time. Shopping malls were the only gun-free zones, and even there, you had to go through those scanners that caused brain cancer. Drones maintained a vigilant watch from far up above and traffic was a mechanical bog. With the upper 405 freeway countless years behind schedule (they'd been working on it since I was born), it was impossible to get anywhere. But I still went out there to see Linda. I had to. She was the prettiest bald girl I'd ever met.

III.

Of course, Shinjee's friend, Hyori, looked nothing like Linda. She had too many tattoos on her head, including that of a mouse fighting a lion and winning. The four of us ordered a green cab and the mechanized operator arrived promptly. Taxis used to have human drivers, but every country in the world (except the

4

U.S.) had changed to mechanized drivers for safety and traffic reasons so that 6-7 passengers could ride. Shinjee ordered, "Waitian Arcade."

Beijing had become a city of vapors, a metropolis of neon calligraphy burning away the surrounding gas. Pollution had become a permanent fixture in the landscape, trapped by the surrounding mountains and aggravated by dust storms. Contours shined like trailing lights, buildings appearing permeable, shifting with the perspective. We veered past cars and streetlights suffering from identity crises. Bikers were waiting at a red light, jumpsuits and WWI gas masks protecting their lungs from contamination. Store names floated in mid-air, Mandarin phrases wandered the alleys like unforgiven spirits, and a sentence cried for redemption, crucified in mist.

I saw Hyori as a mask of colors outlined like a jigsaw puzzle, her thick red lips sauntering through dialectics as quickly as mood swings. She spoke good English, even if she had a slight Korean accent, though it was Shinjee who dominated the conversation.

Shinjee looked like trouble. She wore long black leather boots, a red coat, and had on thick sunglasses even though it was night. A beret flopped on top of her head and the first thing she said to me was, "You bloody Americans are destroying our world for a God you don't even believe in."

"What?"

"Do you like buffalo meat?" Hyori cut in.

"Never had it."

"Supposedly, the Japanese branch makes the best braised buffalo in the world."

"Are we going to have buffalo?"

"Snake-blood wine," Shinjee said.

"That stuff makes you young, right?" Larry asked.

"Virile," Shinjee replied.

Waitian was packed and there were a hundred taxis backed

up, trying to drop off their customers. The attendants were dressed as videogame characters and some of the partiers even had on suits from old retro games like Mario and Zelda. We got out, Larry scanning his credit key for payment. Spotlights were beaming around and I could hear loud drum beats set to familiar game music.

Hyori asked me, "What was your favorite video game?"

"What was yours?"

"Kid Icarus. That's why I brought these!" From her bag popped out angel wings and a fake bow-and-arrow kit. Right in front of us, Princess Peach and Luigi were making out. Some Teenage Mutant Ninja turtles were bumping and grinding with their shells. A God of War stalked a Heavenly Sword. Mega Man was buying different drinks for different women to try to pry his way into their weaknesses.

We had to pick out costumes at the rental booth. I wondered secretly if I was too old for this, but Larry, who was even older than me, didn't seem to think so. He picked out a Final Fantasy character, Kefka, the madman who succeeded in destroying the world. I matched him with another Final Fantasy character, Sephiroth. Shinjee put on the bounty-hunter suit of Samus from the NES classic, Metroid. We were ready to retro boogie.

IV.

It was loud and spacious inside and there were big screens every-where. Several top gamers were playing their games and digital editors cut footage from the sequences together. The music responded to the rhythms on screen and the sound effects responded to the jumping beats. There were thousands of people dressed as videogame characters and our booth had a holographic pad in case we wanted to get involved in the mix. Games were a low priority for Shinjee who wanted her snake-blood wine right away. The menu popped up along with our waitress, a cute holographic dragon who said, "We have a special on soma today."

"I hate soma," Larry muttered. "It's too old school. Doesn't pack a punch."

"Snake-blood wine," Shinjee ordered.

It arrived through a panel to the side. Viscous and gelatinous, I didn't like the look of it at all. Shinjee grabbed her glass and took it down in one shot. The blood dripped off the side of her lip and she said, "I never understood why your Adam and Eve ate the apple when they could have cooked up the snake and spared themselves all the trouble."

"They were vegetarian," I suggested, took my cup, and brought it to my mouth. The stagnant odor was overwhelming and nearly made me puke. It smelled like intestines, tanned leather, and a really bad Bloody Mary.

Hyori downed hers and even Larry made a good effort out of it, stopping a few times, coughing, but somehow emptying the cup. One sip made me nauseous and I shook my head. "No way."

"Oh, c'mon."

"No way," I repeated. "I'll just have an 8-Bit Blaster."

The 8BB was a joke of a drink, tasting like a juice cocktail. But as I saw Larry taking down more alcohol, I realized I'd have to take it easy. He was probably counting on me to get him out of trouble if we had any. Shinjee wasn't holding back, matching drink for drink.

"Nick used to be one helluva cricket fighter," Larry said. "He'd control their little brains through the neural interface. Never saw a guy win so many battles in a row."

"Don't remind me. I hate insects," I said. "Still get nightmares about being a cricket."

"They say the Song Dynasty fell because the ruler was so obsessed with cricket fighting."

"That's because he never had to live as one."

"You have?" Shinjee asked.

"Hundred days is all they have," I answered. "One season to

7

be born and to die."

Hyori was watching me and I could tell she was looking for an opening to say something. But I ignored her and relegated myself to convoy service for the night. Several times, she asked questions about me. I gave pat answers and never allowed it to progress beyond that. Eventually, the two girls decided to go freshen up at the bathroom.

"What's wrong?" Larry asked me.

"Nothing."

"These girls are trained in the art of love. We've got to find out if it's as good as they say."

"I have no interest in my date."

"You've barely gotten to know her."

"She's a spy!"

"What if the earth collapses tomorrow? What if a thousand-year winter arrives? What if some plague wipes out half of humanity? We're living dinosaurs, man. We'll be dead anyways. Enjoy what you got."

"My idea of enjoyment isn't being around spies."

"Expand your horizons, bro!" he declared. "Besides, you want to live a boring quiet life?"

"I do."

Larry shook his head and said, "I have two big regrets in life. You know what they are?" His breath reeked of alcohol and when he leaned into me, he pressed the holopad which brought up the dragon waitress.

She repeated, "We have a special on—"

"My first is Renee," Larry continued. "Holy shit, she had the best body I've ever seen on a woman. She was also damn smart, an architect who only built underwater complexes. Just thinking about her gets me excited. At the end of our date, she asked to come back to my place. I was so excited, I couldn't believe this girl asked to come to my place. We arrive, and guess what?"

"She's a man?" Which wouldn't have surprised me considering how these stories usually went.

"I have to take the biggest dump of my life. My stomach was raging man. I couldn't control it. I said, 'Excuse me,' ran to the bathroom, and felt my ass pour out of my stomach. The farts man; they were like mini gastro bombs. They were *loud*. By the time I got out, she was like, 'Take me home right this minute.' Never saw her again." He had his hands out in front of him like he was cupping something. "I wish I could have seen her naked just once. Not a day goes by without me thinking about what could have been." His eyes drifted to the past.

"What's the second?" I asked.

He looked at me, lost in thought. "It was my first sexual experience. Ever. I'd fantasized about this girl for years. I had the chance to get with her and lose my virginity. But I was so drunk, my little guy wouldn't respond. It was humiliating. I tried my best and I stalled for like an hour and she was like, 'C'mon, c'mon.' Nothing. Nada. I didn't know it was the drink, thought I had ED or something. She laughed it off, but I could tell she was disappointed. I couldn't reveal to her that I was a virgin, try to explain I didn't even know the mechanics of it all. Can you believe I still remember her smell?"

As he spoke, I wondered about my own regrets.

"It's been almost twenty years since both those nights," Larry said, "and I still wish I could have done it differently. A woman ain't just a body. She's a journey. Those moments of intimacy you share. It's like entering a different universe and I thank each and every single one. Let go of your leash, man. I'm not asking you to marry the girl. Just have a little fun."

Larry was an expert at philosophizing his lust and a part of me wondered, what was the worst that could happen? Neither of us had any secrets that would be valuable to them or their government. Hyori was no Linda. But she was still a very attractive woman. The two of them came back, spruced up. I waved at Hyori and asked her what kind of drink she wanted.

It turned out Hyori had always wanted to be a librarian. She loved books and her cover story was that she came to Beijing to work for her uncle because she wanted to experience more of the world's literature. When I asked what her favorite book was, she told me it was the autobiography of their Great Leader. "Every time I read his book and read how much he cares about his people, I cry," she revealed. "He's sacrificed everything for us. Without him, the world would have destroyed the integrity of our culture. Think about your world. You think you have total freedom, but that's worse than restricted freedom because the noise drowns out the truly amazing. It's the loudest voice that gets heard in your country, not the most beautiful."

"The variety of voices has its advantages. You can read and find out anything you want," I replied. "Everyone is heard."

"If everyone talks at the same time, you can't hear anyone," she answered.

A guy next to us moved like a robot and ten guys played a game of fake basketball as they threw out a hovering ball. Some women strapped on jetpacks and were dancing mid-air. All the screens suddenly paused and a spotlight shone at the center stage.

It was opera as spectacle, a brunette in lingerie trying to mimic Pavarotti, or was it Final Fantasy VI and the Aria di Mezzo Carattere? Her staccatos were thinner than her thong as classical tones raged against digital drums. The performers wore iridescent masks that glowed neon and had caricatured expressions carved into them. There was lust, jealousy, happiness— personified emotions.

Larry was entranced. So was Hyori who was also on her fourth glass of wine. Shinjee seemed annoyed that the singer was distracting attention from her and smoked a cigarette, puffing out whiffs of discontent.

"You don't like this song?" I asked her.

"I think love songs are sappy and pointless."

"Why?"

"Whenever you dramatize love, all the mundane stuff gets thrown out. That's 99% of love. It's a lie to only emphasize the 1%." She stood up and said to Larry, "I'm bored. Let's get out of here."

"Where to?"

"My favorite dumpling shop. I feel like some dessert."

V.

Hyori was inebriated and wanted to prove to me that freedom was overrated. "Does freedom really make you happy?" she asked inside the taxi. "It's true, you have more knowledge than people did a hundred years ago. But does that liberate you or just complicate everything?"

We arrived at our destination and as we got out of the cab, Larry whispered to me, "She likes you."

"That's why she's lecturing me?" I said out loud, wanting her to hear me.

"If she didn't like you, she wouldn't be trying so hard to convince you."

The more drunk and dogmatic she got, the harsher the contours in her gestures came into focus. There was something cruel in her eyes, perhaps because she'd suffered too much. If Shinjee was worried about Hyori revealing anything, she didn't indicate it. Her and Larry were discussing the details of their restaurant commercial which he'd generously offered to finance.

"I don't know what they do at my factory, but they make tons of money and I'm always happy to spend it for them. My family has been making wigs for four generations. They've never been rich until now. Who would have thought, eh? The greatest ecological disaster in the world made my family super rich," he said, laughing.

I didn't recognize where we were. We ducked under labyrinthine corridors, crossed short bridges, and came to a busy street filled with pedestrians. A man blew fire from his pipes and an awkward woman with a huge nose swallowed swords. There were long alleys everywhere we turned.

"I've never seen this place before," Larry said.

"It's one of those well-known secrets that's hard to find the first time," Shinjee said. "You just need a guide."

There were puppet shows of dynasty romances playing out in high-pitched shrieks and cymbals. Food was boiled in the cauldron of oil drums, cobs of corn burning with an egg pizza that smelled like cinders. Dice players reveled through their rotting teeth, gums eviscerated by poor hygiene. The street was bursting with lights, a ballet of lanterns dancing to the swell of the night breeze. There was a guy who smelled of garbage with a dog trained to speak Mandarin. The dog jumped on Hyori and barked, "*Wo ai ni.*" I love you.

"I love puppies," Hyori exclaimed.

The owner encouraged his canine to say more, then pointed at the cap filled with coins. His swarthy eyes and his desperate smile depressed me.

"Life becomes more poignant with humiliation," Larry said.

"What do you mean?"

"There's an old Chinese story about a town that was attacked by fox spirits. They hired a Taoist monk to protect them so he took a bunch of paper, wrote his special Mandarin characters, and wha-lah! It came to life as a paper golem that fended off the evil spirits. But it had to be fed all the time and grew so big, it ended up destroying the town it was meant to save."

Shinjee, who couldn't stop smoking, said, "I've never heard this one."

Larry shrugged. "My uncle used to tell me a lot of weird stories. He was depressed because his wife left him after he lost all his money gambling. He was part of the wig business too but hated it, thought there was no future in it, and sold his shares to my dad before it hit big. I named one of my last films *Rennaili* because of a street like this in Beijing he always used to talk about."

"What about it?"

"More than a century ago, the Empress Cixi got mad at one of the merchants and shut the whole street down. After she was deposed, people came back. During WWII when the Japanese took over Beijing, they chased away all the vendors. After they lost, people came back. During the Cultural Revolution, the officials said this place was too capitalistic and closed it down. After it ended, people came back. The place is called *Rennaili*— endurance in Mandarin."

The girls wanted to stop at a clothing store and Larry said to me, "Don't look back, but I think we're being followed."

"Where?" I said, immediately looking in the direction he'd told me not to look. I saw two butch Korean guys sporting Mohawk wigs, trying hard to blend into the crowd. They both wore sunglasses and green striped suits.

"I could be wrong," Larry said. "They've been following us since Wailiau."

Shinjee and Hyori came back out. "Nothing we want," Hyori explained.

We rushed to the dumpling restaurant. It was a crowded hole-in-the-wall that barely looked sanitary. The tiled floors were dirty and there was only one waitress for the whole place. She spoke a guttural Mandarin that was thickly accented. There were old 2D photographs from before the Baldification, though even with real hair, people looked pretty much the same.

Shinjee ordered a hundred dumplings, three hamburgers, five anchovy omelets. "I'm not that hungry," I warned her.

"This is for me and Hyori," Shinjee said. "If you guys want to eat, you'll need to order something yourselves."

I passed and Larry ordered more vodka. The steaming dumplings came out and I was impressed at how heartily the two ate their food. There was no sense of propriety or fake demureness. These women liked their food and I liked how they shed their artifice and devoured their meals. They used their fingers, didn't bother closing their mouths, and chewed loudly. It was the only time this evening I felt like I was seeing a genuine side to them. The burgers were doused with Sichuan spicy sauce and Shinjee offered some to Larry.

"Those peppers make my ass burn when I do my business," he said. "Forgive me for being so crass."

That elicited knowing laughter from the two ladies. "They say they've found a prehistoric crab that used to be the size of a grizzly bear," Shinjee said. "I'd love to have seafood like that."

"Shandong has the best seafood," Hyori said. "Have you visited their shrimp farms? Those shrimp get pretty big."

We both took sips from our vodka and I tried to imagine a crab that was bigger than me.

Shinjee, after helping devour the hundred dumplings, brought up recent movies as they started critiquing various elements from an action flick.

"The Great Leader loves movies," Hyori said. "He would esteem your position if you two came and made movies for our great country."

"I'm not ready to move just yet," Larry said. "I'm working on my next big epic."

"What epic?"

"The one that's going to change everything."

"You never told me about this," Shinjee said.

"I haven't told anyone yet. Until I finish it, or at least start it, I'm not going anywhere. I tell you though, this is the film that's going to change everything."

"What's it called?" I asked.

He grinned at me. "We'll talk when the time's right. Not yet though. I still need to work out the story."

Usually when he had an idea for a movie, he would gush with information. In fact, he usually had too many ideas and it took months just to settle on one out of tens of thousands. Phone calls in the middle of the night were the norm, telling me he knew what his next "epic" was going to be, talking until the morning. Then a few hours later, another phone call from him saying he had an even better idea. He wasn't secretive with strangers either, not in the least bit worried about people stealing his ideas. "It's the execution, not the idea that counts," he liked to say. In this case, his silence was so uncharacteristic, I didn't know what to make of it and I pushed for more information. But he wouldn't budge.

"I still have a ton of research to do," he insisted.

Shinjee whispered something in his ear and talked in a sweet tone.

"Sorry. Not until I'm ready," he replied to her. "If this movie fails, then I'll know I don't have what it takes to be a filmmaker. I'll give up and focus on wigs."

"Your ass is drunk," I said. "This is the third straight film I've heard this threat."

"This time I mean it!" he declared.

"Sure, buddy," I said and burst out laughing.

"Don't laugh at me! Don't laugh at me!" he yelled. "Not everyone's meant to lead. Maybe I don't got the vision."

"Ladies. Larry needs some fresh air. Let me escort him out."

I grabbed Larry and helped him outside.

"No more alcohol," I said, then noticed the two thugs lurking across from us. They were casting furtive glances in our direction and I wondered if they were coordinating something with the girls. I peered inside, but Shinjee and Hyori were still eating. "I have this strange feeling that maybe we should leave the girls and get the hell out of here."

"You mean just leave them in there?" he asked. "I'm trying to get laid, man. She won't even let me kiss her yet. If I leave, it's over."

"And those two guys following us? What if they plan on

kidnapping us?"

"If I get to sleep with her for one night, it'll be worth it. Besides, I got you to get me out of trouble. Remember those girls we visited in the Congo?"

"Don't remind me."

"You saved my life twice that night," Larry said. "That lady nearly cut off my—" and he stumbled. I helped him back up. "All that technology, all those computer simulations, and we're still risking our asses for a lay. Or was that just me? You were a prude back then too, weren't you? I thought it was just Linda that yoked your ass."

"If these girls are spies, they're more dangerous than the girls back then," I said.

"It's a good thing you have your toys to help us." He took off his fedora, unattached his wig, looked at the brand tag that read Chao Toufa. "Everyone says we make the best hair in the world. We have some special chemical that makes the hair super real, better than horse hair. Can you believe these wigs cost a fortune?"

"Hair is the most precious luxury in the world."

"Long time ago, people used to shave their heads on purpose because they didn't have showers like now and lice would get in your hair and make your head all itchy. I can't imagine living with bugs in my hair all day."

"It would make life less lonely."

He laughed and put his arm around my shoulder. "Shinjee is so pretty, it makes me wanna cry. The only thing I want more than her is for my next film to succeed. It's going to be amazing."

"You're not going to tell me anything?"

"Not until it's ready. I promise I'll tell you everything when it's set. Just know it'll be bigger than anything I've done before. Can you please help me tonight?"

When I first met Larry, I didn't know who he was, only that he didn't seem to give a shit about anything or anyone. The military gave him demerits, censures, and reprimands, and he'd just laugh it off.

One day, he charted who downloaded what porn in the base, categorizing them by their preferences. He was stunned that the married lieutenant who always espoused the Church of Peace enjoyed, "Weird animal stuff involving broccoli and purple dildos," while three asshole sergeants strayed towards revenge porn and bondage.

"It makes sense, a lot of them are just angry about (fill in the blank)." He put the list into a document and sent it "accidentally" to the entire cadre. Was nearly court-martialed until a general who saw this gave commendations to Larry for his act of "moral courage."

"What are you doing, man?" I asked in concern.

He laughed. "C'mon, man, it was totally worth it."

VI.

With Larry, it was hard to distinguish between courage and crazy recklessness. Shinjee and Hyuni invited us back to their place for drinks. Before I could answer, Larry replied, "Sounds great."

They lived in the east part of town, out near Sihui. The street lights resembled circular halos that hovered like frozen hummingbirds and a vendor was selling mushroom lamps, pink and green neon sprouts flourishing in the night. There was a pickup truck that had sleeping bags in the back, exhausted workers snoring inside. A group of drunks engaged in a rabid game of Chinese poker, demanding more beer, commenting vociferously on their play. The apartments were high-rises that were mostly twenty stories high, a steppe of buildings compressed as closely together as possible. We entered their apartment building. Shinjee stomped the ground to trigger the light sensor. The elevator took us up to the sixteenth floor and we entered their unit. It was surprisingly spacious. At the center of the apartment was a grand black piano, polished smooth so that both of us were reflected upside down. The keys were ermine, the set of chords looking like an intricate rib cage on a charred torso.

"Who plays the piano?" Larry asked.

"I do," Shinjee answered. "I used to be a musician. I even played once for the Leader's nephew."

"Not a love song, right?" I asked.

She simpered. "Not a love song."

"Play something for us," Larry said, and pressed in closer to Shinjee to try to kiss her. She deftly avoided him as though expecting his move.

"Get us some drinks," she ordered Hyori.

Hyori went to the kitchen while Shinjee sat down in front of the piano. She played a piece I didn't recognize. Larry put his arms around her and she asked, "Do you want me to play something or not?" I could tell Larry wanted to be alone with her so I quietly made my way to the kitchen.

Hyori was getting drinks ready, but there was something uneasy in her behavior. I didn't announce myself, watching to see if she was going to do anything. She used a teaspoon to mix juice and soda with heavy doses of liquor. Then I saw her take a tiny capsule and pour it into both our cups. She turned around, about to bring out the alcohol on a tray.

"What was that?" I asked.

"What are you talking about?"

"I saw what you just did."

"I don't know what you're talking about."

"Then drink our drink."

"You don't trust me?"

"Larry!" I shouted. "Larry!"

"What?" he answered.

"We need to leave."

"What are you talking about?"

"You can't just leave!" Hyori shouted.

"Larry, we need to get out of here. Larry!"

"What the hell happened?" Larry demanded as he approached.

"She was trying to drug us," I said.

Larry stared at her. Then back at Shinjee and grinned. "Can we just put all the cards on the table?"

"What do you mean?"

"We've been pussyfooting around it the whole night. What do you want from us?" Larry asked. "Wait, it doesn't even matter. I'm willing to do it, as long as I can have one night with you." He looked directly at Shinjee.

Hyori was flustered and Shinjee looked confused. There was a loud banging on the door. While I was happy Larry was smart to what was going on, it didn't help our plight any. I was not interested in sacrificing myself for one night with Hyori, especially as my eye kept on going to that dumb mouse tattoo on her head celebrating its victory over the lion.

"You can call off the infantry because you won't need them," Larry assured the two. I knew he was turning on his directorial "I'm in command" voice "You want me to make a film for you? You want money? Name it. Anything aside from the factory, you can have. I'd even give you the factory, except I don't have that kind of authority. My dad knew how crazy I was and since I have no other family left, he put selling control over it to a computer. Even if you took me hostage, you couldn't touch Chao Toufa. So what is it you want?"

Shinjee was surprised and I knew she hadn't expected this twist. "Y-you knew it was a trap?"

He went and kissed her. She didn't stop him. The knocking on the door got louder until the lock turned and the two goons following us burst through the door, getting stuck for a second because they were too big to enter at the same time. I looked over at Larry and his lips were red from lipstick. He gently let Shinjee down.

"Welcome, gentlemen," Larry said. "You guys have been

following us the whole night. Have fun?" He looked at me, then took off his fedora and covered his eyes.

I took a light grenade out of my jacket and tossed it up, putting on my protective glasses. An explosive burst of light designed to cause retinal damage shined with the intensity of a small sun, rays deluging the senses. "If you open your eyes for more than three seconds, you'll go blind!" I warned them. "I wouldn't move for at least three hours if I were you." Larry was still covering his eyes. I grabbed him by his arm to lead him out. Hyori was down on the ground, screaming from visual pain. Both blocky goons were also on the ground, squirming in circles like flipped cockroaches wiggling their legs.

We exited and I shut the door behind me.

Larry removed his fedora. "I can never get used to all that light," he said, rubbing his eyes. Even with the protective contact lenses on, I knew it hurt without the glasses. He patted me on the shoulder. "Man, the evening could not have gone more perfect. Did you see her expression, man? She'll be thinking about that kiss the whole night."

We grabbed a cab and he was humming the Final Fantasy song.

"Three days and she'll call me, apologize, ask to meet me privately."

"If she doesn't?" I asked.

"Then it wasn't meant to be. At least I gave it my best shot." He looked at me. "You're still going to L.A. tomorrow?"

I nodded. "I do it every year. You gonna be okay?"

"Lots of research to do. I'll be busy." He looked at my coat. "You got a lot more gadgets in there?"

"I'd love to go on a date where I don't have to use any of them."

"Oh c'mon, man. I know you had a little thing for Hyori. Don't say a part of you didn't want to." He shook his finger at me. "Oh, Hyori, I haven't been with a girl proper since my ex-wife. Can

20

you remind me of what it means to make passionate love with a woman again? Aw yeah!"

"I worry for the day you actually get married again."

"Just don't let any light grenades go off."

"What do you think they wanted from you?" I asked.

"Probably control of the factories. They don't know how little control I actually have," he said and laughed. "I'm not tired. Should we grab another drink?"

I shrugged. "Only if you promise no more crazy girls."

"You know I can't make that promise. Besides, who's crazier, the one who leads, or the one who follows?"

"One of these days, I'm going to meet a girl crazier than any girl you've met and you'll find out what it feels like."

"Bring it on."

VII.

By the time I got back to my apartment, it was 4:34 in the morning. I was about to sleep but heard my neighbors, a young couple, screaming at each other. There was pounding, cursing, yelling again. My heart raced, my mind zipping back to a time when I was the one screaming at Linda and she was screaming back. Little tatters of regret crept into my mind, splitting open sieves. I tossed, tightened the ear plug in my ear, turned on the radio to drown out sound. I could hear the rage and their love bitterly intertwined into repulsion. They wanted to stop. They just didn't know how.

Eventually, the screaming died down. Did they make up, or did they sleep in separate rooms? I usually ended up sleeping on the sofa.

I struggled through sleep, angry I couldn't rest, wondering about meaningless words that still stung. Pain had an expiration date, didn't it? Before I knew it, it was seven a.m. and I'd slept in a hazy nausea that felt more like being adrift than at rest. *America, here I come.*

2. Do You Believe?

I.

I came to Los Angeles once a year for my sister's birthday. She'd passed away, but her husband was still alive and it was her dying wish I'd visit him every year.

I smelled Los Angeles right after we landed. The pollutants had gotten worse and the ocean smelled like a dumping ground. There were huge billboards of Jesus in military fatigues and a laser gun, a logo above him asking, "Do you believe?" The biggest billboard in the world was a sky board owned by the Church of Peace that played a 24-hour broadcast of *Jesus the General*. *Jesus the General* was the most highly rated show in the United States and a nine-time winner of the GEAs (Global Entertainment Awards). Oddly, the second most popular was the *Real Life of Rhonda*, an ex-porn star who still engaged in crazy sexual escapades and had won eighteen GEAs. She was nearly sixty, but American plastic surgeons were the best in the world and she looked like she was nineteen. Her catch phrase was, "Where have you been?" and she ventured the world finding sex in all its different forms. Jesus versus Rhonda was the biggest ratings war the planet had ever seen.

The plastic surgeons played a bigger role in this battle than anyone cared to admit. They'd gotten so skilled, they could make anyone look exactly like anyone else. People started asking to look like old celebrities. Marilyn Monroe was popular. So were JFK, Richard Nixon, Bill Clinton, and George W. Bush. Scandals arose when random citizens got surgery to look like celebrities and the journalists got them mixed up. Eventually, the government had to pass a law on "Image Facilitation" as plastic surgery officially came to be known. No recreating public figures without a hundred-million-dollar fee (USD).

We were the only country still using the American dollar.

Everyone else had adapted Standard Currency (SC) after the dollar's inflation made it worthless decades ago. An orange juice that cost me 2 SC cost me almost 10,000 USD. In fact orange juice in L.A. was more expensive than Image Facilitation depending on the sale that was going on at the time.

LAX was one of the safest air fortresses in the world. Part of that was because of the huge military presence, soldiers with huge guns watching me at every corner. Outside, Los Angeles had reverted to its western origins. It was literally the Wild West out there. Rather than impose gun control, Americans had gone the way of equipping everyone with arms. You had to wear vests and a helmet in case of stray bullets that might break bones. Hospital bills were super expensive too since they had to work for a profit.

I'd packed my armor suit which was in all grays to let strangers know I was a neutral, not bound up in one of the turf wars that raged throughout the city as indicated by different-colored armor. The glass plating on the helmet surrounded my head and I fastened the armor to cover all major arteries. I'd gotten accustomed to the violence, especially since most public places had gunbots or aerial drones to take down hostiles.

I still hated coming. I always felt like I was being sold something, even on the taxis that were filled with 3D panoramas of advertisements and holobuddies hooked into my credit information to determine what kind of products I'd be interested in. If I opted out of ads, my cab rates would be ten times the normal rate. Endure ads and the ride was partially subsidized. The cab driver was a grumpy old man who asked, "Where to?"

I gave him the address for the hospital.

He didn't turn around and I was glad he wasn't the chattering type asking me a hundred questions about where I was from. I felt exhausted, especially with the flip in time zone and the fact that I'd barely slept the night before.

I thought about my brother-in-law, Ian. He was a snob whose

only obsession was being famous when he had his sanity. He tried real hard to be famous, forced my sister to do a lot of stupid things for him. I remembered the first time I met him, I was just ending gun training class. A young girl named Tina couldn't stop crying after the teacher shot her because she'd cowered at the last second causing the bullet to impact her at an angle that made her bang her head. The teacher forced us to type in our standards (copy/paste disabled) while she chewed out Tina for not following instructions.

We will immediately report any suspicious behavior to the teacher.

Anyone threatening any other student, even as a joke, should be reported.

On and on.

Kelly came in as she was picking me up and said, "You better not tell Mom about Ian."

"Who's Ian?"

I found out a few minutes later. Ian smelled funny and had messy curly hair. The first thing he asked was, "Damn, your brother's really ugly. You think I can rap about that?"

"Rap about whatever you want," Kelly said.

Three days later, there was a rap online called "My Girlfriend's Ugly Brother" that had pictures of me provided by my sister, making me the butt of all jokes at school. This was the jerk I had to visit every year.

Traffic was bad. Helicopters were racing to a gun battle ahead and I heard the sirens from police bikes. Fortunately, helmets came with audio players and visual displays so I could block it out and watch the news. Most news channels were reported by young and attractive broadcasters who were practically naked on-screen and replaced every two months or however long ratings kept up with them. When the necessary one-minute global recap was finished, it was the usual splurge of man wants to marry his dog, woman had an affair with both her bosses, and prodigy can beat any videogame in ten minutes. *Jesus the General* commercials played on every channel and the latest episode declared, "Jesus takes on the Viet Cong and kicks ass."

"You know how it was written, turn your cheek. Well I say onto thee, turn your cheek and aim properly through the scope," Jesus, played by actor James Leyton, declared. "I am the way, the truth, and your life or death, depending on how you answer my question."

"Do you believe?" a female voice asked as the commercial came to an end.

That was followed by a Chao Toufa ad starring an obese young man shunned by all his friends. He bought a Chao Toufa wig and was immediately surrounded by beautiful people who revered him for his full head of hair. "It's the most realistic hair in the world," four attractive women declared.

America was home to the most overweight people in the world. After the FDA got bought out by a fast-food chain, regulatory rules became a joke and the drivel that passed as hamburgers was deemed organic because they came from "living cows." It was no wonder that Institute #38822, officially known as "The Center for Peaceful Recuperation," was filled with the corpulent obese. I wasn't talking a little overweight, but people who couldn't even walk because they were so big. I'd always wondered where all the collective dumps they took went. That was a lot of crap to dispose of, even if used as fertilizer for the farms of the world.

I got out of the cab. It was raining hard. I rushed to the front entrance where I signed in. The institute was a warehouse for people who couldn't work because they couldn't walk. It was as big as some convention centers and every person was allotted a space with a holopad so they could lose themselves in entertainment and commercials. The holopads were hooked into their wheel bikes without which they would have no mobility. Wheel bikes also served as bathrooms. Many had IV needles in them and the stench of junk food was horrific as much of it had been regurgitated or stuck as stains on their clothing. It was a pig sty for humans. Nurses and janitors cleaned up where they could, though most just flirted with each other and gossiped about trivia. Every piece of equipment had a logo for a food brand.

Ian was watching a basketball game and didn't notice I'd come. "Hey, Ian," I said.

He didn't reply. He never replied. A stroke from all those cholesterols clotting his veins had caused permanent brain damage.

Kelly was the only biological relation I'd ever acknowledged as "family." Even though she was stubborn and pig-headed, I could never really be angry with her. She'd had a tough childhood and I understood why she was the way she was. Violence begat violence. A man had to murder his past to destroy the cycle. The whole history of humanity was violence so that this current motion towards peace could be considered an anomaly or quirk of circumstance. Since the early 20th century, Koreans were immersed in violence. First the Japanese Empire, then the North Koreans who sundered families apart. The Korean military rulers who took over after America established the demilitarized zone were a ruthless lot that crushed resistance, especially student protesters who believed they were fighting for a better world. Tie in Confucian ideals of following elders without question, and it almost explained why my biological father was an abusive control freak who beat us mercilessly as children. My whole childhood was a memory of escaping pain, doing my best not to incur his wrath. It was never associated with something tangible, like bad grades or bad behavior. Instead, it was random violence made worse by my mother who would scream that if I didn't stop crying, they would kill me, my incomprehensible life blotted out in punches and kicks. As Kelly got older, she took on the brunt of the pain. When she couldn't stop crying after watching a scary Chinese movie about walking corpses, my biological father beat her to a few inches short of death and locked her inside a cabinet afterwards. Kelly, rather than resisting, sat quietly inside without a murmur. That was even more terrifying. Was she okay? Was she living? Even now, I'm ashamed that I didn't have the courage to check. She came out all right, but she didn't speak for three months. At elementary school, the teachers thought she had a psychological problem and suggested special schools for her. A few convenient bribes silenced the teachers.

Even now, I can't refer to that man as a "father" without shivering, but rather the "biological father" who contributed chemicals to my birth. What makes me burn though wasn't his actions, but the indifference of all those around me. I swore when I grew up, I would escape and make my own family. The Great Baldification meant freedom for me, the death of my past. It was the most welcome event of my life as my parents got divorced and left us in the care of Baochai. In my eyes, they were dead. I was reborn. I'd pave a new path.

For Kelly, marrying this scumbag turned out to be a dead end. She couldn't find herself so it was important to find her identity by reconnecting with our biological parents. That was the last thing I wanted. More than anything, I wanted a new family so that I could branch out on my own. That meant sundering any connection with the past and I did it, not caring what anyone else might think or say. I still hoped for a connection with Kelly, but she kept on insisting on drawing me back into a past I wanted nothing to do with. It became worse with moderate fame from our movies as people came out of nowhere, claiming a connection with my past and the family that I wanted to forget. I realized that the only way to really move on was to literally murder every part of the past. Every part. I didn't talk to Kelly until she passed away, cut her out completely. Even though I missed her, I still didn't regret my actions. My future family would be different. They wouldn't have to suffer for my past. Linda was supposed to be the beginning of that.

I tried talking with Ian for a while, knowing he wasn't

listening. Another pointless trip to feel sorry about myself. I checked my phone and saw Larry had called several times.

"Sorry to break up your personal time," he said when I called back. "Nice helmet." He appeared chipper.

"I'm done. What's up?"

"Can I ask you for a favor?"

"I don't think I can go on another date tonight."

He grinned. "Can you pick up a package for me? I'm sending over an address."

"What's in it?"

"A special gift for a special lady."

I groaned, remembering all the times I'd brought back "special" gifts for him. "This isn't going to get me in trouble with the censors, is it?"

He shook his head. "You're coming back by private jet. It's on standby. I also sent a car for you."

"Where am I going?"

"Only if you're willing. I won't force you."

I grimaced. "Where am I going?"

"The Absalom Institute of Hair."

"What's that?"

"It's a research facility. One of the researchers, Dr. Asahi, will have something for you. But you need to make it before six."

"Why?"

"Someone there I want you to meet," Larry said.

I was already heading out and a driver was waiting in front of the center with a black sedan. The rain had stopped, but it was windy and cold. I hopped into the backseat of the car and removed my helmet. "Someone?" I continued with Larry.

"You said you wanted to meet someone crazy. I thought, why not kill two rats with one spoon?"

"Are you sending me on a blind date?"

"Connection's getting fuzzy, can't hear you," and the communication ended.

As we got on the freeway, I saw four separate apartment complexes on fire. Everywhere I looked, the buildings were dilapidated. I couldn't help but wonder, *Los Angeles, how is it you look worse every time I come back?*

II.

Larry had never actually arranged a blind date for me alone (he always accompanied me) so a part of me was curious what kind of a girl she was, even though I already knew what I was going to tell her. "Thank you, but I'm not interested in dating at this time." Especially not while I was in Los Angeles.

We headed towards the San Fernando Valley via the 5 Freeway and the driver pointed out the new suit and wig that were waiting in the back. I had no interest in either, though I did feel the wig which was a marvel. It was hard to believe they got horse hair to feel this real. I put it back as I never accepted anything from Larry unless it was for official business. He already had a thousand sycophants and I wanted to maintain a line of balance between us as friend and employer.

The Absalom Institute of Hair was fenced off and isolated among a series of hills. We had to go through three security gates, passing by two massive parking lots. I was disappointed that what awaited was a plain-looking building painted brown with curtained windows. *Why was this building so closely guarded?* Aside from a lawn and three people smoking out front without armor, there wasn't any indication of something special. I stepped out of the car and it was blazing hot, even though the sun was going down. The clouds had dissipated. I walked through the front door and came to a lobby with copied Impressionist paintings on the wall. There were metal chairs that looked uncomfortable, several doors in the hallway, and a lady at the reception desk who looked up at me. It reminded me of a doctor's office. "You're late," the woman said. "I've been waiting thirty minutes. You don't need armor in here." She was wearing a brunette wig and had a Eurasian look to her. I didn't know if it was the makeup or her natural complexion, but the texture of her skin was tanned, a brownish hue that made it seem like she'd had been exposed to just the perfect amount of sun. She had a big forehead and a strong jaw that puffed out her cheeks and made her face seem square. She was wearing a dress that looked brand new, a cross hybrid between a yellow cardigan and red skirt. It looked like she'd prepared for our meeting and I wondered if she was disappointed at the sight of me in my armor. She stood up and was several inches taller than me. "Should we go?"

She led and I followed, taking off my helmet.

"Where are we going?"

"To eat," she said.

We went through the third door on the right, then the second door on the left, through the hall, down a set of stairs to a room with ten round dining tables. The food was already prepared on our corner table—salad and tofu steaks. "This is where we usually greet outsiders without security clearance," she explained. "I hate eating out in California. Just to get to the restaurant, you have to pay a parking fee, 35% state tax, and 25% tip on top of the meal."

I nodded knowingly as we sat down and started to eat. "Where is everyone?"

"In the lab, down below," she said.

I assumed the underground structure beneath the building was the reason for all the security. "What goes on down there?"

"Actually, I've never been so I don't know the specifics."

"How long you work here?" I asked.

"Almost three years now but it's very hush hush. Still, I've always wanted to work in hair so I don't mind."

"Why hair?"

"My mom used to own a chain of hair salons but after the Baldification, all her stores were finished. We grew up real poor like everyone else in the hair industry and I just wanted to understand what caused the whole mess. Larry speaks very highly of you. He tells me you film all his movies?"

I nodded. "He saved me from a life of mediocrity."

"Oh?"

"We served together in Africa and after I was discharged, I got a job working as a digital pusher at SolTech. It was hell. I mean, the army, I got that I had to follow orders. But the politics were even worse at SolTech. Larry gave me a chance to be independent and I enjoyed shooting his films."

"I like Mr. Chao's films. The lighting and the cinematography are beautiful."

I was surprised that she had seen them. "Thank you. Do they-do they study the Baldification here?" I asked, curious about the facility.

"Mr. Chao didn't tell you?"

I shook my head. "He just told me to pick up a package."

Confusion flitted across her face. "He told you about this dinner though?"

"Actually, he mentioned it while I was on the way here."

She sighed. "Mr. Chao and Dr. Asahi spent the last month hounding me about this. I finally agreed because she told me you were begging to meet me."

"I'm sorry, but that's not true. I gotta be honest. I-I just got out of a marriage," by which I meant a few years, "and I'm not ready for a relationship. I've told Larry that several times."

"I have no interest in relationships either," she said. "I'm focused on my career. But Mr. Chao told me you were so depressed that if I didn't meet with you, you might do something extreme. I can see that isn't true. Besides, you're too short for me. I don't like short guys."

"I don't like women taller than me," I replied, peeved by her comment.

"That's settled then. I don't want to waste my time. Why don't we just eat dinner and go?"

"Why even have dinner? I can just take the package and go."

"Even better. I was only being respectful to the chefs because they prepared the food." She picked up her plate, said, "Stop by my desk after you're done," and left the room.

I called Larry.

"How'd it go?" he asked eagerly.

"I was expecting someone a lot crazier."

Larry laughed. "You know I like messing with expectations."

"Is that why you told her I was depressed and begging to meet her?"

"Rebecca's as stubborn as you are," Larry answered. "She's been divorced four years and she still hasn't moved on. Just like you. I needed to give her motivation."

"My situation is different."

"Oh c'mon, man. You know you've been moping too long. You haven't even been with another woman since Linda. That's a really long time. I can't imagine what that's like."

"Hey, man. That was in confidence. You can't use that against me," I protested.

"I'm not using it against you. I'm just stating my—amazement at your abstinence."

"Forget it," I said. "What is this place?"

Larry shook his head. "Can't tell you over the phone. I'll tell you when I see you. You have the package?"

"Not yet. I was about to go grab it. You want me to drop it off when I get in?"

"Yeah. I'm visiting the factory today so I'll have someone pick you up." Larry stared at me. "Bro, at least give her a chance, will you? You worry me."

"We had an argument."

"Over what?"

"Over nothing."

"Haven't you learned there is no such thing as victory in an argument with a woman?"

"Too late," I said. "See you later."

I ate the tofu steak by myself. Despite my irritation with the situation, it tasted really good which lightened my mood.

III.

Back in the lobby, Rebecca was finishing her meal.

"Is the package ready?" I asked.

"It'll be coming soon," she said. "You can take a seat and I'll let you know when it comes."

I sat down and the seat was so hard, it hurt my butt after sitting about a minute. I stood up and put my helmet back on to watch some news. There was a special on serial killers that had never been caught in California; the Zodiac Killer, the Red Wig Snatcher, and the Yearly Killer. I got tired of the perpetual advertisements and took the helmet off, rubbing my scalp because it was itchy.

"You live in L.A. or you fly in?" I asked Rebecca.

"I fly in on the weekends."

"From?"

"Shanghai," she answered, then went back to reading a document on her holopad.

"How do you like L.A.?"

She simpered up at me. "I really hate chit-chat. So unless you have something important, let's skip it."

Her phone rang and she picked up. "He's here." She nodded several times. "No, nothing. I'm sure of it." Shortly afterwards, she hung up. "Dr. Asahi's on her way up."

Dr. Asahi was an older Japanese woman who didn't bother with a wig and wore square glasses which was a surprise as almost no one in Los Angeles wore glasses other than as a fashion accessory (everyone got their eyes lasered). She wore a leathery yellow overcoat that looked like it was assembled from snake scales and she was carrying a small capsule that was about the size of my thumbnail. Her nose curved inwards to form tiny nostrils that made her face seem almost noseless.

"I'm completely stumped how he got this," she said. "I can understand why he sent you to pick it up directly. That's all the data he asked for." She turned to Rebecca. "Give him your card."

Rebecca stared at Dr. Asahi with a glower of protest, but the doctor ignored her.

"Tell Larry to call me as soon as he gets this and if you have any questions about anything, feel free to contact Rebecca." She left without a farewell greeting.

Rebecca handed me her card; Rebecca Lian, it read, Project Manager at AIOH. Her phone number was a series of sevens and twos that were comically easy to memorize. I wouldn't have bothered to scan it in even if it had been hard and we both knew it was an empty gesture. I placed the card in my pocket and said, "Good luck. Maybe I'll see you in Shanghai sometime."

"Has anyone told you that you have a very strange-looking scalp?"

"Not in those words," I replied.

Outside, it was raining again. At least I didn't have to take a shuttle flight back where I'd be packed in with thousands of others, standing on the plane like we were in a train, hoping to grab a seat, holding onto the rail if there wasn't one available. Rainy days were the worst as everyone's clothes and shoes were wet. Traffic had become a quagmire and we were at a standstill on the freeway. The clouds vanished and the sun came up. Climatologists speculated the capricious weather swings in L.A. were just part of the mood swings the earth underwent after both poles melted. I knew the East Coast got it worse, though they adapted. New York was a sea city with underwater tours of the old ruins. Greenland was now a tropical resort.

I saw a naked man running by on the freeway. Followed by hundreds of others. The nude herd of men and women rushed through the freeway like a stampede of deer, pounding people's stationary cars, hammering them with their hands. It was a stark contrast, these armored cars with armored drivers to the fully bare men and women running without any worries. I asked the driver, "What's going on?"

"They call it the Free Run."

"What are they running for?"

"I think freedom. But I've never been sure. Nice view though."

The shriveled penises and the perky nipples hinted at how cold it still was outside. Perhaps they were tired of living in paranoid vigilance every day. Eventually, the mass moved on and the roads cleared up.

As we arrived at the airport, I knew the real reason I always came back was Linda Yu. She still lived in the city, and even if she hadn't, the memory of her lingered here. She'd moved on, ironically, by staying put. I lived halfway across the world but was still stuck here. I examined Dr. Asahi's capsule. It was tiny. Probably a data chip with some information related to sexual performance. I appreciated Larry's attempt to arrange a date, but I much preferred to experience life through a camera lens, upon the screen, long after everything had played out, rewinding to watch over and over.

3. Acid Reflux

I.

I'd been dreaming about thirst almost every night. I'd get really thirsty, feel how dry my throat was, grab a cup and fill it with water. No matter how much I drank, the thirst was never quenched and I couldn't swallow without feeling a desiccated lump. That lump was me trying to wet my throat in real life. Fantasy could not overcome the physical necessities of thirst which would make me in turn realize I was in a dream.

Gastroesophageal reflux had been the cause. I kept on coughing in the middle of the night, my throat feeling irritated. The doctor told me I shouldn't eat before I slept and needed at least three hours between drinking water and sleeping. I was waking up in the middle of the night with a dry throat or, as in this case, a drive to the Beijing factory of Chao Toufa which was located on the outskirts of the capital city. I felt like I needed a whole day of sleep to recuperate.

Larry greeted me and burst out laughing as soon as he saw me. "Way to make an impression," he said. I was about to hand him the package but he said, "Hold it for now."

The factory was huge, taking up over thirty buildings. The campus had a lake, verdant knolls, and two big amphitheaters where various concerts took place. Larry's father was an admirer of the philosophy of treating his employees well ("Heaven's Mandate," he called it) and had established a company culture that espoused, "Work Hard, Play Hard." The buildings were divided by categories. One of the buildings only did eyelashes. Another, brows. Hair types were divvied; Chinese style, Brazilian, European, and custom hair. Machines did much of the hair preparation, sorting them to maintain direction and avoid tangling. The ventilating needles knotted the hair into the foundation material and also carried out the stylization. The machines still needed human supervision as we walked through and saw several huge mechanical arms with miniscule needle points at the end creating the wigs. Larry's favorite area was the pubic hairs, especially as most of them had to be customized to individual orders with personalized scans. Larry liked to muse, "What I wouldn't give to see a woman with natural—"

"Have you met Russ Lambert?" he asked in the present.

Russ was the rotund Manager of Operations who kept things running in Larry's absence. He had the tattoos of Mandarin characters on his head and had shifty blue eyes that averted direct contact. He always seemed to be looking down at my belly.

"We've met. How are you doing, Nick?" he asked with a squeaky voice, sharpened by the rolls of fat under his chin. He had on a pastel-blue suit with a kilt underneath, long blooming jacket covering his back.

"Fine, thanks."

"You just got back from Los Angeles?" Russ asked.

"Yeah. Visiting family."

"I spent two years there," he replied. "Got shot twice. Fortunately, the armor held."

I told them about the naked runners and Larry was fascinated by the idea, asking all the details, focusing, of course, on the lurid aspects of which I knew nothing.

I was introduced to forty other people who were managers of various departments. They were polite as I was the owner's friend, though their cordiality didn't go beyond that. I wondered where we were going and why we were checking in on all the buildings. We walked for almost two hours and I knew beyond the factories, there was a huge span of farmland devoted to animals who could graze freely; horses, goats, peacocks, and others that required an army of caretakers just to keep everything spick and span.

"George said hello," Larry suddenly said. "Why don't you stop by and see the old man? I have a meeting I gotta run to, but we'll do brunch after that."

George served in the African Wars with us, though as a mechanic. He was part of the UN Peacekeepers and we went to him whenever our computers had problems. He was a master with hardware, though his specialty was cybernetic parts and tank assemblies. I still remembered the first time we met in Africa—he was working on a drone engine. I noticed his overwhelming beer belly, abetted by his passion for Russian beers. He wore an afro for his wig, though he switched that up with a handkerchief as hat. The top two buttons on his uniform were unbuttoned and his hands were greasy. I'd brought a computer that a foreign virus had destroyed. It was an older machine and I wondered whether it was time to retire it.

He put the part for the drone down, whistled, then said with a thick Russian accent, "I have not seen 300XVA since I graduate from university. They used these babies for robotics."

"Robotics?"

"The military vanted to build huge robot to fight in Africa. Top secret project. Ve had military officer overseeing everything. Idiot supervisor, vanted all the credit. Ignored all mechanical problems. Too heavy to valk. Engine burned out. The fourth year I vorking on it, ve had goal to make it take a step. Fell apart before first step. They vere huge, taller than skyscraper. Ugly and boxy looking. Ve built them in big factories and whole place smelled like burnt oil. I hated smell but vas stuck. I built small gauge to measure heat levels. Funny thing. Modern cars veeth' computers are more advanced than our million-dollar robot. Hard to keep up veeth' the computers they put in cars these days. Military shut us down. Twenty years later, here I am," George said. "Fixing drone bots to kill our enemies."

"How's that make you feel?"

He grinned, his two gold teeth gleaming. "Too bad var can't last forever."

After the war ended, Larry hired George to modernize many

of their factories and he'd done an amazing job. He also provided us with gadgets like the light bomb I'd used earlier. He was currently working on a pet project that Larry financed, a construction robot designed to expedite the building of structures. It was an ugly robot that looked like the ED-209 from the old *Robocop* films we loved, though with a sleeker design and no artillery. I marveled at the sight of the machine now as I stood waiting for him to finish up what he was working on. He struggled, cursed, and beat one of the bigger parts until he spotted me. Laughing, he came over with a yellow afro on. "Larry tell me you no like girl he introduce to you."

"He already told you?"

"Both us vorry 'bout you."

"I'm just not ready for a relationship."

"You a young man. It's no good to be alone. Need sweetheart, cuddle and hold at night. I have Mrs. George, I'm an old man. But you. Young-blooded, need voman to love." He gave me a jocular punch to the shoulder that actually hurt. "The internet stuff," he said, making a hand jerking-off motion. "Not healthy for brain or heart. He have too much love. You have too little." His knowing grin made it clear Larry had informed him of my state of abstinence. *Thank you, Larry.*

"It might be a good thing," I offered, knowing how weak it sounded. "I can't tell you how many times I've had to save him from trouble. If it wasn't for your light bombs, I don't know where we'd be."

"Vhat kind of ladies you meet, you need all these gadgets for? Every time Larry talks about Rome, I nearly get a heart attack."

The memory of the trouble that rained down during our Italian trip when Larry tried to steal away two actresses from their politician husbands brought shudders. "We wouldn't have testicles if it weren't for the light bombs."

George laughed and put his arm around my shoulder. "Machiavelli said a prince should not touch another man's land or vomen."

"That was before the prince changed his name and became an artist."

We spent the next hour swapping stories before Larry arrived. "Brunch? I'm starving. Might be a little business though."

"That's fine," I said. We both looked to George.

"Mrs. George cooked my lunch. Have fun and try not to vaste light bomb."

II.

Russ, Larry, five other executives I didn't know, and myself ate in a room in the west dining hall. There was a circular table with a Lazy Susan. Larry was at the head as host, Russ across from him as secondary host. I was to Larry's left, a Chinese executive I didn't know to his right (he might have been a government officer?). We were served fried duck with dasheen, braised turtle in brown sauce, fish roe with scallop dumpling, wutong tea-smoked chicken, toasted rabbit legs with cumin, jellyfish head with mixed vegetables, radish cake with assorted preserved meat, sliced ox-tripe, and duck blood with chili sauce.

Russ asked after each of the families of those present. One of the executives cut in: "The Colonel is giving us a beating. We got to do something before she destroys our Chongqing factory. She already tried poisoning our horses three times."

The discussion became heated and I realized this was a full-fledged business meeting under the pretence of a meal. Most of the frustration came from the figure called the Colonel who was a rival trying to establish her own wig company. This Colonel was ruthless in her pursuit to achieve her objectives, resorting to military tactics which had to be protested with the government. All heads turned towards the man next to Larry who hadn't spoken the whole time. He was an elderly man with a wart on his right cheek. He had calm and soothing eyes which didn't waver as he ate the duck meat on his plate.

He spoke back in Mandarin, saying the government was well aware of the tactics of the Colonel and that there was a line she could not cross. There were complications because she was stationed in Thailand, though those could be circumvented if needed. *Zou hou men* was the Chinese saying—through the back-gate dealings.

"It's a good thing your father never had to deal with a woman like her," Russ said. "She fights business like war."

"She served in Africa. You heard of her," Larry said to me. "Bloody Rina."

Bloody Rina—the officer who took Harare, capital city of Zimbabwe, by sending every troop she had, resulting in a disastrous number of deaths. She was heavily reprimanded and discharged, although she expressed no shame, publicly stating, "Even if it meant a million deaths, I would still have sent them for victory." She was now apparently rival to Larry's company.

Larry was jotting down notes in his holopad and seemed intensely absorbed. I wondered what was going through his head as the discussion moved onto the actions a number of smaller rivals were making, the huge volume of petty lawsuits being brought against the company, as well as negotiations that had to take place to secure various organic materials. At one point, he tilted the holopad and I could see what was on it. He'd just been scribbling, drawing random patterns, squiggly circles and squares overlapping each other in a haphazard diagram. He wasn't even paying attention. I chucked inwardly and zoned out as well, especially when everyone started speaking in Mandarin which was hard enough to follow without all the business jargon.

"What do you think, Larry?" Russ asked at one point which snapped me out of a reverie I couldn't remember even though it was a second ago.

Larry put down his chopsticks. "I think my dad hired you fine folks to make the business decisions and didn't want me to interfere. We had a good year. I'm not worried."

"We had an excellent year," Russ said. "But that'll evaporate if we don't take a stand."

"So make the stand," Larry said and got up. "You gentlemen continue. I have some business to attend to."

"Larry."

"Russ. You get paid the big bucks for a reason."

We bid farewell to those at the table and stepped outside as the meeting continued without us.

"If I have to go to another meeting, I'm going to shoot myself," Larry stated. "I'm done for the day. Do you mind going shopping with me?"

"It seemed like a serious meeting," I said.

"It's always a serious meeting with these guys. Everything is the end of the world. The world is big enough for rival wig companies."

We got into his car and he input directions for a shopping center.

"What are we buying?" I asked.

"A gift for some of my ladies. Also, you need to send Rebecca an apology gift."

"Huh?"

The automated taxi took us to a shopping complex about an hour away. Larry was engrossed in a long phone call about various business updates which consisted mostly of him saying, "Uh huh, uh huh," while making lewd gestures with his fingers as he pretended to take the conversation seriously with the camera flipped off.

"This Colonel doesn't got you worried?" I asked after he hung up.

Larry grinned. "She's a scary hag. You know she had all her teeth blown out during a bombing? She picked up her teeth and made a collar of them and they say she wears it to sleep. She has that tattoo of the King of Hell on her scalp too which doesn't help.

Anytime I see her, I just want to hand her the keys to the company and tell her, *don't kill me please.*"

"Why don't you?"

"I told you. I don't have the power to give it up," he answered. "It's up to the master computer, the *Zhuge Liang*. All selling power is controlled by the AI. I just reap the benefits. My dad could be an asshole, but he could read people. He knew I wasn't a businessman and knew he couldn't leave control of the company in my hands. I'm glad, because if he had, I'd be broke and I'd probably have signed my company away to some hottie who batted her eyes at me and said, 'Oh, Larry, can you give me shares in your company?' It's something way bigger that's got me concerned."

"What's bigger than that?"

He rubbed his forehead. "Did you notice anything strange during the lunch?"

"Like what?"

"Anything unusual?"

I thought about it. "No. Should I have?"

"I was hoping you would. That's why I invited you. Sorry if it was boring. I have to do about twenty of those a week."

"It's all right. Kind of interesting actually." I thought back on the conversation and while the topics were foreign to me, I didn't know if there was something specific Larry was referring to. "Was it when we were talking about the Colonel?"

Larry shook his head.

"About the lawsuits?" I asked.

He shook his head again. "It's actually related to that chip from Dr. Asahi."

I got ready to take it out when he stopped me.

"I've been avoiding it all day. I'm hoping I'm wrong."

"About what?"

He placed his thumbnail in his mouth and chewed it nervously. "About a whole lot of things."

The first shopping center we arrived at was packed and there were cameras everywhere along with a stream of fashionably dressed patrons. Turned out they were filming a show called *Fashion Addicts* where the eponymous contestants had to go through shopping malls for a year without buying anything in order to try and cure their disease. Larry decided we should go to a different shopping center that was fifteen miles further. It was practically empty despite being five floors tall and taking up a massive space. There were all sorts of stores on the first floor selling clothing, books, shoes, herbs, sunglasses, and kitchen appliances. The second floor was full of odd products that had never caught on; talking mannequins, robotic pets, books that yelled their contents, pens that wrote themselves, clothes that changed color depending on the emotion of the wearer, and clocks that counted fiscal irresponsibility. I didn't know if it was the location or if it was because the place was so old that it didn't have dazzling lights and advertisements, but there were no patrons. There were some stragglers here and there, but not enough to be able to finance such a big area. As a result, the store owners had a desperate gleam to them, watching us expectantly, hoping we would stop in to make a purchase. I couldn't imagine spending my whole life waiting in one of these stuffed stores, trying to make enough of a living to survive. They existed customer to customer, haggling over pennies that made no difference to those arguing but meant rent to those fighting to maintain that slight margin of profit.

"What's on this disk?" I asked. "Dr. Asahi said she was stumped."

"The answer to a puzzle," Larry answered.

"If you're going to tell me this is somehow related to a girl you're in love with—"

"She hasn't called me yet," he said. "But no, this isn't related. You reminded me though. Why hasn't Shinjee called me back yet?"

"We did disable her bodyguards and expose their attempt to knock us out."

"She's just making a living," Larry said, shrugging it off.

"I'm not trying to question you, man, but should you have paid more attention at the meeting?"

Larry laughed. "Do you know what the real point of the meeting was?"

"It wasn't to discuss business matters?"

"The other managers wanted to embarrass Russ by pointing out all the problems and supersede his authority by talking directly to me. I had to act like I didn't care so they'd understand Russ was still the man and talking to me was pointless."

"You guys planned this?"

Larry nodded. "He's really big on expanding into garbage disposal which has caused a political nightmare. The others think it's a fool's game and part of me agrees with them. But hell, diversity can't be bad." He cleared his throat. "Russ also thinks one of the managers is working for the Colonel. Had to be careful what we said in there. Anyways, thinking about all this business stuff stresses me out. I sometimes think about giving it all up and just wandering the planet."

"Why don't you?"

"I'd miss all my ladies."

I laughed. "You can meet new ones."

"The ones I'm chasing now are way too attractive for me to give up without at least trying."

"You mean Shinjee?"

"Plus two new ones I met last night."

I sighed. "You're in love?"

"Not yet. But the Austrian-British lady I met last night reminded me of this Greek statue I once saw in San Francisco. She's actually the niece to our regional manager in Mongolia. We talked about quantum mechanics as love made into mathematics."

"What about the other one?"

He waved his finger at me. "I'm not kidding you, she looked like an elf. Perfect body proportions, cute like someone from those fantasy-book covers. All she needed was pointy ears. What about you? Did you at least find Rebecca attractive?"

"She was—nice."

"I didn't ask if she was nice."

"She told me she doesn't like guys shorter than her—and I'm shorter than her."

He pointed out some flowers. "Roses have a funny way of equalizing uneven heights. So do coats. How do you think these look?"

He had lifted up some red winter coats that appeared cheap, embroidered with flowery designs.

"I don't like it."

"I love it," Larry said. "*Duo shao qian?*" he asked the owner.

"150 SC," was the response.

"I'll take ten."

The owner appeared shocked.

"You sure you don't want to haggle a little?" I asked.

"You know I never haggle," Larry replied.

He scanned in his credit key and the owner examined it multiple times to make sure it wasn't a fake.

There was a jade store which sold some incredibly detailed jewelry. There was one of a jade fox that was particularly stunning. I examined it, impressed by the craftsmanship.

"How much?" I asked.

The response was ridiculously high and I tried to haggle, but he wouldn't budge.

"This is of the finest material and I personally crafted it," he insisted.

"You don't want it?" Larry asked. "I think Rebecca will love it."

"Too expensive."

We went to ten more shops buying more clothing that he was either going to "donate or use as costumes in the next movie." The look on the faces of the shopkeepers was a mixture of wariness, surprise, and bliss. I could tell they thought Larry was a wasteful buffoon for paying so high, though they didn't mind one bit.

The bags became too heavy and I told him, "I'll take these downstairs."

"I'll see you in a bit."

I put the bags in the car and thought about how much Linda used to love shopping. We couldn't afford any of the good stuff, especially not at the expensive shopping malls in California, but she loved finding places like this where she could haggle for amazing deals. As much as I tried to enjoy shopping, I couldn't, my body becoming tired, yawns escaping me, my attention shifting to the internet to read useless trivia. We used to fight because I'd want to go home and she wanted to spend a little more time shopping. To her, it was a game as she navigated her way through merchants who thought they were smarter. Beating them was the challenge and the only place where she could feel a sense of control as we had so little with our overwhelming debts. I knew that now. Why didn't I back then?

When I got back upstairs, Larry was running straight towards me. He had on a woman's wig that was colored green and was dressed in a blue dress, bra wrapped around his neck. As he zoomed by, he yelled, "Help!"

Behind him was a middle-aged Chinese man with a beaver hat and a bat swinging at everything in his way. "Stop him!" he was screaming. "STOP HIM!!!"

Just as he was about to pass me, I stuck my foot out and tripped him. He crashed into a rack full of ear muffs. He tried to lift up his bat, but I stomped down on his wrists. He let out a yelp. "What are you doing?" he protested in Mandarin.

"Larry!" I shouted. "Larry! What's going on?"

Larry sheepishly came back. From the direction that the two of them had been running, I saw a young woman in tears.

"There's been a huge misunderstanding," Larry said. "I didn't sleep with your wife. I didn't even know she was married."

"Then why's she pregnant?" he demanded. "I haven't been to bed with her in almost a year!"

I looked to Larry, then back at the woman and noticed the bulge in her belly.

"Ask her, not me," Larry said. "I just talked to her about buying some dresses."

The man started crying and looked silly with his hat shaped like a beaver with two buck teeth. "Why are the heavens so cruel to me?"

Larry signaled for me to take my feet off the guy. He stooped down and said, "If you need a divorce lawyer, I can help you. Just give me a discount when I buy thirty dresses."

"I don't want to divorce her. I've already forgiven her five times. But now she's gotten pregnant. I love her so much, I'd rather die than part with her."

Larry peered over at the woman who still looked coquettish, biting her lips, demurely watching us. "You picked the wrong girl to love," he said.

III.

Very little was sacred for Larry. Marriage was one of those exceptions. He hated people who cheated. One of his top producers, Limeng, was having an affair while his wife was in the hospital with breast cancer. No one minded much because he was such a likable guy (and as people pointed out, he hadn't gotten laid in years). But after Larry found out, he fired him instantly and not only that, made sure he was blacklisted with any company he had contacts with. "A man who doesn't respect marriage can't be trusted," Larry declared. "Especially when his wife is dying in the hospital."

In this case, he asked me to stay outside while he talked with the beaver man. I reminded Larry that just a few moments ago, beaver man had tried to bash his head in.

"If you thought your wife was cheating on you, wouldn't you do the same?"

Of course, he had no respect for relationships outside of marriage, frequently stealing women from men they'd been dating. Likewise, even if he was dating a woman, he'd meet many others. But married women were strictly taboo, even if it was just a matter of semantics.

IV.

I received a number of calls for a photo shoot I'd scheduled for the evening and coordinated with the individuals involved. Once Larry got back out, he handed me a case. "What is it?" I asked.

"Open it."

It was the jade necklace with the ornate fox.

"You think Rebecca will like it?" Larry wanted to know.

"Man, this is too expensive."

"It's nothing," he shrugged it off. "Record a message for me and I'll have it sent ASAP."

"I can't take this, man."

"Take it. You saved my head from getting bashed in," he said, then rubbed his head. "I like my head the way it is."

I thanked him and asked, "Do you think it's a little too much to send when I barely know her?"

"Extremity is the only way to get things done in this world," Larry answered. "Guess what?"

He seemed especially exuberant. "What?"

"Shinjee called. She wants to meet for a private date. I get shivers just thinking about the possibility of holding her."

"Is that safe?"

"I can handle her. Also, we need to start preparations."

"For what?"

"We're filming a documentary about my factories and I'm giving you full access to record everything."

"Is this your new film?"

He winked and made a guttural sound that sounded kind of like a mean chuckle. "Maybe. Just know, this is going to be bigger than anything we've ever done before. Can you give me the disk?"

I handed it to him. He took out his digital monocle, scanned the contents in, and perused them.

"So?" I asked.

Inside the package was a small lock of white hair. Like most of the other wig samples from Chao Toufa, it looked like authentic human hair.

I saw a flash of anger flit across his face as his upper lip curled. He restrained himself with a sigh and sealed up the package, putting it inside his pocket.

"What's wrong?" I asked.

"We'll talk about this later. I need to prepare for my date. Besides, you look tired."

"I actually have a photo shoot tonight. Couple models coming over."

"Maybe I should change my plans and join you," he jested.

"Feel free. I think they'd love it."

Larry laughed. "Gotta stay true to my love. I'll see you at the factory in the morning."

"You sure you don't want me to come along? I can delay the shoot."

"And keep the models waiting? You'll crush their egos and I can't allow that. Plus, I think I can handle it this time. Just keep your phone on."

He ordered a car to take me home. I recorded a message to Rebecca thanking her for an interesting time. He zipped back to wherever it was that he was heading.

My cab arrived five minutes later and I jumped into the backseat. I dozed off and dreamt about a big python controlled by an Indian trainer for a circus. I got too close and the snake struck, biting my testicles. The pain from its fangs woke me up and I realized I was finally home. I hoped the dream didn't symbolize any unconscious woes I wasn't aware of.

V.

I hated recreating and resculpting violence on the camera as that was all I did during the African Wars. So I strayed from violence to the societal anomalies that invisibly lurked with us for my photography. The shoots I did changed depending on the propensities I was having at any given time. Recently, I'd been recreating American urban legends. I wanted to cover a gamut of smaller urban legends like the woman who got bit by an iguana at a supermarket, a cactus exploding with an army of tarantulas, and an AIDS Mary who infected hapless men and sent them letters welcoming them to "the world of HIV." Most nights, for every ten thousand photos I took, I discarded 9900 of them. As I got ready to click away, I wondered, like love (as Shinjee put it), if a person could discard 99% of their life and experience only the best 1%, would they think life a grand and beautiful thing?

Those ten thousand clicks were a tricky affair. I had to imprint, then selectively discard the images that were no good, luridity and sensationalism ignored as passé, wiping the model down with body wax to produce a shimmer of sweat reeking of demystified lust. Ten models arrived of mixed gender and race. Jimi looked like she was 15 but she was 29. Darlene looked like she was 26 but she was 18. Neither suffered from anorexia. They simply didn't like the taste of food. Once, it was poverty, war, and hunger that were the great evils of society. Now, it was white bread, carbs, and sweets.

I overheard three guys talking about how certain creams and soaps were good for tone and fleshiness. They exchanged recipes, talked about ten magazine covers that were like the Ten Commandments to them; *thou shalt look like me or suffer the damnable fires of mediocrity.* It was self-induced abandonment as they lamented the fact that they were two pounds overweight.

Zim Frog, as she called herself, encompassed a gallery of emotions; defiant, seductive, onerous, contemplative, indolent, rambunctious, and lethargic. She also smelled terrible as she refused showers. I had two assistants and three makeup artists to deal with her.

None of the models had tattoos as that would mean career suicide. Designers and photographers wanted to paint their own temporary head tattoos to match the outfits. I had to work with the designer to pick out the costumes and make sure the lighting fit. The makeup artists went with the typical statuesque look that resembled most shows and magazine covers. I hated it and had to show samples from my portfolio to indicate I wanted something with both less and more panache, the way Linda so masterfully balanced her talents.

I despised over-complicated cameras. Aperture, exposure, f-stops all meant nothing without the right model. Give the right woman jeans and a shirt, and she'd look a thousand times more striking than any woman in the most elaborate costume. Plus, post-production technology was so powerful, I could do anything after the fact except masquerade a lack of character. Swapping lenses helped, but a vacuous personality couldn't seem interesting with the best lens in the world. I used to run shoots with Linda all the time, do freelancing work for a variety of venues. She used to regale me with the intense drama between models as they competed for photographers and face time. Sex was just the stepping point and insecurities abounded. Plastic surgery had changed the landscape of fashion. Anyone could be a model if they were willing to lend their faces and bodies to image facilitators. Magazines had to start posting disclaimers that said, "None of our models have been image facilitated," when in fact many had, leading to a few scandals and editorial resignations.

I switched my camera on, then off, running about trying to capture a frame of a doctored moment that was really an embellishment in a chorus of discordant harmony. The world was a square frame and I played my part as visual scrivener, my fingers set to autopilot. This was the way I experienced most of my life, unable to change things, trying to maintain control through the visual canvas. I adjusted the level of flash to overcompensate for the monochromic palette that consumed the fake house set. Wine was being passed out to encourage drunk emanations in dizzying bouts of dazzling delirium. Phones of different shapes were distributed, a collection of old cell phones made into a costume on top of Jazz, a model who never spoke during shoots.

Handling the tarantulas was painful and the wrangler had to be particularly delicate as the two male models were terrified arachnaphobes. I used a Pinlighter 1887 for this scene, a camera that was slightly bigger than a pen that recorded images remarkably well. It was my camera of choice when recording Larry's movies as it gave me complete flexibility. If I had one complaint, it was that it was too light, even with automatic motion-stabilizing, so that the footage had to be corrected in post. Conveniently, I could position it anywhere and have it feed directly into my eye scanner. Automated hover lights with shifting brightness moved into place and seven additional cameras recorded the scene in 3D, projecting it onto a digital environment which I could shift and mold as I pleased. Any tree I wanted to download, any famous site I wanted to shoot against would be automatically recreated. If I wanted to get especially fancy, I could use a printer to create the physical environments, though that was time-consuming and wasteful. The tattoo artists could either map their designs in 3D and project it onto the model or do it live, though the latter gave less flexibility. My current design was in a desert with a whole lot of cacti.

After that scene wrapped, I saw I had a few missed calls. Most were from friends who wanted to hang out (well, to be more accurate, they wanted to hang out so I could help them be a contact to Larry who they wanted to ask for money). I was surprised to see a series of sevens and twos that I recognized as Rebecca Lian's number.

"Hey," I said as I called her back. "How are you?"

"Busy?"

"I have time to talk."

"Lovely necklace," she said. "It was a kind gesture and totally not necessary."

"You liked it?"

"My mom used to read me stories from Pu Songling about fox spirits who would seduce men and steal their souls."

I laughed. "There was no hidden meaning in my gift."

"I can't accept it."

"They had a no-return policy," I said, not actually knowing if they did. "And I wouldn't know what to do with it. Like I said in my message, consider it a thank you gift for lunch. We are business associates after all."

She looked at me, then simpered. "I'll be in Shanghai next week. Give me a call." She hung up.

"Nick! Nick!" The designer ran to me. "We have a problem."

In the dressing room, the mirror had been shattered. There was a male model that had been restrained by three others, his face a bloody goulash.

"I hate myself, I hate myself," he kept on repeating. "I'm so ugly, I'm so ugly."

"What happened?" I asked the designer.

"He tried to cut up his face, but the others stopped him," she told me.

They'd called the medics who arrived a few minutes later to roll him away. As they did, I saw his eyes. There wasn't fear or regret or even pain. Only self-loathing and repulsion aimed at himself. Acid reflux wasn't just limited to the physical.

4. Divine Humor

I.

"Hey, mister. That's quite a rod you got there. You know what would make a girl like me even happier?" I snapped awake to see a buxom nurse in a skimpy outfit talking to me. "An even bigger one. They have a special going on for penile enlargement at—" It was one of those 3D advertisements and I tried to ignore it. "Possible side effects include erectile dysfunction, severe hypotension, photophobia, prolonged erection, heavy migraines, stroke—" It'd been a long night. Magus, the model who mutilated himself, was in the surgery unit. Normally, it would have been a quick patch up, but this was the eighth time he'd had surgery in the past year and insurance was balking at paying. "—and sudden death. But isn't it worth it to get with a girl like me?"

Waiting here in the lobby, I was half-awake, half-asleep. More advertisements played and I tried to shut them off but was kindly told, "If you opt out of advertisements, there is an hourly fee for waiting in the lobby. The—"

I rubbed the mucus out of my eyes and fought back yawns. "Are you tired of having to watch your diet? Well, now you can eat all you want if you sign up for our specially bred tapeworms that can be fully financed—"

There were ads about the new fashion trend, "man-boobs." A few marketing dentists pointed out things I didn't need to protect myself against possible cancer if I didn't floss three times a day and coat my teeth with protective sealant. I'd already had enough work done on my teeth to last a lifetime and I still wasn't sure if any of it had been necessary. I hated the thought of spending even a cent more on them.

They finally approved Magus's insurance and took him in for image facilitation. "I want to look different this time around," he said and was told, "You've used your premiums for the year. Wait until next year."

I slept in the lobby, drowning out the ads. They used subcortical rays to invade my dreams. I was all right with that even if I dreamt of surgeries I didn't need just as long as I could sleep. Around eight in the morning, the doctors wrapped up and Magus looked like a brand new man. He gave me a fist pump and asked, "So when's the next shoot?"

II.

Outside the factory grounds of Chao Toufa, fifty protesters were keeping vigil. None of them wore wigs as they were a religious cult that believed wigs were immoral and encouraged sexual deviancy. I wondered if the bribes to the Ministry of Religion were late this month for them to allow this rally.

Security was extensive with tall walls, guard drones, and personnel around the perimeter to protect against people trying to steal wigs. There were fifteen gates and each required an eye scan, fingerprint key, voice identification measuring throat ululations, olfactory substantiation, and credit report. I didn't know why I was rushing. I was supposed to meet Larry at ten a.m. but he was nowhere in sight and wasn't picking up his phone either. No big surprise there. Fatigue overwhelmed me and I took a nap in one of the bunks, trying to get the subconscious images of dancing nurses pleading with me to get a "physical upgrade" out of my mind. I hated the way the hospital marketing department scrambled my neurons.

My phone rang late in the afternoon with a message from Larry that he would arrive shortly. Larry arrived at 5:32 in a custom-made sports car that was so exclusive, it wasn't even part of a brand. I'd never actually seen it before but I knew it cost him millions and was too expensive to get insured. It was sleek and aerodynamic, a titanium coat that gave it the appearance of a stealth jet on wheels.

"Can I take a picture of this thing?" I asked.

"Absolutely. You wanna go for a ride later?"

"Are you kidding? Of course." As he got out, I saw the bounce in his step, his joy pronounced in his beaming smile. "How'd it go?" I asked, already knowing the answer.

"She was a goddess in bed," he replied. "You have no idea how incredible she is. She's everything I could have hoped for and more. Just the way her body moved. It was the perfect shape." He placed his hands against his heart. "If I were to die right this moment, I'd die content."

"Everything worked out then?"

Larry gleamed. "I don't want to bore you with details of our debauchery, but it was a wild night. We're heading out to Xi'an later. She hasn't seen the Terracotta Warriors yet and she also loves lamb and they have that lamb at that specialty house I love. Her terracotta pie was incredible, best I ever had."

Vulgarities aside, I laughed too. "I guess that means no filming?"

"Just a slight delay. Work has got me depressed."

"Aren't you worried about her associates?"

"She wanted to come clean, but I told her not to bother, that I didn't care. You want to do an early dinner? I had a huge brunch, but I'm still starving. How do crab legs sound?"

We went to the private restaurant near the western lakes. The lakes were filled with ducks and swan. Larry pointed out the mandarin ducks who, according to folklore, always lived in pairs as they were monogamous. When one died, the other would die soon afterwards. I could see four of the factory buildings from our seat and many of the workers were leaving early as it was Friday, general policy set by his father so that they could get some rest as long as there were no pressing deadlines.

"She speaks seven languages fluently, man," Larry said. "Never made love to a woman who could start a sentence in French, continue in Japanese, Mandarin, Spanish, English, then finish in Korean. She's been trained you know, so she's learned advanced techniques to multiply pleasure. I'd heard rumors, but man, I—" and he started giggling.

"Calm down, you're scaring me," and I laughed as well.

Several old Chinese women brought out the crab in spicy sauce that was mixed in garlic, lemon, and a whole lot of Cajun pepper sauce. Gumbo soup was served on the side as well as buttered rice that was steaming hot. Larry got up and hugged one of the old ladies. A rotund woman with a ruddy face, she was in charge of the kitchen. Larry affectionately called her *Laolao* and told me, "When my dad used to send me to bed without dinner, *Laolao* sent me up sweet honey biscuits that were the best I ever had."

She giggled. "When you have a son, I'll make the same biscuits for him."

The crab legs were huge, hard-shelled, and juicy. I doused them in the sauce and ate them with the rice. My tongue burned, but it was culinary heaven.

"Did you know king crab leg fishing used to be one of the deadliest professions in the world?" Larry asked.

"Are they dangerous animals?"

"That's not why it's dangerous. But yeah, they are to each other. If you leave them in a tank together too long, they'll cannibalize each other. And if one dies while it's held, it'll release toxins that'll kill the other crabs."

"I thought people were bad to each other."

"Nature is brutal. But not as much as hypothermia and drowning in the ocean." Larry cracked apart a shell and bit into the white meat. "These are so amazing. The best ones used to only be in Alaska. But these days, crabs can only be raised in farms. Did you know we own a farm in Shanghai? They're hellishly hard to maintain. But the crabs taste so good." Larry took a sip of wine. "I used to hate crab when I was a kid. Hated seafood in general."

"Me too. Especially sushi. I thought it was gross."

"Same here," Larry answered. "How'd you get over it?"

"Linda. She loved seafood and we ate it every chance we had." He waved his crab leg at me. "Mine was a girl named Venus."

"You told me this one."

Larry laughed. "Well I still don't love sushi. I hear fish used to be fresh, but these days, all the farm-raised stuff tastes terrible raw." He snapped apart some tough shells. "On the way here, some show host was talking about how the galaxy is getting bigger faster than they thought. And I wondered, what if the galaxy weren't getting bigger, but we're actually shrinking? I mean our entire planet, and we just didn't know it."

"I think it'd make for an interesting film."

"You remember we were thinking about making a universe shot in 58 Random Deaths?" *58 Random Deaths and Unrequited Love* was the first film Larry and I worked on. He wanted to make parallels between the death of galaxies and the death of random individuals.

"I still think we should have put it in."

He nodded. "I can't believe how many films we've made together. You know what all of them have in common?"

"We made them?"

"They all failed."

"How do you define failure?" I asked.

"They failed to make back the money they cost and they failed to get critical acclaim," Larry answered. He put his food down. "Do you ever wonder if maybe I don't got what it takes to be a filmmaker? These days, it's all about multiple choices, sexual encounters, and virtual scenarios. I loved films back when they were just on a screen and the director made the story and camera choices."

"Some of our films did get critical acclaim," I said, knowing Larry was his own harshest critic. "And even if they weren't box office successes, at least you got to tell the stories you wanted to."

"Yeah. Isn't it ironic? Chao Toufa provides the hair for all the stars that are gonna show up at the GEAs (Global Entertainment Awards), but none of my films have even been up for a nomination. I mean, literally, we provide the wig for Jesus Christ." He took sausages out of his gumbo, chewed on two shrimp. "Shinjee's only 21 years old. You should have seen the way she acted. She was just a kid to me. I'm about to turn 40, man, and I'm trying to act like I'm 21." He scratched his forehead, his temples taut with wrinkles. "Did I ever tell you my dad sent me to a high school in Sweden?"

"No."

"I'd been kicked out of eight schools already. He wanted to teach me a lesson. He took away all my privileges and sent me to this poverty-stricken school without anything. It was a brutal six months man. Kids bullied me. I got my rib bones broken three times. I lived in this old apartment and the toilet used to break all the time. That was when I caught that rare strain of typhoid that nearly killed me. Before that, I used to be so picky about food. But then, my mouth got puffy with blood and all my shit was bloody and I was feverish for two weeks. I learned to appreciate even the cheapest food. The nurses finally got to me and saved my life. I tried to reach my dad, tried to reach anyone, but there was no way to get out. He would have left me there to die. I learned my lesson, man."

"Without money, life can be pretty shitty?" I guessed.

He shook his head. "Don't let others have any say where you go. That's why I got sent to the army. My dad wanted to teach me another lesson."

A part of me wondered what exactly had transpired between him and Shinjee.

"I've spent all this money and have nothing to show for it," Larry continued. "My friends are secretly happy. They all pretend to support me, but deep down, they want me to fail. You know why? Because none of them followed their dreams and they're stuck doing dreary business jobs they hate. Yeah, they're rich, but they can't even enjoy it because they always want more. They don't even watch my movies. The other moviemakers want me to fail too. They think I'm just an upstart trying to buy my way in. Which is true to a certain extent, but I don't care. They're so snobby. How many millions did they spend going to film school instead of just getting out there and living life, you know? All of them kissed my ass when things were looking good but as soon as the critics turned on me, none of them returned my calls until they needed financing and then it was like, 'Your films are brilliant.'"

"It's not personal, man," I answered. "You said yourself there was a Chinese general who lost 99 battles but won the hundredth one which was the one that counted."

"How many generals lost everything because they didn't know when to retreat?" he pondered. "Chao Toufa has been having lots of problems over the past year. Maybe I should be more involved here."

"Did that girl hit you in the head or something?"

"Why?"

"Yesterday, you were saying you wanted to leave everything behind to Russ."

He seemed puzzled. "Was that yesterday?"

I nodded.

He laughed. "Maybe I'm being a touch melodramatic. Beautiful women always do that to me. Let's give it one more shot. This new film I was mentioning. It'll be the biggest ever."

"Can you give more details?"

"At first, I thought maybe I'd do a documentary about my family. Or maybe I'd make it into a film about a rich family with an idiot son who squandered everything. Would that be too cliché? I don't want to be that idiot," he said. "I'm starting to settle on one idea."

"What is it?"

"I've always wanted to do an epic about the Baldification.

Maybe call it *Bald New World*. Do a film about the people in it. It'll be massive. I guarantee you. This'll be the film that everyone notices."

"No one's figured out what exactly happened yet."

"That's what the businesses would like people to think," Larry said. "What if I told you people like my father knew exactly what happened?"

"What do you mean?"

"Well—"

Behind us, one of the factories exploded, blowing the plates off the table and knocking us both back. A second factory blew up, the fire blasting against our faces. My ears were ringing and the smoke made everything hazy. I heard a third boom but couldn't tell where it was from. Sirens were ringing.

"Larry!" I called. "Larry! Are you all right?"

Larry got up, his face smeared with Cajun sauce. He looked at me, then at the factories. He wiped his face and ran to his car. I followed and saw him change into a white uniform that clung close to his body. It appeared plastic, a shiny post-modern sheen about it that made me think of a futuristic punk rocker.

"Does it look cool? It's fire-resistant," he said.

"We should get out of here," I replied.

"There might still be people stuck in there. Get somewhere safe."

Larry hopped back in his car and I jumped in the other side.

"I don't have an extra suit," he said.

"I'll be careful."

Both doors shut and he switched the car to manual control as we sped towards the factory.

"See how smooth it drives? She's a thing of beauty. How is it Germans build the best cars in the world?"

The first factory to explode was still partially standing, though the conflagration had consumed most of it. The heat was scorching and the smoke was drowning the building in debris.

The doors were sealed shut and several people were outside, wailing and crying. One of the women had heavy burns and her face was a sooty mask.

"Why are you all still here?" Larry demanded as he stuck his head out the window. "Get away from the fire!"

"There's still people inside."

The factory doors were sealed shut and the fire was preventing people from getting too close.

"Get out of the way," Larry ordered the people standing about. Then to me, "Get out."

"You can't go in there."

"This is not a discussion. Get out!"

"I'll come with you."

He looked at me. "You want to die?"

"Maybe I want to get some footage for our new documentary."

He turned to me. "What would you do if I gave up the film business?"

"Make seven more films that'll fail at the box office. I'll dedicate all of them to you."

He laughed. "Hold onto your seat."

He hit the accelerator, but before it hit the building, the car shut down. The AI notified us, "Safety protocols have overridden manual control. Please—"

"Can you go to the back and deactivate the AI?"

"How?" I asked.

"Press the manual-override button on the panel," Larry said. "I'll pop the hatch."

I stepped out, but before I could ask where it was, Larry sped forward, crashing his expensive car through the front doors.

Damn him.

All three stories were burning and the throng outside watched helplessly. Various bystanders were trying to dial the fire department, but phones were offline. It smelled of burning machinery and the stench was hard to bear.

"—was a big bursting sound. I turned around and the whole mechanical arm fell down," a woman described the scene. "I ran for the door and right when I got out, the whole thing collapsed behind me. There was no warning anything was wrong and none of the machines detected overloads."

Billows of smoke fumed furiously up. Part of the building crumbled and all the remaining windows on the west side burst. I coughed from the smoke. A few people tried to push me back to a safer distance. I insisted on staying put. My eyes were glued to the door. *Where's Larry?*

Visibility was dampening. The fire was intensifying and it resembled a living force, devouring everything in its wake, gorging on itself and swelling with fiery cholesterols. I wanted to rush in, but the blaze was too strong. Segments of the roof caved in and the fractals within the fire bisected, sundered, and expanded. There was a raucous creaking sound. I forced myself to step forward, covered in sweat. My hands were sooty. I loosened my shirt, wiped my forehead. "Larry?!!!" I shouted. "Larry!"

A speaker with a mellifluous voice declared, "Fellow brothers and sisters, please calmly head to the central building. Everything is under control, everything is well. We are suffering technical glitches that will be resolved shortly." Soothing classical music from the automated emergency record was blaring to the image of decimation in front of me.

The explosions were too coincidental to be an accident. Was it an attack? During the African Wars, scenes like this were so common, I got inured to them as I spliced and edited them to resemble action films. I'd never actually seen burnt people without the digital barrier. In front of me, a man was screaming in pain, rubbing his charred arms that looked like they would crumble. Another woman's hair was cinders, her mouth starkly vermilion against the blackened skin. I hated the smell of burning. It was consuming my nostrils and Larry was nowhere in sight. A dozen people rushed out the door and were immediately taken to safety by the ambulances that had arrived. A pair of automated hovercopters (a hybrid form of a helicopter and airplane that didn't have rotors but used engines for more stability) descended with huge buckets of water as they hosed the factory.

"Where's Larry?" I asked them. "Have you seen Larry?"

"He's back there trying to save Mr. Foster."

"Where's Mr. —?"

There was a boom, a tempestuous swirl of fire that was formless, burning in irregular spasms. The building was collapsing. Through the door, I could see one of the conveyor belts melt. The smoke intensified and I was coughing to try to exhume the ashes. Someone tried to drag me away but I pushed them off, wanting—needing to stay. "Larry!" I shouted again. I wondered if I should go in but there was another blast and it looked like the building was going to implode. That's when I saw a white figure through the smoke, forming like someone was molding the shadows into a sculpture. Something was galloping forward with a scintillating bell—a cow, mooing and running. Behind, it was Larry. He was carrying an old man. Several hospital workers were ready with a gurney to take the man to safety. Larry's face was charred and his white suit was covered in streaks of black. He placed the man on the gurney, looked around and spotted me.

"Are you all right?" I asked and put my arm on his shoulder only to flinch as it was still hot.

Larry petted the cow. "Thanks to this fellow, I am."

"And the car?"

He waved it off. "I put it to good use."

"You're crazy, man. Aren't you scared of anything?"

"Are you kidding me? I was scared off my ass," Larry declared. Behind, we heard the fire sirens of a fleet of hovercopters. The full rescue team arrived and carted Larry to safety.

III.

Russ was apoplectic. Five of the factory buildings had been targeted and four of those were beyond repair. The first few hours had been spent putting the fire out. Once that had been done, it was damage assessment in the conference room. While the police continued their investigation outside, Russ targeted his rage at the heads of security. "How could something like this happen?"

"We warned you about the Colonel."

"Do we even know it's the Colonel who did this?!"

The guy who couldn't look me in the eye was ripping into these security chiefs that were twice as big as him. Larry had asked me to sit in while the doctors checked him for burns. What I gathered from all the yelling was that no one had any idea what had happened.

A nurse came in and told me, "Larry asked for you."

Russ said, "If Larry's okay, tell him I need to see him immediately."

I followed her out and was expecting to go to the infirmary, but she led me through the lobby and outside where we crossed the field. It still smelled of ash and the speakers were still playing the soppy classical music of violins and pianos. "Where are we going?" I asked.

"To see Larry."

Larry was waiting at the southern gate with a new car.

"Are you going somewhere?" I asked, surprised.

He leaned in close. "There's a traitor and I don't know who it is."

"Working for the Colonel?"

He shook his head. "I got the report back. There were no casualties, even though there were a lot of injuries. Whoever did this waited until most of the people cleared out. That's not the Colonel's style. She'd want to maximize violence."

"Who do you think it is?"

Larry stared at me somberly. "We have too many enemies. It could be anyone. I've been away too long and neglected my duties. I wanted to be a filmmaker. But when it comes down to it, I'm a wigmaker."

"There's nothing stopping you from being both."

"Except these huge explosions."

"You're not hurt?"

"The suit worked perfectly. Thank George for me if you see him. He has a bunch of crazy suits he's been working on," Larry said. "All cancelled military projects."

"I've heard. Skeleton projects."

He seemed amused by what I'd said. "Most wealthy people have skeletons."

"That's not just the wealthy."

Larry took out the capsule from Dr. Asahi. "If it's someone against us, then we can fight back. But if it's related to this, then we deserve it."

"What are you talking about?"

"A part of me wishes I could have lived up to my dad's expectations. And a part of me repels from that idea. It looks like I got to either go my own way and give it all up, or fight for his dream and rebuild the factories. I feel I should apologize to you."

"Why?"

"I've dragged you along in my dream. Don't be too disappointed."

"Why would I be disappointed?"

"There's things about my family, about my past that—well, just don't be disappointed."

"Are you kidding, man? No matter what happens, it doesn't change the fact that the last decade has been the best time of my life," I said, and I meant it.

To my surprise, Larry appeared to tear up. "Kind of you to say that, man. I-I should get going."

"Going where?"

"I gotta take care of some business."

"Is it safe for you to go alone?"

"If whoever planned this wanted me, I'd already be dead."

"But—"

"I have some stuff I got to take care of and honestly, I don't know who to trust in there."

"Let me come with you."

"Not this time. I'll explain everything later, but right now, I have some stuff I have to take care of on my own."

"Lar—"

He stopped me. "Can you stop by my place later tonight? I'll explain everything then."

I saw the cold obstinacy in his eyes. "Yeah, of course. What should I tell Russ?"

He shrugged. "Nothing. Don't go back in there. Don't take any calls from anyone until we talk later. I have to go now." He was about to get into his new vehicle when he stopped. "Did you ever talk to Rebecca again?"

"She called me about the gift," I replied. "I might see her when she's visiting Shanghai."

"Don't argue with her, please."

He got in and drove away.

IV.

I headed home and turned my phone off to all calls except from Larry. I kept on hearing the explosion in my head and my ears were still ringing. The water in my bath was set to a comfortable heat and I scrubbed the soot off my body. The soap wasn't very effective and I made the water hotter to try to alleviate the soreness. Some of the black spots on my knees turned out to be bruises from the initial blast when it had flung us to the floor. Every time I took a sniff, my nostrils smelled of ash. What had Larry been talking about? What skeletons was he hiding?

There had always been some high-ranking officer to tell me

what to do with the footage in the past. Even on our shoots, Larry told me what he was aiming for. Now, the film was rudderless and I didn't know where to point the camera.

The news stations were covering the factory explosions from a bird's-eye view. Investigators still hadn't uncovered anything (at least they hadn't announced anything publicly). The memory of the explosion suddenly provoked the smell of burnt gumbo and Cajun sauce. It was disgusting. I turned off the news after the focus turned to the garbage epidemic in the Western nations and the images of the mountains of radioactive trash no one knew what to do with.

I tried taking a look at the digital photos from the photo shoot but felt an unexpected dread. The prospect of touching up all the pictures and adding post effects to make the models more beautiful seemed burdensome. Why was I always working so hard to make people more beautiful than they really were? When images of Magus popped up, pretentiously happy with two other women, I shut off the computer.

Linda always knew the right thing to say in moments like this. She didn't even need to say anything. Just having her by my side could calm my nerves. Now, I didn't have anyone I could talk to. I never thought I'd long for the hospital lobby and their holographic advertisements. Moments of weakness like this stirred the flesh in me. I flipped to a channel I knew I shouldn't, turning on the holographic cameras.

"Need a friend?" an attractive Asian woman asked. A second for the memory to upload. "Oh it's you, Nick. Are you ready to do more than a preview? We have everything here for reasonable rates and we even have specials, direct interfacing at—"

I shut it off. These virtual girl addictions were a disease and I knew I shouldn't be drawn in. I had friends who had given up their marriages for computerized companions. No matter how bad the isolation felt, I couldn't replace it with artificial affection. Who could have guessed advances in technology would make prostitution obsolete and endanger so many relationships?

I went back into the shower for an extra scrubbing. I turned the water super hot. It pounded my head like burning rain. But it still couldn't wipe away the memory of fire.

V.

It was late when I got to Larry's penthouse. His place was on the top floor of a high-rise located within the second ring of Beijing. I knocked but the door was open. "Larry?" I called. "Larry." I entered as he often left the door unlocked. Took my shoes off knowing how much he hated shoes inside. There were posters from all of his movies, various props including model spaceships and alien costumes lining the living room. A gallery of mannequins that looked human were on display, adorned in erotic outfits. Larry was sitting naked on his sofa, watching one of our old films. "Can you explain what you were talking about earlier?" I asked, but he didn't answer me.

There was the tattoo of a big frog right above his belly which he'd gotten after his mother said that was her birth dream. It was colored sapphire and there was a Mandarin character for *frog*, though one of the lines was misspelled. There were beer cans to either side of him and I was about to grab one when I saw his face, mouth agape, bloody holes perforating his neck and legs. They were tiny and looked too small to be knife wounds or bullet holes. It was as though he'd been needled to death. But by what? He was pallid and resembled an FX mask we'd made of him. Only, I saw the veins within and there was a level of muscle detail there we'd never put in a fake. My legs wobbled and my arms shook. *Larry, you idiot. Why did I let you go alone?* Random memories sprang to mind; chasing a pair of religious girls and running away from their religious co-believers when they found out what we were after; playing strip poker with strangers in the snow; the nights he took me out drinking after my divorce because I was so depressed.

I remembered him explaining, "I make movies so I can try to change fate. Doesn't work very well though. Anyone who isn't a fatalist doesn't get the joke."

"What joke?"

"That God created death as a joke on humanity for feeling so self-important."

"Isn't a joke supposed to be funny?" I asked.

He mused on it. "One day, I'll tell you the answer. Promise me you'll laugh?"

I shook his hand playfully then.

And now, here was the joke. Only, it wasn't funny and I couldn't laugh.

It appeared his body had been dragged here because there was very little blood on the sofa. But from where? That was when I heard a scuffling sound. Looking over to the side, I saw Shinjee with four big North Korean goons.

"You-you did this!" I shouted, then charged straight at her.

Two of the thugs tried to impede me, but I punched one in the face and kicked the other in the groin. I grabbed Shinjee by the hair, but another thug bear-hugged me from behind and choked me. "I'll kill you all!" I threatened. "I can't believe he trusted you!"

"You think I did this?" Shinjee asked, outraged. She reeked of perfume and false indignation. "I found him like this!"

"Sure you did!" I yelled, trying to get the big guy off me.

Another thug approached and slugged me in the face. I tried to fight but the pain was getting too much for me. One of them threw me to the floor and kicked me in the belly. More feet swarmed my way and I suddenly had a flashback to my childhood. It enraged me and I laughed defiantly. "You guys should do feet massages." I felt an explosion inside my gut and four pairs of legs assailed me until I saw a huge fist coming my way and—

VI.

I tried opening my eyes but it was dark. I was blindfolded and felt a cold chill. There was nothing covering my body. I was naked and my arms and legs were tied behind me.

"Are you up?" I heard, immediately smelling strong perfume. Shinjee.

"What do you want?"

"I'm trying to help you."

"I don't want your help!"

"Keep your voice down," she whispered furiously. "If you don't listen to me right now, you will live a life of misery and die without anyone knowing you've disappeared."

"What?"

"They're taking you to a labor camp, either in Russia or near the Manchurian border."

"Why?"

"It's too complicated to explain. Take this," she said, and put a key in my palm that stuck by an adhesive. She stuffed a pill in my mouth. "Eat this."

"What is it?"

"They're going to inject you with something that'll make you pass out for the whole trip. This'll wake you a few hours after you get knocked out. Swallow quickly."

I was tempted to bite her fingers, but realized I didn't have any other choice than to trust her. "When you wake up, free yourself and get out of the truck within thirty seconds or they'll release sleeping gas. It'll be an automated driver so you'll be all right as long as you get out quickly. If you do get out, disappear so no one finds you. Think of it as a second chance to be whoever you want to be."

"If I get out, I'll find you," I warned her.

"I don't blame you for being angry. I didn't want this to happen to him either. He was too naive to survive in a world like ours."

I was already plotting my revenge when I heard her abruptly make her exit. I heard grunts, then heavy steps. Something sharp pierced my elbow. Nap time.

It felt like I'd blinked and I was already up. I was groggy. My body was encased in something cold and metallic. I was standing upright. From the bouncing and heavy engine noises, I knew I was in a vehicle. The key was adherent to my palm. I used it to unlock my manacles, then removed my blind. I was in a truck with about seventy others, all of whom were restrained naked against the slabs. They were unconscious prisoners and a part of me wished I could help them. But as soon as I stepped forward, an alarm blared. I had thirty seconds before they released the sleeping gas. I felt for the poor slobs who were being shipped off to a life of slavery. I sprinted for the door and opened it, jumping out, then tumbled off the road, scraping my elbows and the side of my back. The harsh reek of asphalt wracked me. It was freezing and I was buck naked. I wondered if I should follow the road back but then saw a car coming from behind, an escort in case of any mishaps. This constituted a mishap. Someone ordered from a speakerphone on the car, "Stay where you are!"

There was a forest a few meters from the road and I ran into it. My feet hurt as they had no protection against the stones, branches, and dirt. Still, the pain was no match for my desperation. I ran without thinking, ran without any specific destination. I was running to run. There were too many trees, tall, goliath bark, shadowy skyscrapers that formed this wooden city. A panoply of leaves above provided an umbrella, though the moonlight cast an eerie luminescence. Parts of my body were feeling itchy and I realized mosquitoes were swarming me even though I couldn't see them. I swatted away my invisible foes and as I did, I remembered that Larry was dead. My skin, already numb from the cold, became even more frigid. My eyes were blind to the geography. Poor Larry. Shinjee called you naive. I thought you were too brave. I never should have let you go alone.

Even if I couldn't have done anything to help, at least we could have died together, brothers in life and death. You were the closest thing to family I had. *If there is a God in Heaven, please help me escape so I can avenge Larry.* I hadn't been expecting anything like a literal salvation. But I saw a bright light in the distance that made lined contours of the forest, vertical strips of black backlit by a shining halo. Was a miracle awaiting me? Had some higher power come down to give me aid, perhaps a mission, some super powers to allow me to overcome my foes? *After I avenge Larry, I will undertake any mission you send me on. Have some heretics you want me to deal with? Send me and I will be your avenging angel! I will make the punishments of the Old Testament seem merciful in comparison. Just save me please. I am useless to you as an angry forest spirit wandering pointlessly about.*

When I arrived at the light, I was shocked to see a huge glowing cross. It was a building of some sorts. Perhaps a church? I launched myself through the front door, ready to receive my mission from God. This was as close to a burning fire as I was going to get and unlike Moses, I was willing to take my divine commission. Desperation demanded total humility. To my surprise, the pews were filled with mid-aged women who looked at me and gasped. I looked down and remembered I was naked. Screaming ensued.

"I'm here to answer the call of God!" I declared.

"The Devil cometh in many forms!" a man at the front altar declared. "Arrest him!"

"No no no, you don't understand. I prayed for a miracle. I prayed for this—"

"Beware of the wolf in sheep's clothing. But this wolf doesn't even bother with his clothing!"

A bunch of men rushed towards me and tied me up, afraid I was going to corrupt their womenfolk. Had I just exchanged one prison for another?

5. Thou Shalt Not Live on Bread Alone

I.

I never missed sleep so much. They had me tied up against the wall with rope. The room was freezing and lit by candles. It smelled of befoulment and blood. A bony man approached. His lips were dry and I wished I could use lip balm to get rid of the dead skin hanging from his mouth. He didn't have a wig on, though he wore a hooded cloak like a wizard from those MMORPG games I used to play. The skin clung tightly to his cheeks and the jaw muscles stretched when he spoke, giving him a skeletal facade. He had large blue eyes even though he appeared Asiatic, and he leaned on a staff, elderly in age.

"My name is Elias Mardi," he said. "Most people call me Mardi. What's your name?"

I figured I'd make one up. "Terrence Kang."

"Mr. Terrence Kang. Why are you here?"

I explained briefly about the North Korean spies, the labor camp, and my escape into their church.

Mardi pounded the ground with his staff. "I've heard a lot of crazy stories, but none like that. Let's try again. Why are you here?"

"I told you, I was—"

The old man flung his wrist with a speed I didn't expect. A thin whip sprang out of nowhere and slashed me across my chest. Red ripped apart my skin and the piercing sensation forced me to howl.

"What are you doing?!" I demanded.

"The first step to absolution is confession. You have lied to me twice already. I won't tolerate a third."

"What am I lying about?"

"Your name is Nicholas Guan," he said. "Why are you here?"

Had they checked my fingerprints? Had they scanned my

blood? There were a hundred ways they could have checked my identity and now they had me at a disadvantage. What kind of answer was the old man looking for?

I decided to ask him directly. "Why do you think I'm here?"

He lifted his staff and pressed it against my neck. "You're like all the other sinners, hoping for a moment of perverse pleasure by corrupting our innocents with a display of your genitals!"

They took me for a flasher? It was such a strange accusation I didn't know how to reply.

"How did you find out about our service?" Mardi demanded. "How much do you know about Yillah?"

"What's Yillah?"

A lash came for my arm and it felt like it tore off flesh. "Don't pretend to be ignorant! I know you've heard of our village. You're not the first to try and corrupt our maidens! What stories did you hear? That we were a village of women ready to be taken for your carnal desires?"

I recognized the glow in his eyes all too well, the illogical fury, the insecure fear of being proven a fool, and the small brained idiocy. It was what I'd grown up with, saying whatever I could to stop the beatings my biological father inflicted. Something inside of me hardened. "That's right. I came to steal all your women. I knew once they saw me, they wouldn't be able to resist. So what? You think you could provide pleasure for them, old man?"

He seemed taken aback by my change in tone. "At least now you've spoken the truth."

"Where are all the ladies? I can't wait to introduce them to the ways of the world."

"Is that why you made films that were pornographic and a corruptive influence on the innocents of the world?"

"I never filmed a porno," I said, realizing that if he knew my name, he could have easily searched the movies I made.

"Your recent film," and he consulted a list. "*Rodenticide* featured a prostitute in the leading role, did it not?"

"She was a good prostitute," I said. "She helps the main character in his protest to save the lives of rats."

"You would value the life of a rat more than a human being?"

"The movie wasn't putting a value on rats versus men, but saying when you devalue any life, then—" but I was cut off by another lash.

I gritted my teeth.

"The list of your films goes on as does the sexual explicitness and gratuitous violence. You are a man that specializes in beautifying violence and shamelessly exploiting what should be kept private between a man and woman. Are you a married man?"

"I was."

"So you divorced your wife?"

"Yes."

"Was it for marital infidelities?"

"No."

"Then why did you divorce?"

I stared at him. "What?"

"Don't you even know why you divorced your wife?"

"I know why I divorced her, but it's none of your business."

"I already know why. All you movie types are the same. Lust, desire, envy. You wanted other women, did you not?" My fists tensed as he continued. "It is against the laws of God and Yillah for man to be with more than one woman! Marriage is a sacred oath you take before Heaven and you desecrated it. For that, you deserve death a million times over."

"Don't bring my ex-wife into this."

"What do you care? You divorced her."

"Shut up."

"Does the truth bother you?"

"What do you know about the truth? You're a coward who hits a man that's tied up," I said. "You don't deserve my breath." I tried to spit but my mouth was too dry and all I could do was make the gesture.

Inside, I was fuming, so angry, I could barely contain my breath.

I guess my gesture pissed him off because his whip lashed me again. I wanted to scream, but I bit my lip and glowered at him. He whipped me again and again. I guffawed as hard as I could. "Go ahead. Kill me if you have to. I've already corrupted all your women. Secretly, they're fantasizing about me. Oh, Nick, take me now."

"Shut your blasphemous mouth or I will rip your tongue out!"

"Go ahead! You think I'm afraid of death!"

He was about to lash me again but stopped. "Your will is still strong. Let's see how long it lasts." He put out the candles, leaving me in darkness. He slammed a door shut as he left. I was relieved until I thought of Linda and I tried to remember why exactly our marriage had fallen apart. All that came to me were memories of the good times we enjoyed together. Her fingers used to quiver when she slept. She'd watch Chinese drama shows until six in the morning, addicted to the historical whimsies of some ancient dynasty with princesses and consorts vying for power. She didn't like pillows and sometimes in the morning, she used her hand to make a small pillow for her head. Often, she'd be smiling in her sleep, and every morning, she had an unusual tale to tell from the meanderings of her subconscious during the night. I wished I could hold her the way I used to, feel her legs against mine, rub her back and hear her breathe softly. At least Mardi's exit meant I could dose off.

II.

The itching and my burning stomach woke me. I had to use the bathroom really badly and the mosquito bites over my body were tingling. I wanted to scratch them but I had no way of relieving the itch. As for my stomach, it felt like it was going to explode. I hadn't eaten anything in a while and I could feel the chemicals in my stomach burning their way through excess. There was no other option other than to piss on the floor in front of me. My bowels pushed and tugged and I tried to hold back. But eventually, the muscles in my stomach couldn't contain themselves and a stream of diarrhea splattered down the wall and my legs. It was disgusting and smelled terrible, the liquid waste forming chunks along my calves. But it warmed my cold legs so I was grateful for that reprieve. Countless others must have suffered the same fate here if they were imprisoned in the same manner.

Now that my stomach had relief, the itchiness aggravated. There were bumps all over my skin and the allergic reaction was causing me to tremble. I shook and twisted and tried anything I could do to make it stop. But that only made things worse. These tiny blood-sucking insects made my life hell by a hundred itches. I had to think about something else, had to divert my mind. Except the only question that came to mind was, *are you ready to die, Nick Guan?* I didn't know the answer. Yes, earlier, when Mardi had been whipping me, I didn't care and would have invited it. But now that I was immersed in darkness, I wondered about the things I should have done in my life. The pain from his lashes stung bad enough. The cold numbed the lacerations.

My stomach grumbled—hungry. *You just took a dump*, I protested. But the growls made its grumpiness evident. I was also thirsty. I tried to remember the torture-preparation classes we had in the army. It was a classic technique to enervate prisoners, deny them food and water to weaken their will. I could probably handle a day or two of this, but more? What would happen, covered in this pitch black? They'd warned about hallucinations. Who would I see? The last time I ate was that crab and the memory of that sauce still brought back the burning sensation. *Larry, man, what am I going to do?* But Larry was dead. Would anyone be looking for me? Maybe some of my photography crew. Then again, they knew I tended to go on trips with Larry and vanished for long periods of time. After they found Larry, would they search for me? But who would think to look out in the middle of nowhere? It was times like this I wished they'd have allowed the credit agencies their way, adding computerized chips under our skin to track us. The religious groups had fought fervidly against their implementation, certain it meant the mark of the beast, 666, the sign that a person had turned against the Church. It was meant to make shopping easy but so many of the fanatics burned themselves and committed sacrificial suicide, the companies gave up. Is that what John dreamt of two millennium ago when he wrote *Revelations*? At least with the chip, anyone looking for me could have found me with a simple scan.

If I were to die, was there anyone I would contact, anyone I would have anything left to say to? It relieved me to know the answer was a *no*. Even with Linda, nothing had gone unspoken. We'd said too much to each other, which had always been the problem. We analyzed everything to death, every stupid word.

It was too bad I didn't have a child. There were no many things I could have taught him, like how everything everyone tells you growing up is bullshit. Don't believe anyone except your own experiences. I could tell him about how insane my biological family was, how cruel and selfish they were and how even after all they did, they still couldn't let go, only thinking about themselves. He wouldn't have to have a chip on his shoulder about family the way I did, ashamed of the way I was, eager to please, afraid of censure. He'd be more confident, do things with ease that I struggled to achieve. He would know how to treat family with respect and thoughtfulness, the little things I never knew when I married Linda because no one ever treated me with kindness and respect. Instead, I grew up learning family was a terrible thing, wanting never to go home, wishing they would all disappear so I could have my freedom. I even resented elderly people in my youth because they rebuked me for my terrible family, telling me to stay away from their children (my "friends") as I was from a bad family. When I first met Linda's family, I was so taken aback by their kindness, I got suspicious. Why were they being so good to me? They were much wealthier than I was and there was nothing I could give them. Had they mistaken me for someone else? Were they secretly going to get rid of me while smiling in my face? Linda laughed at my wariness and assured me, "This is what family is."

No yelling, no beating me when I didn't want to do something, no castigations saying I deserved death for not listening. Instead, an inexplicable kindness and thoughtfulness, calls asking after my health. I'd endured a poverty-stricken childhood and thought I could bear anything. But I wasn't prepared for this sort of kindness. I felt undeserving, unworthy. Was that the beginning of the end of our marriage?

My unborn child, you'll never have to worry about my illogical fear of death. You'll never have to grow up being told every day that if you didn't please your biological father, you would be beaten to pulp and die a dog's death. You'll never have to have a dumbly narcissistic mother who only chased after other men and didn't care what happened to you as long as she was happy. You won't have to have a brain-damaged sister who took pride in lacking common sense and never listened to the fact that I wanted nothing to do with my biological family and insisted on bringing them back into my life even though I asked her a thousand times not to do so. You won't have to rely on fake friends you thought were family because your definition of family was so pathetic and then get disappointed when they left you over nothing and then came crawling back when they found out you were famous. You would think me pathetic for the way I sought so eagerly to call people who didn't have the faintest idea about relationships family. *It's all right though. I won't hide my foibles. You should know the truth about your father.*

Linda broke my heart, but she also liberated me in ways you couldn't imagine. She's my only family. Larry was family too, but he's dead now.

In the end, I failed him just like I failed Linda. I let him go alone when every instinct in me told me not to let him go by himself.

I deserve everything I'm going to get for the next few days.

III.

"Have you no shame?" Mardi asked as the light caused my eyes to cringe. I hadn't slept, but I hadn't been awake either. "Get a hose in here."

Two men entered with a hose and fired water at me. The spray hit me like a kick to the chest and they wiped the feces away with the water blasts. I stuck my tongue out, trying to get a lick. The water was sweet and tasted better than any nectar.

"This is a special town," Mardi told me. "Divinely inspired 30 years ago to be a bulwark against the madness of this world. Yillah was our prophetess, the great messenger who brought us hope by creating a village here to be protected from the outside world. She taught us that the only chance for salvation was cutting away the cancer, chopping off our arm if we needed to protect ourselves against iniquity. There's no hope in the world you're from. Nothing is sacred. Everyone would damn the world rather than sacrifice just a little bit of themselves."

Like all zealots, he was a preacher and he loved hearing himself speak. He went on and on, first about the strange miracles Yillah performed. Then he proceeded to lecture me about how evil the world was. According to him, Yillah was God reincarnated in womanly form and one of the proofs was that she never had a period.

"Son, I have a job today, a mission if you might," Mardi explained. "Have you heard of the Inquisition?"

"Don't call me 'son'," I said.

He ignored me and leaned on his staff. "The Inquisition was a nasty, but essential, part of the Church. Guillotines and other tortures were brutal, but nothing compared to the executions developed in China over 5000 years. There used to be a death manual for executioners and killing was an art. I have no interest in killing you. We are in the business of saving souls. But we've adapted various punishments to help temper stubborn spirits. Spare yourself the agony. Bare your soul before Yillah so that you can be forgiven your transgressions. That is the only way you will be allowed to stay."

"Stay? Who said anything about staying? I have to get back to Beijing."

"Out of the question. After you are redeemed, you will never want to leave."

"What if I don't want to be redeemed?"

"Either you seek mercy from Yillah through us, or you will present your case to Yillah directly in person."

"I have too many transgressions and I'm guilty of all of them."

"Let's be more specific."

"How?"

"Why don't you tell me why you divorced your wife?"

"My relationship with Li—" and I hesitated, not wanting to tell him her name.

"Linda Yu. I know her name. Don't try to hide it from me."

"My relationship with Linda is none of your business."

"It is every bit my business. You come from a broken family, is that not correct?" he asked. "Families often get into a cycle they can never break. The children learn from watching their parents that marriage is not inviolable. They learn bad habits that they repeat. Even if you didn't know it, they influenced you negatively. You divorced Linda because your parents never taught you that—"

One of the most unbearable things for me was when people brought up my past to condemn my present. How many people had done that to me growing up? I could feel my teeth chattering and my fingers quivering. *Breathe deeply, Nick. Breathe 1, 2, 3.* "My parents had nothing to do with my relationship with Linda."

It had everything to do with my belief in the American Dream, the idea that any man or woman could reshape their destiny regardless of their background. In a world full of false idols, it was my one true belief.

"If you had come from a healthy family, do you think you would have divorced Linda?" he asked.

"Define 'healthy family'," I replied.

He took his staff and poked me in the shoulder. "You were one of those clever lonely boys growing up, weren't you? Compensating for your insecurities with a smart lip. I know your type. It's sad that such intelligence is wasted. I'm not your enemy. I just want you to come to terms with who you really are."

"Who am I?"

"A sinner. You were born into a life of sin. You were tainted by a life of sin. You perpetuated your life of sin."

"My marriage with Linda had nothing to do with my past."

Mardi appeared irritated that I'd given him an answer he wasn't satisfied with. "Your whole life was predetermined by your past. Accept that first. Tell me more about them. Then we can work through it together."

I answered, "I have nothing to tell."

"You have nothing to tell?"

"Nothing."

"There is a trial for those who claim to have nothing to say."

"What is it?"

"If you are still of the same mind at the end of the week, then I will explain it to you. For now, listen to this." He turned on the religious hymns of an audio player and left. The music constantly shifted timbres and any time I was about to fall asleep, the shift in tone caused me to wake. They were singing in Latin or Hebrew—I wasn't sure. I pissed and relieved myself on my leg again. My stomach was growling for food. I felt dizzy. Part of the shadow moved and asked, "Why do people's nails grow?"

"What?"

"There are millions of cameras in the world but none have captured definitive proof of either a ghost or an alien."

"So what?"

"Why assume there is only one type of light that can reveal all the digital layers of reality?"

"What other light is there?"

"Earth has a hundred suns, but you only see the dimmest bulb that requires the most energy to burn."

"Can you leave me alone so I can sleep?" I asked.

"You've been asleep your whole life, waiting for this moment."

"What moment?"

The shadow orbited around me. "When you become one with your shit."

Don't break down so easily, Nick. You've been prepared for this kind of thing. Resist the chemicals in your mind. There is no voice speaking to you. It's yourself.

Suddenly, the lights came back on.

It was Mardi. "You can't even control your bowels anymore!" he yelled. "It smells terrible in here. If you act like an animal, you force me to treat you like an animal!" Mardi whipped me twice across the legs. "Dogs have better sense than you! At least they've been potty-trained."

"W-where else am I supposed to go?"

"Did I say you could speak?!" he yelled and gripped me by the neck, his fingers pressing against my esophagus. His rubbery gloves grated against my skin and my breath became constricted. He let go and shook his head. "It's disgusting touching you."

There was a pungent smell that reminded me of chicken. A maid brought in a plate of food. My stomach cried out and my mouth started to salivate. Mardi lifted up the dish and took a bite. I pressed against the rope and tried to struggle free. My only commandment was to eat.

Mardi handed the plate back to the maid. "I'm not hungry. Take it out of here." I stared at the food. He saw my gaze. "Wait."

He grabbed the piece of meat and as he was coming to me, he threw it on the ground in my waste. He lifted it back up, herbal sauce mixed in with crap. "Do you still want it?"

"This is how the religious treat their prisoners?"

"This is how we treat unrepentant sinners."

"I'm repentant."

"Of what?" he asked.

"Of immorality and perversion."

"Because of your family?"

"My past has nothing to do with who I am now."

He took the chicken and rubbed it in my face, smearing it all over my nose and cheeks.

"You think shit can be wiped off so easily?" he asked.

"With a strong enough hose," I answered.

"Spray him!" he commanded.

The hose came at me full burst again, knocking me against the wall. This time, I couldn't see who it was that directed the water and wondered how many people there were in the room beyond the candlelight.

"Did you ever go to church?" he asked after the water stopped.

"When I was young."

"Why did you stop?"

"I got bored with the sermons."

"I can't blame you there. God bless all pastors, but some are extremely tedious."

I could sense another speech coming. My mind drifted. Most times, I went to church to chase after pretty girls. But I got real tired of people using religion to suit their agendas. God became a mental genie that could be called upon to justify anything. It was a shame because I always thought religion was a beautiful thing with some of the most moral and wonderful stories ever told. The idea that the poor and the weak were more powerful than the rich and strong was so riveting for me—a reevaluation of morality. In many ways, the fundamental concept of the American Dream would not have been possible without the idea of salvation for anyone who sought it. Having come thousands of years ago, it was a radically liberating idea that still resonated with billions of people and I knew how poor a substitute science was for hope and spirituality. It couldn't help being misused. Religious protesters used to rally against Larry's film and people would tell me in a pitying tone, "I'm praying for your soul so you don't suffer in Hell." None of them ever protested vices like greed, violence, and child abuse. But show a few naked teats on screen or a woman with tattoos over her scalp, and nothing less than the end of morality was at stake. If we were to make another film —

And then it came back to me. I was never going to get to make another film with Larry again. I couldn't believe it. How could Larry be dead?

"—can't remember how to speak anymore?" Mardi asked.

Was he asking me a question?

"To show we are merciful, to show we are just, I will allow you to take the trial."

"What trial?"

And then the lights went out again. Or were they back on? I saw Mardi. He was holding curry soup. I loved curry. How did he know I loved curry? Whenever Linda cooked curry, our apartment would smell for days. Same when I cooked kimchee soup. Her favorite were dumplings. One Chinese New Year, her mom cooked us so many dumplings, I stopped eating them for almost a year. I craved those little *jiaozis*. Even one bite now, and I would have traded away my birthright.

Ropes slithered around my wrists and hissed at me.

Lights out again. Where did Mardi go? He was asking me a question about stealing. Or was it lust?

I lusted all the time. But after the divorce, I refused to go near any other woman. It'd been so long since I'd even kissed a girl.

Did a part of me wish Linda might come back?

I knew that was impossible. She'd already gotten remarried. I didn't know to whom, but I hoped he could take care of her better than I did. After being discharged from the army, I got involved in a scam where a real-estate agent promised special veteran rates for a mortgage. It was an adjustable loan that would jump from 1% to 19% after two years. "Not to worry," the old Korean businessman with slick hair told me. "The price of the house will go up so you can refinance your loan." He took me out to dinner several times, told me I was a brave soldier fighting for their rights. I lapped it up and bought an apartment I couldn't afford just like everyone else getting in on the housing frenzy.

Only prices plummeted after the bubble collapsed and my credit was ruined while my savings evaporated when the banks sent debt collectors after me.

We were always on the move because the owners would kick us out for whatever reasons. "I can pay for an apartment," she offered. "It's not a big deal and at least we won't have to keep on moving every few months."

I couldn't accept her money. Shouldn't I be the one providing for her?

"Are you here?" Mardi demanded.

"Wh-where???"

"Hose him."

Doused in water, doused in urine, doused in unusual memories, I heard my toes complaining about all the blood gathering in my calves. My legs were tired of standing upright and my body was drooping against the wall. I dreamt of hair. I was a little boy again with a full head of hair. It was covered with dandruff but I still hated using shampoo because soap got in my eyes and made them sting.

"God is merciful, but only to those who seek His mercy. Did you ever cheat on your wife?"

"Never!" I shouted.

But when I stared carefully, no one was there. Had anyone asked me a question? Other lovers were never part of our equation. It might have been easier if they were. My problem was that I believed in the idea of unlimited opportunities. I believed that no matter what happened in the past, the future could be changed. Had I been overly optimistic?

"It's a common fault," Mardi said.

"If only I could have provided the basics."

Stuck in a cubicle for SolTech wasn't so bad, but all everyone around me did was complain and moan and that made me miserable too and we fed off our negativity until all of us hated being at work and compared it to digital prostitution when prostitution in its old form was a horrific nightmare nothing like what we had to endure. The corporations wanted to maximize profit, so in my second year they reduced our cubicle space to the size of a box. We had to stand in an area smaller than my closet at home, vispads over our eyes and optical keypads we could type on using audio, mental stimuli, or our fingers. Standing all day made my feet hurt the same way they did in the present except it was worse now because at least then, I could go home and lie in bed with Linda and she'd scratch my back to put me to sleep and I'd pat her on her shoulders until she got droopy. She used to joke she was a fox fairy and asked if I wanted to see a magic trick, her best being her ability to splay her toes. SolTech was deemed one of the top ten happiest places to work in the world, and they maintained that by continually monitoring everything we did through cortical sensors and paying us only for the minutes we spent actually doing work. Even bathroom breaks were docked which made every urge a financial dilemma.

Candle lights out. Light back on. Light off.

I had to use the restroom but I didn't want to lose out on fifteen minutes of pay.

It was Larry to the rescue. "You want to be my cinematogr—"

"Those films were filth!" Mardi clamored.

Whispers were everywhere. I remembered all the hair that had fallen out onto my bed. Politicians were telling us not to be afraid. Panic had set out. The days right after the Baldification were scary. Buildings were in blazes, eaten by flames that were slowly chomping them up. A variety of screaming cried out in a variety of languages. I recorded everything I could, particularly the gangs of people running along the sidewalk and destroying property. The army jumped in with their armored suits and gunships, and it was also the beginning of the 24-hour drone watch above the skies. I thought it was so cool and wanted to join the army because it reminded me of the videogames I played.

"Did you take to liquor?" Mardi asked in a harmless tone.

Was he really in front of me? I needed a drink. I'd have drunk my own piss if I could have shot it into my mouth.

Larry took me out every night after the divorce. I didn't want to talk about Linda, didn't want to tell him anything. He didn't ask. He just chased after women, all sorts of women. Skinny, buxom, short, tall. Different nationalities, different religions, different politics. He was a paragon of equality. Didn't mind that I would moan and whimper and get so drunk that I wanted to curse the world. I didn't want to talk to any other women. I just wanted to see Linda again and any woman that talked to me received my wrathful scorn. "Leave me alone. I don't want your company. I don't want to talk to you. I don't care about your problems!"

"You're stuck with me," Mardi answered.

"How many days have we been here?" I asked.

"Not enough," he replied. It felt like a month. It might have been less than a week. Every time I blinked, Mardi was there, or he wasn't. I thought of Larry taking me out despite my grumpiness, despite the fact that I ruined the mood for many of the women he was interested in.

"Sorry, man."

He'd grin and wave it off. "I didn't like her anyways."

IV.

The hose woke me again, but this time, it was different. They were putting clothes on me. They dragged me outside, carried me up some stairs, then through a hallway. I felt like I was made of straw and my bones were mush, although it was a boon to finally have the restraints removed from my arms. When we stepped outside, the sun attacked me with light and my eyes felt overwhelmed by brightness. Even with my lids shut, the light tore at my sockets and tried to burn their way in. I felt nauseous until they put me on a stage.

"For three weeks, this infidel has resisted our attempts to lead him toward the righteous path. Let it never be said we don't offer a fair trial!" Mardi yelled into a speaker. There were guards to either side of me holding whips. I saw the contours of people, heard them jeering, except I couldn't see their faces because it was too bright. I never hated the sun so much. It was my enemy. Scientists said the sun had something to do with the Baldification, the burst in radiation, solar spikes that disrupted our telecommunications periodically. I just wanted to punch the sun in the face, let it feel my hands as nuclear implosions, scrape away the hydrogen bursts and swallow it like an overly spiced jalapeno, spitting out the seeds. The seeds would spring from the dead earth and form flowers of discontent that would blossom into a hundred reborn stars outlined as constellations of vagabonds. We'd rage a war, sun versus the stars of the earth and duke it out. Not for dominance, but the darkness of anonymity, the billions who sacrificed themselves so that other suns could burn more brightly.

Mardi lifted a stone that was the size of my hand and a whole lot thicker.

"You refuse to repent. Fine. We leave justice to God. If you can carry this rock with your mouth all the way to the end of our main road without using your hands, you are free to leave. But if you fail, then you must repent of your sins. You will be given three chances. Do you accept?"

Was he serious? Carrying a rock in my mouth seemed like an easy enough task. "I accept," I replied.

A guard tied my hands in front of me. Mardi stuffed the stone into my mouth and it barely fit. They had sanded the rock to be slippery and I had to clamp down hard with my teeth to keep it from slipping out. Its size was already taking a toll on my jaw. My strong clench caused pain to shoot up my gums and my teeth felt sore within ten seconds of biting. Tooth pains were the worst and were already giving me a headache. They may as well have put needles in my mouth. I could barely focus and when the people started jeering me, the migraine intensified. Distracted for a moment, the stone dropped out of my mouth onto the dusty road. I was whipped twice.

"Do you repent sinner?!" Mardi asked.

My back felt like it'd been burnt and I dropped to my knees. My joints creaked and I picked up the rock. I tried to stand, but my legs betrayed me. They were too weak. I focused on the scalding pain in my back, and willed myself up. The rock was covered with dirt, but I had to put it in my mouth. The coarse particles of dirt rolled in my tongue and I wanted to gag, but I thought of that whip and I thought of having to surrender to these nutcases. I clamped down with my teeth again and took a step forward. Another. I'd just taken a total of two steps when I needed to make thousands. The thought horrified me. I forced myself to put it out of my head. *Don't think about the end. Just think about the next step.* It was a cliché, but it was all I had.

Linda, you always joked Larry would get me into a whole lot of trouble, but I never imagined it would be like this. I would rather die than live a life of forced subjugation. That's the household I grew up in, forced to repent for imagined crimes. I struggled so hard to leave that life behind. *Nick. You fought to get out. Now fight to stay out.*

I knew my teeth were upset. I implored them: *I know it hurts a whole lot, but help me now. Help me and I swear I will get you the best dental treatments in the world. I'll drink a hundred bottles of wine and only pick out the most select teas in the Chengdu chaguans. Want ice cream? Which flavor? Warm broths, huo guo, mapo tofu, anything you want, you'll get. I wish I could have taken more calcium for you guys, given deeper fortifications to you laterals and cuspids. Canines, I know it's been a long time since you've been pointy fangs, but I need you to clench as though we were in the wild. I need you to be ruthlessly bestial on this rock and obliterate it.*

The villagers started throwing fruits at me. A tomato hit the side of my head. Apples, which were much harder, started coming my way. I decided to take a risk. I let the rock fall out of my mouth. Two lashes hurtled against me.

"Do you repent?"

I got down again, but this time, rather than the rock, I picked up one of the apples and took four rapid bites. I swallowed without chewing and by the time Mardi realized what I was up to, he tore the apple away and yelled to the crowd, "Don't throw any more food!"

An apple had never tasted so sweet and savory. I felt energy swell from within. It was the best apple I'd ever had, even if it was covered with dirt.

"Thank you," I whispered to the crowd.

I put the rock back in my mouth and stood up.

Five, six, seven, eight.

I clenched harder, felt saliva dripping over the rock. Only I saw red slithering over the rock and realized it was blood. I heard a chip, felt my teeth compact.

"We are a society that believes good morals are the foundation of a family. How dare you enter our village and try to corrupt everything we hold dear?!" Mardi yelled. "Look how hard he resists. Look how he struggles against the righteous path. All he needs do is repent. But he would rather die than turn away from his life of sin!"

If it was sin I was turning away from, I would have gladly given it up. Sign me up to be a monk. What did I care? I hadn't even touched a woman in years. Priests and monks were guilty of every vice but sex, and even that, they often violated. I had no beef with God or their Yillah. I had a beef with the sun, with the religious freaks, with the gravity that was pulling on this stone. God had never done me any wrong. Only humans misusing God and every other idea in the universe to exact their petty creeds. I realized the only way for me to get to the end was clamp even harder and destroy my teeth. Break through until it was gums and blood to cement the rock so I could hold it in my jaws. No one ever said the American Dream was free.

I no longer tried to protect my teeth. I pressed down, pressed like I was trying to cause fusion in my mouth. My laterals gave way first and the pain nearly caused me to drop the rock as I felt the pieces tumble on my tongue. I let them leak out the side of my mouth and bit harder. Sanded as it was, all the blood and saliva was soaking in. They whipped me because I was standing still, trying to break my teeth.

"Keep moving!" Mardi demanded.

I complied and kept on exerting force until my cuspids broke and my canines shattered. The rock had more space in my mouth. The pain gave me an adrenaline rush and surged my exhausted body awake. I cursed the sun and at the same time, begged my feet for the energy to get to the end of the path. *Shine your beams elsewhere!*

I didn't know why I fought with Linda so much when I never loved anyone as much as her. *You and me were going to change the world.* Instead, we became the butt of jokes, all the idiot friends who were secretly pleased that we'd become a car wreck just because their lives were the flotsam of selfish idiocies. Like any of them had such amazing relationships, like any of them knew what it meant to have family. I wished I could have been more patient. I wished I had a voice repressor that censored words that

I'd program in beforehand. Any sentence starting with a *but* had to go. "Shut up shut up!!!"

I walked because I loved Linda. I walked because I loved Larry. I walked because I should have been dead but I wasn't so now I had to walk, walk until I died. Accept that there was no future. Accept that I had nothing to look forward to. This was a matter of dignity. Self-respect. To die a worthy death, not scared like prey hunted down by wolves. Death made cowards out of the most courageous of men. I was never a courageous man. Not even close. I was a born coward. If I'd have had guts, I wouldn't have left my destiny up to other men, executives and corporations that dictated the measurements of my life. If I'd have had guts, I would have prevented Larry from going alone. If I'd have had guts, I wouldn't have let Linda leave that last night by herself.

"Mardi," I heard. "He's more than halfway."

"No one else has made it this far."

Mardi didn't reply, or if he did, I didn't hear it.

There was no bright light at the end of a tunnel. I was seeking the darkness. I was yearning for death. I waddled, I straggled, I pressed on, feeling the rock split apart more teeth. Pain nerves fired up and forced my muscles to contract violently. Let it never be said I died an easy death.

There were no more sounds. I saw figures walking ahead of me, translucent, white garbs. For a minute, I thought I saw Larry. He was flirting with some girl and I wanted to warn him to be careful, that the zealots might hang him up for it. He seemed amused. "Let em' try." Then went back to the cute girl with chubby cheeks.

Mardi approached closely. "You think I don't know what you're going through? I do, brother. I know I've been harsh and that's because I understand your obstinacy personally. This is a test to forge your heart. Don't fight the way I did. Give in. Surrender yourself."

I ignored him and focused ahead. There were houses, I think. There were also intersecting roads. This was a village hidden inside a forest. But I didn't recognize the architecture, and the streets were old. I noticed a river running rapidly through the village. I didn't know how much further I had to go. But I had no delusions about them actually letting me go. At least with the river, I might die free. I'd heard drowning was the worst way to die. But whoever said that probably hadn't been tortured to death—you know, skin being scalded off, bones torn off, sliced into thousands of pieces, and getting a hole drilled in his head.

I tumbled into the river and felt it sweeping me away. It was cold but cleansing, even if the river was most likely full of toxic pollutants. Drowning, or having my flesh melt from poison. They didn't seem like such bad options now. The water tossed me about and I took the stone out of my mouth, gripping it. That was until a rock hit me in the head and a series of waves pressed over me. I no longer fought inevitability.

V.

When I woke up, my teeth hurt like crazy. I was surprised to find myself head down on a river bank, the forest spanning ahead. Had I really escaped? I remembered what had happened and knew I had to run. I could barely stand up and my legs cramped after I forced myself up. There was a rustling sound that made me pause. It was Mardi.

"You're finally up," he said.

"What do you want?" I demanded. "Trying to take me back?"

He raised up both his hands. "I honor my word. A man like you would rather die than turn away. If that is the will of God, there is nothing we can do. I figured you'd wash up somewhere along the shore."

I would have spat at him except I had to save every drop of water in my body.

He went for his bag and I stepped back, wary of what he might get. If he tried to take me back, I'd have to jump into the water again. He took out a bottle of water and some rice porridge in sealed containers. "You'll need these."

"I don't want anything from you," I said.

"You won't survive without these."

"I'd rather die than accept anything from you."

"You think I don't understand your position?"

"How could you?"

He put his hand in his mouth and took his teeth out. They were dentures.

"That's why I'm still here," he said and grabbed the water again. "Don't think with your pride. Think with your head. You'll need these to get to Gamble Town."

The name sounded familiar. "What's Gamble Town?"

"It's twenty miles north of here, a terrible gathering of vice and sin. You'll be able to find a phone there along with anything money can buy. But you won't get anywhere without these."

I looked at him, a pensive glint in his eyes. "You were originally from Gamble Town?" I asked.

"No one is from Gamble Town. But I was an addict. After I squandered everything I had—all my wealth, sold my wife and kids into slavery for my debts—I came here. They took me in. But not before they destroyed who I was. You could have had a home here, you know? We need more strong-willed men like you here."

"No thanks."

He left the water and porridge on the ground, took out a small bottle of pills. "Painkillers. Take it with lots of water."

"You expect me to thank you?"

"No."

"What were you hoping to achieve?" I asked.

"Redemption."

"You failed."

"No. *You* failed." He looked at me again, took off his shoes and his poncho, placed them on the ground, then walked away. I waited a few minutes, making sure he was gone. Then I took the bottle and drank the whole thing down. I devoured the porridge, greedily chewing. Almost immediately, my stomach growled but I ignored it. I had to eat. I felt tears in my eyes as I felt so desperate. I fought them back and welcomed the temporary burst of rejuvenation. There were three more containers left. I grabbed them, put on the poncho. His shoes were a bit tight, though better than nothing. I made my way towards Gamble Town.

6. Gamble Town

I.

The humming sound was the first thing that struck me as I approached the glitzy lights and tall buildings that reminded me of Las Vegas, albeit with a much grungier facade. Firecrackers were going off, music blasted, and women in lingerie danced in a troupe. Drunks were passed out in the corners while other drunks were dancing as hard as they could. As I got closer, I saw the source of the humming. It was a massive glass cage filled with flies. Insects were everywhere. There were spider fights between female orb-weavers, roach races in elaborate tracks, and caterpillar leaf-eating contests. Cricket fighting was also on display, and there were hundreds of simultaneous matches. The crickets were screeching like a war cry and obsessed crowds cheered for their favorites. Cricket pilots were at their booths, interfacing with their crickets through a neural feed, fighting with a degree of precision and endurance that would have been unthinkable decades ago. This was how I used to burn the long hours between shifts during the African Wars.

There were five tall buildings around a central strip and I could tell from the faded logos that they used to be big casino hotels, targeting rich tourists and gamblers. Times had changed and it was the seedier elements that were welcomed now, the g-rated veneer discarded. 3D billboards for strip clubs and gambling saloons blasted gaudy advertisements. Workers making minimum wage passed out business cards for prostitutes that had naked pictures with little star graphics to cover the "secret" spots (standard 2D, no 3D, suggesting they had no budget to waste). Slot machines rang continuously with chimes that were addictively satisfying, although it was insect gambling that had the rapt attention of most of the patrons. I distantly recollected hearing about a place like this. It was subsidized by the government and became a booming casino town until the subsidies got pulled. Overnight, it turned into a ghost town. A few enterprising entrepreneurs decided to take a risk and rebrand it. Was this the result?

I needed to make a phone call. My options were limited and when I asked a few people if I could borrow their phone, I was refused. While the river had wiped most of my smell away, I could see from the disgusted looks of those passing by that they assumed I was a waif. I didn't get far before plainclothes guards grabbed me and warned, "Don't make a fuss. It'll be easier for both of us."

Actually glad for their presence, I went along. Perhaps they would allow me to use a phone and get out of this mess. The prospect of home gave me a glimmer of hope. I longed for my apartment, would have done anything to lie in my bed, smell my favorite pillow, sleep for a week straight, and eat Chinese food. But the hum of the insects was making me queasy. I hated bugs. When I was growing up as a kid, I slept with a mat on the floor. Big roaches would crawl up my leg and I'd wake up, feeling them run along my thighs. I'd sweep them away, turn on the light, and see them dashing madly for cover. It made me squeamish to see their wet black shells and their multiple limbs.

We went into an alley full of trash. One of the guards, a stocky fellow with menacing eyes and a chin that resembled an ass, asked, "Do you have any money on you?"

"It's a long story," I started. "If you can let me use your phone, I'll have—"

"Do you have any money on you right now?" the ass-chin asked me.

"Not this minute, but—"

"We don't take kindly to vagrants here."

Seven of them swarmed me like locust on corn and were getting ready to strike. *Here we go again.* I shut my eyes, wondering how much more my body could endure, when someone asked, "Nick?"

I looked up and saw a man in the raggedy uniform of a two-bit security guard. He had a belly, was unshaven, and his hair was an oily mess. I almost didn't recognize Dan. We served in the African Wars together and I helped him a couple times while he was shooting *American Murder*, a popular documentary filming real-life murders sanctioned by the government for popularity ratings.

"It is you," he confirmed.

"You know this guy?" ass-chin wanted to know.

"Yeah. We served in Africa together," Dan answered. "He was one of the best damn cricket fighters we had. Ain't that right?"

"I was all right."

"Don't be modest. What the hell happened to you?"

"Like I was saying earlier, it's a long story."

"Can you still fight with crickets?" he asked.

His teeth were a yellow mess and his breath reeked of garlic. Even though he was smiling, I realized if I didn't tell him what he wanted to hear, he'd let the goons eat me alive. "Been a while, but I can manage." I'd won my fair share of fights through the neural interface. Crickets were in many ways simplified versions of us: born, fed gruel, mated with a lover, fighting for their survival, then left to die.

There was a greedy glint in his eyes. "If I got you some healthy crickets, you think you can win a few fights?"

"I can try. It's been a while. I'll need some practice."

Dan huddled with his guards and I heard them whispering to one another.

He came back after a few minutes and inquired, "How would you like to make a deal?"

"What kind of deal?"

Dan took out a capsule from his jacket. "A lucrative one."

I heard a chirp and recognized a cricket. I hated crickets—not as much as roaches, but they were still a visually disgusting lot. Which is probably the reason I fought so well as one.

II.

"What the hell happened to you?" Dan asked.

He'd taken me up to his place, a hotel room with a king-sized bed and a single bathroom. The room smelled of tar and nicotine. There were tons of hooker cards scattered next to the bed stands as well as empty beer bottles. Eleven different knives hung on the wall.

I was about to answer, but he stopped me. "It doesn't matter. All I care about is the fights. The favorite this season is a brutish little bastard we all call Zhou because of his short master. The pilot is a kid who calls himself Tolstoy."

"Does he like Tolstoy's books?"

Dan ignored my question and explained, "His little bugger has gone undefeated in fifty fights so far, favored to win every match a hundred to one odds. He's just a kid and he's beating everyone. But he ain't ever fought a soldier before."

Kid fighters worried me. They had less mental clutter, more focus that allowed them a purity in their connection that adults struggled with. Still, he was right. I represented the army in cricket battles. With practice, I could fight against the best.

I had to be honest with him. "I'm not in the best condition right now. I—"

"I called a nurse for you. I see those scars. Don't know where you've been, but we'll get you patched up. I have the night shift anyways so I gotta get back. Get some sleep and we'll start tomorrow."

"I need a few days of practice." More like a few months.

"We set up a match for you against the kid. Not a real one, just a warm up. He'll probably kick your ass, but it's a feint."

"A feint?"

"Throw everyone off their guard and dismiss you when you lose."

And then when I came back for a rematch a few days later, naturally, everyone would bet against me. It was one of the oldest cons around.

"Heidi will be here in a few minutes," Dan said.

"The nurse?"

He grinned. "She'll treat you."

I wanted to understand the terms that we were arranging. "What's the deal?" I asked outright.

"You beat him, we make a boatload of money. You take 5% and go wherever you want."

"If I fail?"

His eyes tightened. "Don't," he answered, and left. I followed behind him and tried to open the door. It was locked to prevent both entry and exit. All I needed was a phone call, and now, I couldn't get out of the room.

As a natural habit, I checked the mattress. There were blood stains everywhere and legions of moving critters. Bed bugs. An infestation of them. I was tired and I knew they would have welcomed my presence. Try some fresh meat, suck on new blood. There was an armchair next to the bed that appeared safer on inspection. I was about to take a seat when I heard a knock.

"Who is it?"

"Heidi."

A redhead in a tight nurse's outfit awaited. She had enormous breasts that were accentuated by the revealing low cut of her uniform. She had puffy lips and fake brows. Makeup was all over her face, but not enough to cover the wrinkles on her neck. Even with the powder, or maybe because of it and the dark purple lipstick, she reminded me of a clown. It always depressed me when I saw someone try so hard to look beautiful and fail. "Heard you need some healing," she said lasciviously.

Was this Dan's idea of R&R?

"Do you have salve?" I asked her.

"What do you mean?"

I took off my shirt and turned around. I think the sight of my whip-lash scars shocked her.

"Do I want to know who did this to you?" she asked. "Because Dan didn't pay for this kind of thing."

"It doesn't matter who did it."

"I can make another part of you feel better," she said, forcing herself to act professional.

I stopped her and said, "Not right now. Could you give me a few minutes to nap? I'm really tired."

"Sure," she answered. "Do you mind if I watch TV?" Before I could answer, she plopped herself down and turned on *Jesus the General*. "I love this show. Don't wanna miss any episodes. Last week, Jesus went back in time and caused a temporal anomaly so he could beat the Mongolians before they invaded Europe. You like the show?"

"Haven't seen much of it."

"Are you serious? You need to. Jesus is my hero."

She watched raptly for a few minutes. My back was aching and I tried to sleep but she started crying.

"What's wrong?" I asked her.

"Sorry. I get really emotional when I watch the show," she answered.

"Can I use your phone to call a hospital?" I asked her.

"Dan said no phones."

I knew she'd have one on her. The only question was, how to get it from her? I approached and she had enough instincts to sense what I wanted.

"I can watch Jesus later," she said. "I think we'll call it a day, sugar." She stood up. I grabbed her, lunging for her bag. She karate-chopped me in the shoulder, forcing me to stumble back. "Don't touch me!" she warned. "I've been trained to deal with assholes like you!"

"I just need a doctor."

"That's not my problem," she said, then rushed out the door.

I felt stupid and craven. She was most certainly going to report this to Dan. For now, the best I could do was rest. I sat down in the armed chair and dozed off.

III.

Dan didn't mention Heidi. He brought me my first cricket to test. The cricket was in a glass cage with a removable top. The interface was a small square chip I placed on my right temple. It translated my thoughts into electrical impulses the cricket could understand and gave feedback of his own senses into my brain. Dan fired the chip gun with its needle point near what little brain the cricket had. I always gave them nicknames and this one I called Crick for lack of imagination. In my first plunge (interlink was the official word), I had a hard time remembering how to move his six legs and felt gross being inside the body of a cricket. The world seemed alien through his eyes and I could barely make sense of my surroundings. I had to vomit, and brain fatigue hit within two minutes. I jumped out, ran to the toilet, and barfed.

Dan laughed.

"How long's it been?"

"Almost a decade," I answered, having forgotten how much mental discipline it required.

"Your first fight is tonight."

"What? I'm not ready."

"Then get ready."

Crickets had to spend their lives finding a home to attract a mate. Once their territory was claimed, they sang every minute using their wings. I wondered what it would be like if people to had to sing for their lives. Just as each human had a unique voice, so did the crickets. Some had talent, others didn't. It was like one of those reality shows. Only, your survival and the next generation depended on it. The worst part was they only had a short time to fulfill their genetic destiny and the females were really picky.

Would a female cricket who wanted a male with the best

house and voice be considered superficial? I felt Linda deserved better than what we had, living in cheap rental units, moving with every lease expiration as the property agencies jacked up rates 25%. I couldn't afford the new prices and constantly worried about being laid off from SolTech. I had quit Larry's movies after marriage because the hours had been so rigorous and I wanted to spend more time with Linda. But going back to SolTech didn't help things as the hours were equally long. Maybe cricket songs were lamentations, working all day and night for what? An impossible cycle that, depending on the species, could end up with their being devoured like cannibalized katydids. Was it better to be a dragonfly? Live underwater as a nymph for almost three years to emerge, undergo metamorphosis, and fly for a few weeks before dying. At least they could fly.

Clear your mind! I thought to myself.

"I brought you some peanuts," Dan said, dropping me a bag.

Peanuts helped clear the mind, rich in vitamin B6 and protein. The tricky part of interfacing had to do with the shock. It wasn't hard linking with a cricket as their brain patterns were so simple. Survive, eat, mate, survive. It was their relationship with the world that was tough. They were completely oblivious to humans who were as alive to them as a hurricane would be to us. Their perceptions were limited and trying to inject them with new thoughts was impossible. It was like trying to do calculus using only 1 through 10. I didn't have direct control over Crick's muscles. Only impulses like attack, run, or mate. I once went through the mating process with one of the crickets during the war. Worst mistake I made. From the cricket's perspective, sex was a mechanical process, devoid of any pleasure, as routine as eating, though it stirred up a strong sense of protectionism over my mate. Being so near the cricket and feeling her intimately left me nauseous and viscerally disturbed. Bugs scared me when I looked down on them from above. Copulating with one left mental scars. I hated bug sex. We normally mated the male with as many females as possible before the fight to arouse his hormones and his combativeness.

I dived back into Crick, focused only on enduring as long as I could. I didn't try to control or affect his movements. I just tried to stay along for the ride. I lasted seven minutes before a splitting headache caused me to get out.

"I have to take a nap," I told Dan.

Dan was reading news on his phone and ignored me. He was never the talkative type and I knew almost nothing about him, probably because he didn't have much to tell. I ate a few peanuts before I went to sleep, using a tooth in the back of my mouth that could bite down without too much pain.

I dreamt about bughood and woke up to a bloody nose. Wiped it clean, ate more peanuts, took a piss, washed my face, and dived back into my interlink. My brain was still exhausted and I jumped out within three minutes. Achieving synchronicity was proving difficult, especially with my back aching.

"You should have let Heidi do her thing," Dan said. "She's a pro. Plus she's clean. Believe me. I call her all the time."

"Why don't you pilot?" I asked.

"Causes seizures in me," he replied. "I've tried. So have the others. I'll be the first to admit it's not as easy as it looks. You're doing way better than any of us did. You want me to call you another girl?"

"How about a real nurse?"

"Too expensive. After you win, you can get one. In the meantime, there's plenty of Asian women that are cheap too, if that's your thing."

What I needed now was rest in the form of a long sleep.

"No thanks."

"C'mon. Ain't nothing like a good lay to rev up the engines."

Was he treating me like a cricket?

IV.

My first match was in Cricket Alley. There were long rows of cricket bouts. Most were smalltime fights used as practice arenas to warm up stronger crickets. Wagers were limited and gamblers came to scout crickets to bet on. Dan accompanied me in plain clothes and I carried Crick along. He told me to lose the fight. Not that I needed encouraging. Even if I tried, my brain would have had a hard time holding on.

"That's Tolstoy," Dan whispered.

Tolstoy had pale skin. But it was his wig that caught my attention. It was white, but it flowed naturally with thick strands, better than any imitation I'd seen. Did he have them grafted onto his scalp? He was a short teen, wearing a gray coat that went down to his knees. His limbs were wiry and he had a caustic snicker curved into his lips. His light hazel eyes methodically watched everything, less out of caution, and more, curiosity, as though everything were new to him. We were both surprised when he approached me.

"You look familiar," he addressed me.

I would have recognized someone with as distinctive a look as he did. "I think you're mistaking me for someone else."

"How many fights have you had?"

"This is my first."

Tolstoy stared at me, even after Dan led me to my seat.

Maybe he'd seen me on some of the behind-the-scenes footage with Larry? "Looks like the champ's taken a fancy to you," Dan said.

Tolstoy was watching my fight.

My mind was focused on my opponent who was also a young fellow, a paunchy male with freckles and a wig of curly choppy hair. He shook my hand but seemed disdainfully sure of himself. "I'm Nick," I introduced myself.

"That's nice," he answered with an arrogant air that suggested he'd already dismissed me as a competitor.

The table had a glass cage separated by a partition. Cameras were hooked to either side and connected to the gambling decks in case anyone wanted to wager. I softly dropped Crick in while my opponent selected from his gallery of ten crickets. Although he didn't say, I knew he probably picked one of his weaker fighters in an attempt to boost their confidence. As a final insult, when one of his compatriots asked, "Do you want us to bring dinner back to you?" he answered, "I won't be long."

"Three rounds, five minutes each," the computerized referee informed us.

I took a seat, grabbed the arm rests, and interfaced with Crick. Mental metamorphosis commenced. I pushed off with my legs and saw an ugly cricket ahead of me. Hesitation would be the worst mistake now. I rammed him and bit his head with my jaws. In my human body, my lungs swelled and a cold sweat broke out. I hated the taste of cricket, hated biting their heads. My opponent finally fought back, pushing hard against me. But it was too late. I had the advantage and felt a rush of adrenaline. He was mine and I wanted to wipe the smirk off the pilot's face. But then my head throbbed and his cricket leapt on top of me. Before I could respond, he bit onto one of my antennae. I tried to feel him out, but I started smelling peanuts in my breath. Or was it me, the pilot? I was already losing track of who I was. It was a good time to surrender. Except I couldn't stand the pilot's look and the way he dismissed me. I rammed him again and kicked off my feet. My whole life was a long bug-hood, surviving by any means necessary. Even if I was supposed to lose the match, I wouldn't surrender. Not yet at least. The fight continued as our crickets locked heads, neither side giving in. If only I had more endurance, if only I wasn't so out of shape, I would have destroyed him. Now, I was barely keeping up. The good thing was, he'd severely underestimated me. I saw an opening because of an injury and flipped his cricket, about to pounce. Suddenly, the match ended. I'd been forcibly disconnected.

"You looked like you were—" Dan was saying, but before he finished, I vomited on the ground next to him, coughing up peanuts.

The other pilot said, "That's disgusting man. You shouldn't be here."

I stared at Dan. "Why'd you disconnect me?"

He didn't answer but I knew it was part of his plan.

I shook my head. Noticed Tolstoy watching me.

Then looked at both competing crickets. They'd been brutally beaten. Before interfacing, cricket fights were rarely mortal. Now, they almost always were. In this case, we'd thrown a white flag and spared both. But as I looked at the two fighters, battered and bruised, it was apparent they would never fight again. I knew exactly how they felt.

V.

Back at the room, Dan seemed ecstatic. "I knew you were good. Less than a day and you were fighting like a pro."

"Barely."

"In a week, you'll be in good shape. I got you some good crickets. I'll bring them by tomorrow. Get yourself a long sleep."

I went to the shower, wanting to clean myself. Several roaches scurried along the bath. The water was too cold and had a brown streak in it that smelled like rust. I was afraid to brush my broken teeth, though I rinsed with water to try to get the smell of peanuts and blood out. Dan was asleep when I emerged from the bathroom and I wondered how he dealt with the bed bugs. The scars on my back hurt and the migraine intensified. I was mixing up smells with sounds and sights with tastes. The ceiling was blurrily fractured and I tried to move a third pair of legs I didn't have, fumbling awkwardly to the ground as a result. It was only one day and I was already a mental mess. The partition between cricket-hood and humanity would come with time. Just as I was about to go to sleep, I felt something crawling on my leg. I looked down and saw three roaches which I brushed off.

What the hell am I doing here? I should be tracking down your killers, Larry, not trying to win a cricket match against some dumb kids.

I looked over at Dan, then at the knives on the wall. Almost three decades later, I was reliving my childhood again. A violent desperation filled me. Despite our facade of civility, we always had too many roaches in our home, a physical manifestation of the rot my biological family suffered. Would I be able to endure this again? I took a deep breath, tried to think about something else. My eyes kept on creeping back to those knives. Would I murder a man while he slept so I could escape? Even though I couldn't stand the smell of food, I was starving, having been unable to keep anything down. I reminded myself that I was no longer a cricket, driven by hormones. I was a human being with reasoning.

I'd have to reason with Dan in the morning. Ask him for a day off so I could recover. Maybe ask if I could stay in a room without roaches. That wasn't too much to ask for, was it?

VI.

"I need you today," Dan insisted. "I've scheduled two matches for you."

My voice was raspy and my eyes felt swollen. He was sharpening his knives. "I need to get some food in me."

"I brought you peanuts."

"I need porridge and ice cream."

"I'll get it for you after the match. The first fight, I want you to lose in the third round. For the second one, fourth round." He repeated it several times.

That was a total of 35 minutes linked. I didn't know if I could even handle a minute.

"Look," he said. "Toughen up. I spent good money getting

you these crickets and buying what you needed. Don't make me regret my decision."

"I need more time to recover, man."

"You don't got time," Dan replied. And from his menacing glower and the way he held his knife, I knew he meant business. So much for reason.

VII.

The first fight wasn't too bad. While I hadn't got enough sleep, the 12-hour break allowed me to recuperate enough to the point where I could dive without immediately feeling exhausted. It wasn't a good fight by any means and I spent most of it either on defense or running away while pretending to be positioning myself. Fortunately, my rival, a mid-aged woman, wasn't an aggressive type and fought askance, not sure why I was running when most men pounced. She was so focused on the match, she probably didn't notice my sickly hue or the fact that my neck muscles were cramping. Getting to the third round was a tough stretch, but I managed. When her cricket flung me into the corner, I signaled my surrender.

It was the second fight that really screwed me up. Dan got me a decent fighter with a big head, in turn meaning bigger mouth. This one had sprightly thick legs which were essential for kicking. He might not have been top of the class, but he was still a damn good fighter. Both crickets were weighed in. My head started to spin. My toe fingers shook uncontrollably.

"I'm not feeling so good," I said to Dan.

"You'll be fine. Don't worry."

I had good reason to worry. My brain was fried. Within ten seconds of diving, I knew I couldn't handle it anymore. I smelled the other cricket's hormones, his face bulgingly big. Electrical currents rushed through my nerves. Every sound was a thousand times louder. Humans were storm fronts passing by. I took off the interface, stumped to the ground. It felt like my head was in a vise and someone was squeezing. Was my head on my neck? I tried to spring, tried to shake my wings, warn other crickets away. But they were missing. What happened to my wings? I was naked and exposed. Chomp, chomp, sing out your warning! They would come upon me at any minute. Even if I wasn't much of a singer, I still had to shake them. I used my hands and rubbed them rapidly together. There wasn't any sound. I shrieked, cried out loud.

"He's still synced," someone sang.

"How long has he been interfaced?"

"Only a few minutes."

"What are you doing bringing amateurs here?"

Why couldn't I fly? Why couldn't I move? My thorax was cemented to the floor. I tried to sense out with my antennae but they'd been chopped off. The earlier fight had—

"Nick! Nick!"

VIII.

"You humiliated me out there," I heard someone say. "It was perfect. Now they think you're a joke. When you beat Tolstoy, we are going to rake in the cash. Aw, man, I can't believe how well it played out. Yeah, I lost a couple bucks today, but we ended up ahead 'cause I bet more on that first match. I had a feeling you wouldn't last that second fight." A chiming sound.

I could smell a woman. She hovered near me. I had to prepare my song, beat my wings together to impress her. But I couldn't feel my wings and had no idea if she was just going to move on without me.

"What's he doing?"

"He thinks he's a cricket."

"Will he keep on shaking like this?"

"It'll pass."

"What should we do?"

"Ignore him and come over here."

She made a song back. I didn't recognize the music, but I knew I had to reply. Damn the wings. I'd have to use my legs to kick the ground. There was someone else after her. I'd have to get louder, make more sound to warn him off. This was *my* mate!

"That's really annoying," she sang.

"Just ignore it."

"It's hard to get in the mood when he's making all this ruckus."

"That's what I'm paying you for."

"Can't you send him out of the room?"

"Will you just shut up and get back down here?"

Her song was getting louder. I would have to get even louder. I could smell her. She wasn't ready for mating. There was something sickly in her. It made me pause. Maybe it was better to let this one go, better to focus on other mates. Needed to scavenge for food. Find some shrubs and fungus to eat.

"Why's he digging under the bed?"

"He thinks he can find food down there."

"This is really creepy."

"You'll get used to it."

"You've seen this before?"

"His brainwaves are meshing with the cricket. It'll pass. Now, can you shut up please and get to work?"

"I'm not the one making all the noise!"

Just needed some food, hungry, felt weak. She was singing louder and I could smell her hormones, but there was something terribly wrong.

"I'm not feeling it."

"What do you mean you're not feeling it?"

"He's burrowing under our bed!"

"You've never seen a pilot get wired?"

"No. You have?"

"I lived through it. Mine was way worse than him."

"You were a pilot?"

"Tried to be."

"You never told me that," she cooed.

"Yeah, I wanted to be a pilot so badly, it was sad. This guy used to be one of my heroes in the army."

"He was a pilot?"

"A damn good one, long time ago. I was envious of him. After the war, I came out here to try to make my way as a cricket pilot. But I couldn't stay interlinked longer than a minute without getting seizures. I had a defect in my brain lobes that prevented it."

"Why didn't you go back home?"

"And let everyone know I'd failed? No way. I made my living out here any way I could. It's been eight years since I first came out."

"I never knew you had your dreams crushed."

"Some people have what it takes, some don't. I didn't. But I'm gonna win big this time. No one'll laugh at me after my pay day."

"Come over here."

"I am here."

"Closer."

The singing got louder.

IX.

It was two hours later when my senses returned to me. Dan was sleeping naked with Heidi. Both were snoring. I knew my body condition. If I went through another day of this, I'd either die, or worse, get permanently wired. That was another way of saying I'd get lost inside the mind of a cricket forever. Many pilots had been locked away in one of those convention centers similar to where my brother-in-law was. Spending too much time under or not having enough breaks between the fights was the most common cause. My eyes returned to the knives on Dan's wall. I didn't know if I even had the strength to stab them. But if I failed, he'd probably kill me anyways which was a better fate than living out the rest of my days as a human thinking he was a cricket. During the war, Dan had been the quiet type. He was always meticulously cleaning his knives and Larry joked, "Don't be surprised if he's secretly a serial killer."

I'd never killed a man. Even during the wars, most of the killing was done by drones and machines. In Los Angeles, where gun fights were common, gun groups had gotten the government to change laws so that if you fired at people wearing armor, it was considered aggravated assault rather than attempted murder. Many of my acquaintances had been brought up on aggravated assault charges, but I didn't have a mark. Murdering someone was against everything I believed. But at this point, it was a matter of kill or be killed. As sick as I was, I started shaking.

He brought this on himself, I kept on telling myself. But I still had a hard time justifying it. I was more than a cricket, wasn't I? Didn't know anymore, couldn't tell the difference. I was about to get up and head towards the shelf of knives when there was a knock on our door followed by several more.

Dan, groggy and tired, answered. I lay on the carpet and pretended to be asleep. He opened, talked with the guest at the door, then came back to me with a confused look. "Nick. Nick! Get up."

"What is it?"

"Tolstoy wants to meet you."

"The champion?" I asked.

"Yeah."

"Why?"

"I don't know. But he wants to see you right away."

"Is that all right?"

"No one refuses the champ," Dan replied.

I went to the door and saw a young lady that had white hair similar to the champ. She had an aquiline nose, brown eyes, and wan cheeks. I couldn't take my eyes off her. Her skin was so perfectly crafted and unblemished, it looked like porcelain. She wore a lacy black dress and carried an umbrella by her side.

"My brother would like to speak with you," she said, presumably making her Tolstoy's sister. "If it's not too much trouble."

"Sure," I said.

She grabbed me by the arm and led me out without waiting for Dan's approval. Next to her were two blocky bodyguards. They looked the same as bodyguards I'd seen everywhere else in the world; human golems that specialized in inflicting pain.

"What's he want to see me for?" I asked.

"He wanted to say hello."

"Why?"

"You can ask him."

The champ's hotel was two buildings over and it was much nicer than Dan's.

"Do you like cricket fighting?" she asked me on the way.

"Do you?"

"I hate it."

"Me too," I confessed.

"Then why do you do it?"

"Same reason crickets do. To survive."

She covered her mouth with a handkerchief. "Is that why so many people are taken with cricket fighting?"

"What do you think?"

"I think people like to see others suffer," she answered, though I couldn't see her expression.

"I've heard your brother is the best fighter around."

"He has cause."

"He likes to see others suffer?" I asked.

"Suffering can become an addiction."

"Only to those who don't know any other way."

"Do you know any other way?"

I shook my head. "I'm looking."

The lobby was full of people with suitcases, checking in for a weekend of revelry. We had to walk through a scanner that zapped any bed bugs on our clothes and was embarrassed when they found over thirty on me. Prostitutes hung around the bars and martinis were being doled out quicker than canned food at a shelter.

"Does the champ like Tolstoy's writing?" I asked, curious about his name.

"I don't like Simone de Beauvoir, but I have her name."

"It's your given name?"

She nodded. "I misunderstood *Anna Karenina* the first time I read it. It was a comedy, not a drama like I'd initially assumed. Once I got the joke—all the characters were selfish, suffering-addicted, idiots—I realized it was brilliant. Everyone in the book was intentionally a farce."

The champ had a penthouse suite and it was almost as massive as Larry's apartment. The paint was fresh, there were maids who regularly cleaned the rooms, and there was no rank odor in the air. The first thing I heard upon entering were the crickets. Hundreds of them in a clashing choir, chirping love songs in an attempt to silence their rivals. His sister led me into the living room where Tolstoy was talking with a fat black cricket. I assumed that was Zhou, the prize winner. The room itself had brown walls and brown furniture. There were also huge piles of junk-food wrappers in the corners.

"It makes me sad," he said, petting Zhou. "He only has a few more weeks."

Zhou was huge and I realized that even prepared, I would have had no chance against his prize specimen.

"The best crickets come from the Shandong Province," he continued. "But this boy was raised right here in Gamble Town."

"Hello," I said.

"Where do I know you from?" Tolstoy inquired.

"I don't think we know each other."

He put Zhou back in his cage. "Why are you working for that lout?"

"You mean Dan?" He nodded. "I have no choice."

"Do you owe him a debt?"

"No."

"He's set you up against me at the end of the week. I've seen your three fights. You're in no condition to be fighting, unless you're the best faker I've ever met and you're pulling a scam. Even if you were, I'd still crush you."

"I used to fight a long time ago."

"I know," he said. "You use older techniques based on older interfaces. But there's no way you'll be ready for me in a week."

"We'll find out."

"Don't kid yourself. One more dive and you're going to get wired permanently."

I wasn't sure how to respond. He was stating the obvious, but why? He was an 18- or 19-year-old teenager, just a kid who barely knew the ways of the world. Was he gloating, trying to scare me away, or just showing off his superiority?

"You'll be the fifth he's done this to," Tolstoy continued. "He makes just enough to keep him going until the next sucker."

"Unless you're willing to let me make some phone calls, I don't have a choice."

"Who would you call?"

"It doesn't matter."

He held out his hand and in it was his phone.

"What's that?" I asked.

"Make your calls."

"What's the catch?"

"There is no catch."

"Are you setting me up?"

"For what?"

"I don't know," I replied, confused by his generosity.

"Make your calls."

I took the phone, stared at him, then at Beauvoir. Tolstoy was tending to his crickets again while Beauvoir watched me with concerned eyes.

I tried to access my account's phone list on a centralized computer, but the authentication wouldn't go through. I didn't remember my passwords because everything was hooked into my own phone which was long gone. I tried typing in numbers I'd memorized, called an old friend, Stan, who had often called me when he was having financial woes. "Stan, I'm in a lot of trouble."

"Nick, I'd love to talk right now, but I'm in trouble with my girlfriend."

"I thought you were married."

"Exactly. Can we talk later?" Before I could reply, he hung up. I tried calling back but his phone was set to off.

I called four other friends and all of them were too busy for me with my friend Dominique being the biggest disappointment as he'd told me so many times, "You can always call me for anything."

"You having trouble there?" Tolstoy asked.

Who else could I call? No other numbers came to mind. Except one.

Rebecca Lian with her 7s and 2s.

"Nick!" she exclaimed on the phone screen once the call patched through. "You finally got my messages."

"What messages?"

"I tried calling after I saw the explosion on the news, but your phone kept on going to voicemail."

The worry on her face surprised me. "I-I need help," I said, desperate.

"Of course. What do you need?"

It took me a second to register her affirmative response. "I-I don't have anything. I'm stuck in this place called Gamble Town."

"I have you on the GPS. Just stay put."

"What do you mean?"

"I'm in Shanghai so I should be able to get there in an hour or two. Can I call you at this number?" I looked up at Tolstoy to confirm and he gave me the number of the hotel instead. She told me she'd be here soon.

I gave Tolstoy his phone back.

"Thank you," I told him, sincerely meaning it.

He put his hands through his hair and the way it flowed off his fingers, I could have sworn it was real. "I know what it's like to be enslaved. We're all slaves in one way or another."

There was a loud banging on the door. "Open the door!" I heard Dan shout. "Open the door right now! I want to see my investment!"

The guards answered and when the three of us went to meet him, Dan seemed surprised.

"What's going on, man?" he demanded of me.

"I'm leaving," I told him.

"What about our agreement?"

"The agreement is off."

"You cheating sonuvabitch! What about the money I wasted on you? I'll take this to the board! I'll have you arrested and sent to debtors prison!"

Tolstoy was about to say something to the guards, but I put my hand on his forearm.

"We fight for it," I said. "Your cricket against mine. If I lose, I'll come back. But if I win, you go away. Tolstoy, could I borrow one of your crickets?"

He seemed amused. "Of course."

Dan looked irritated as he fiddled with his fingers. His eyes kept on darting back and forth between the guards and me. He finally blew up. "We had an agreement! You can't take that back!"

"He just challenged you," Tolstoy said. "Either accept or get out of here before I have you thrown out."

Dan's eyes constricted. He was calculating in his head if he could do it.

"You're going to regret this." He sat down, taking out one of his crickets.

Tolstoy gave me one of his better fighters after jacking me into the interlink. The cricket was easy to control, being in top shape and brimming with hormones. He was ready to take on any combatant and attracted female crickets everywhere he went. I could smell the lust and envied him for being everything I was not. I shook my head, telling myself, *I can't afford to get distracted by jealousy for a cricket.* I had to block out all thoughts—fear, longing, the desire for the things I didn't have. *Blank it out. There is no future or past. Only death for the weak.*

Filters were essential for mental survival, swaths and gauges that acted as memory swipes for distractions and irrelevancies. Everything became irrelevant in death. Beauvoir put her hand on my shoulder, easing my shaking. My mind was getting dizzy and I knew this would be a fight of endurance. I reminded myself that Dan didn't have the stomach to handle this too long. If I could just outlast him, even in my condition, I knew it would screw up his brain enough for him to have to surrender. Talent could sway things, but Dan was no pilot. I'd lived through too much to surrender here. When he plugged in, I saw his cricket and realized it was the one I'd used earlier. He was no match for Tolstoy's cricket. My own was ready to attack, annoyed by the presence of this outsider who'd encroached upon his harem. Still, even with the physical advantage, my mental links felt shredded. The leaps and attacks were making my head feel scrambled. I was nauseous and my intestines were unraveling so they could crawl their way up my esophagus. *Who is this stranger? How dare he try to take part of what I've fought so hard to earn?* I leapt out but something held me back, an electric current making my membrane twitch. Something was commanding me to refrain. Six legs to march, hind legs to thrust. Everything smelled, especially this cricket that was trying to ram me. I knew he was hungry and didn't have the will to fight. But Dan was driving him. I finally felt the grip on my muscles loosen as the sync went into place and charged the other, kicking him with a thrust to his torso. That knocked him back and I bit into his antennae to try to rip it off. He smelled of fear and death. I reveled in the miasma of violence that we both were waddling in. I tore the antennae off and bit into his face, ripping off the mask. He made a sharp shriek, tried to withdraw. I lunged onto his back and attacked his shell. Right when I was about to split his back apart, water doused my head. I blinked and was human again, only everything seemed globular and nebulous. Next to me was Beauvoir. I could smell every part of her and it aroused me. I grabbed her and bit into her neck, wanted to rip her clothes off and take her. My hands searched her body in maddening lust and I tore off the top of her dress. Her breasts felt like plums for me to squeeze and I bit into her chest, wanting to merge myself into her. "Don't hurt him! He's still synced!" someone sang. Was it her? Did she sing? But her voice was shrill. I could wing her a song, reverberate along my wings.

I couldn't control my breathing, I wanted to ravish and consume her. She did not flinch, but clutched me tight, arms around me. There was a sharp pinch on my neck. The dizziness became circular before dancing away. I saw that blood looked a hundred times more crimson against her white skin. The intense smells dampened.

"Are you back with us? Nick. Are you back with us?"

I stared up at Beauvoir who was half-naked and looked more beautiful than any woman I'd ever seen. "I-I think so."

I remembered the fight, remembered the crickets. Tolstoy was holding a syringe. They must have given me some kind of stimulant to break the sync. I looked over at Dan. Dan was on the ground in a seizure, his pupils where his lids were. Vomit and spittle were ramming their way out of the corner of his mouth.

He was shaking in uneven tremors, his body a discombobulated mess.

"Get him out of here," Tolstoy ordered one of the guards.

I wondered how much of Dan's memory would survive. They dragged him out and even though I was disgusted by the way he'd treated me, I hoped he'd recover.

I looked back at Beauvoir. "I-I'm sorry."

She shook her head. "You were crazy to fight him in your condition."

I averted my eyes. "Probably."

"What if you hadn't been able to break the sync?" Tolstoy asked.

It all came back to me in one swoop. "I would rather have died as a cricket than go back to being his slave."

"As a cricket, you would have been my slave."

I hadn't thought of that and he saw the acknowledgement in my face which caused him to laugh. His phone rang and he talked quickly before hanging up. He looked to Beauvoir. "I have to go. Will you be okay?"

"Of course," she replied.

Tolstoy put on his coat and as he was about to leave, asked, "Do you know a Larry Chao?"

"Larry Chao is dead," I answered.

He smiled a sad simper. "So I've been told." He raised up his cricket. "Say goodbye to our wandering stranger. This'll be the last time you see him."

Zhou chirped an indifferent farewell. He had more important things on his mind.

X.

I could barely stand and Beauvoir, who'd changed her clothes, led me to the sofa. "Do you need anything?"

"Don't ask me that," I said.

"Why not?"

"You don't want to hear my answer," I said, and felt stupid. I was still raging with hormones and even though I knew I was under the influence of the cricket sync, I wanted her more than I'd wanted anyone. The way she moved, her effeminate steps, the rosiness in her cheeks. My thoughts shamed me, especially as she had been so generous and kind. *It's the cricket in you, Nick, the cricket.*

"I've seen others who've suffered worse syncing issues than you," she said.

"I'm still sorry."

"Don't be," she answered with a pleasant smile.

It took all my discipline not to reach out and grab her and tear off her clothes again. Instead, I tried to focus on the victory. It wasn't much of a victory, but I'd survived. *Dan is gone. You will be able to go back home.* But my mind couldn't stay anchored as lust was swelling through me and my pants felt uncomfortably taut.

"Do you want one of these?" she asked, holding up a pill.

"What is it?"

"It'll help you sleep until your friend comes. You need some rest or your brain will stay a mess."

She gave it to me along with a cup of water. I swallowed the pill. She placed her hand on my cheek. "I didn't mean to question your sanity back there. You were very brave."

"No. You're right. I was crazy and stupid. I didn't need to fight him."

"You did. For yourself."

"Great good it did me."

"That's the only fight worth fighting," she said intently.

Right as I was about to reply, I fell asleep.

She woke me a minute later.

"I'm sorry," I was saying. "I don't kno—"

"Your friend is here," she said.

I shook my head. "How long have I been out?"

"Three hours."

Rebecca was across from me and I almost didn't recognize her. She was taller than I remembered and from the look in her eyes, I gathered how sorry I must have looked. "We have to get you to a hospital."

As we left, I turned around and looked at Beauvoir. "I owe you and your brother my life."

She shook her head. "Neither my brother nor I believe in debts."

"I do. I'll pay you back one day."

She looked like a doll as she regarded me with plaintive eyes. I wondered what I looked like to her.

7. Shanghai Intrigues

I.

Stasis, a freezing feeling, my chest congealed. Thoughts were still active during the dreams of hibernation. I argued with a guy named Cleaver who carried a chainsaw wherever he went; a tsunami of soda threatened to destroy dinner with old colleagues I hadn't seen in decades; I was back in Hong Kong in my friend's tiny studio, overwhelmed by monsoon season, wishing there was more space to stretch as moths ate their way through my skin to my liver. Dreams were melting into reality and reality was a forgotten dream that seemed distant and unnervingly vague. Why was it for all the money researchers spent studying DNA and nerves, they still didn't have any idea what dreams really were? Could they possibly be subconscious replays formed by bored brain neurons playing with memories the way people played with golf balls? My awareness of my split consciousness made me realize I was about to come out of a deep sleep. I'd been put under. How many imagined conversations had I had during that time? How many forgotten epiphanies?

Cryogenic healing was the way of contemporary Asian medicine. Nanobots and regenerative chemicals stimulated the nerves, allowing the body to naturally heal as much as it could. Microbacteria ate my crap and recycled it into nutrients that succored my skin. This wasn't Los Angeles with their tubes and million-dollar surgeries that made me feel like a machine-grafted chimera perpetually addicted to surgical fixes that never fixed anything and became dropping palliatives to fatten doctor's wallets. Miniscule organic machines were collaborating with my cells to make me better, communicating in quantum entanglement that stirred cellular rebirth in what others might have mistaken for telepathy. Doctors acted as guides rather than technicians meandering through the clumsy schematic they deemed an operation.

I'd asked them to use the best treatment possible for my teeth. I wouldn't have them removed no matter how much the dentists insisted. Even if there was only a bit left of my teeth, they'd suffered for me. I wasn't going to have them pulled and replaced by artificial crowns, damn root canals and teeth pains. I had them all capped and given calcium reinforcements. *I promised you tea and wine, and you'll get it.*

Rebecca awaited my awakening. The first question I asked was, "Did they find out who killed Larry yet?"

She ignored my question and informed me, "They want you to stay under for two more days. You have no other family, do you?"

"Why?"

"They needed someone to sign for you, but there wasn't anyone listed."

I nodded gratefully. "I don't know how I can thank you for staying here with me like this."

"Get better."

A two-day dream passed in what seemed like minutes. By the time they pulled me out, tested my muscles, and checked my organs ten times, I felt like a new man. Rebecca bought me clothes; a thick yellow coat that thinned with the seasons, jeans, and a striped collar shirt. I looked like a typical Shanghai student.

It was time for the inevitable bill. Even with insurance, my treatment cost a fortune. I didn't care. I was alive and I was starving. I could have eaten a hundred buffets, though I would have been content with one. Hamburgers, Peking *kaoya*, Chicago-style deep-crusted pizza, medium-rare prime rib covered with pepper, ahi tuna, green curry, anything but king crab legs and that hot sauce that still reminded me of burning. As Rebecca escorted me out to her car, taller, and I suspect, much stronger than me, I felt her body against mine and I thought of my reaction to Beauvoir. I reminded myself that not only was Beauvoir nowhere near, but I was with Rebecca.

It always rained in Shanghai. Many called her Venice of the East. I'd been to Venice, and it never looked as glamorous and ritzy as Shanghai. I generally based my perception of futuristic cities off of what I'd seen in movies. Shanghai was kind of like them, except with a higher budget and a whole lot more advertisements. New buildings went up every week. Entrepreneurs waged bragging wars to see who could build taller buildings (and no, it wasn't just a cock fight as women were equally aggressive in their construction races). I always got snobby treatment in Shanghai. I loved the city; it just didn't love me back. I looked over at Rebecca, the most unlikeliest of saviors. Why had she come to my aid?

"Did they find Larry's killers yet?" I asked her.

"You asked me that before and I don't understand what you mean."

"Larry was murdered before they kidnapped me."

"Who kidnapped you? And what are you talking about? Mr. Chao is fine."

"I saw Larry's body."

She turned on the television in the car. "Larry Chao," she said. It brought up a hundred feeds of Larry escorted by various models. "That's from a party two days ago."

"That's impossible. W-what about the factory explosions?" I asked.

"Generator malfunctions. Several managers were arraigned on incompetence charges and imprisoned."

"Those were terrorist attacks," I said.

She looked worried. "The doctors told me you took a lot of physical trauma. They said your memory might be affected."

"If Larry were alive, he'd be looking for me."

"How could anyone guess you'd been kidnapped?"

I still couldn't believe he was alive. "Can I use your phone?"

She handed it to me but I realized I didn't know Larry's number.

"Do you have his number?"

"Not on me. Just at the office," she said.

I'd have to get home and log into my network.

"You can log in at my apartment. You also need some food. I'll order ahead. Anything specific you feel like?"

"Everything," I replied.

II.

I attacked my food, became a garbage disposal of everything coming my way. I chewed softly, letting my teeth and gums savor every bite, the juices dripping on my tongue. My body had endured oblivion. I didn't know how long my resurrection would last, but I would appreciate it while it did. I was thrilled by the taste of garlic bok choy, braised pork, and steamed fish. I went over and held Rebecca's hand and jumped with joy and drank down two glasses of wine like they were water. My stomach had shrunk and I got full quickly but I kept on stuffing it, unable to countenance limitation. *Eat stomach. Eat like it's the last meal of your life!*

Rebecca was amused by my boyish giddiness and said, "You eat like you haven't eaten in years."

She'd taken off her white coat and wore a white dress that emphasized the contours of her body. I was surprised to see the jade fox necklace that I'd gotten her around her neck. Small gold chains held them in place and my mind had a sudden flash to the torture room where I'd been chained up. I would have groveled for a taste of anything then. I forced back the memories, took generous portions of the onion-grilled kale and sweet shrimp. My eyes went back to the necklace and the way it lay on top of her skin. I was drunk, my knees wobbly. I could feel the hair along the back of my neck bristling and turned away from her. She asked, "You full?"

"I was full twenty minutes ago."

"Is it time for dessert then?"

Salt-caramel ice cream and chocolate-mocha cupcakes. "How'd you know these were my favorite?"

"I looked up your profile the first time we met."

Food coma sort of described my feeling, though as I'd just come out of a semi-coma, I was acutely aware of the differences. *Larry, are you really still alive? If so, does this mean everything can go back to normal?*

I would have to deal with those questions later after I let my stomach digest the food.

"What else was in my profile?" I asked.

"That you're naturally a follower."

"Anything wrong with following?"

"Depends on who's leading."

I nodded and asked, "Were your mom's salons in Shanghai?"

"You remembered," she said, seeming genuinely impressed. "Shanghai and Hangzhou. But after the Baldification, we were lucky just to have a home. Is Beijing home for you?"

"I don't know if I have a home anymore after everything that's happened."

"Do you want to talk about it?"

I tried to explain in brief, but as I remembered the forced cricket interlinks and my teeth fighting against the stone in my mouth, my heart started racing.

"We can talk about something else," she offered.

"Sorry. It's a long story."

"When you were under, the hospital told me you used to have a different name."

"I used to be Gene Liang until I joined the army."

"Why the name change?"

"Another long story."

"You have a lot of those."

"Don't you have your share?"

There was an air of melancholy about her as she nodded.

"Do you ever miss your hair?" I asked.

"I like the freedom of wigs. You?"

"No. But I guess we'd all look different."

"You look like a different man since the last time I saw you."

"I feel like a different man," I answered.

"I like it. You look more handsome skinny."

"T-thank you. And you. You look lovely."

She simpered.

I looked around her apartment. She had a thing for white; white sofas, white shelves, and white marble floors. Even her rugs were ermine. She lived above a prison, making her studio one of the safest places in the world. Residential properties above jails were the most sought-after places in the world for multiple reasons, the principal being security. Even if a riot broke out, prisons were safe, stacked with the meanest police guards in the world as well as the security drones that never faltered.

Cameras were inside most residences and it had all begun with nanny cams placed by caring parents to make sure nothing was going awry in their absence. After a few break-ins went bad but were recorded by these secret cameras, people started requesting internal cameras as part of the property. At first, private companies were in charge of installations, and then it expanded to a government service. Within a decade, everyone in the world wanted a camera in their home, so much so that it became a crucial part of the realtor's negotiations. A United Nations agency was set up to regulate domestic security and while some jokingly referred to them as Big Brother (an arcane reference to an ancient writer who couldn't understand how crucial surveillance was to the survival of the individual), most just knew them as the Vid Coppers.

Vid Coppers were watching our meal, making sure my drunken state wouldn't turn into something that might go against the request of my hostess. Mostly, it was an AI machine that measured hormonal levels and motion activity to interpret possible criminal behavior. I guess my hormonal levels were suspect as Rebecca got a phone call. She picked up, *uh huh'd* a few times, then hung up.

"They're telling me you're horny and I should be careful," she said and laughed heartily.

"What?" I asked.

"Your face is red."

"I'm sorry," I said, completely embarrassed.

"The doctor warned me you'd be like this," she replied. "It's the increased hormonal activity from your therapy. Don't worry. I won't hold it against you."

I knew if Larry were here, he would have said some suave line, turned things in his favor, then swooped her off her feet. I couldn't get over my initial shame at being found out and asked her if she minded me using her computer to log into my network. "Sure, go ahead," she told me. She put her palm against the wall which turned into a 3D display.

I sat down, logged on, and tried to determine if anyone had stolen my identity.

We all had one global identity number, confirmed by a passcode, voice-identity test, and several random algorithms hooked into the credit agencies. While I'd forgotten my password, a scan of my eye, fingerprints, and voice unlocked my account. I reset the basic codes and went through a list of all my financial accounts as well as my personal communication number. Everything was intact. No unusual activity, not even the leech-ware that sucked one to two cents every month and wasn't worth reporting as that invited reprisal from hackers who'd get upset that their tiny tribute exacted from millions could encounter resistance (our modern-day protection racket). I had to delete spam and block out news updates about the garbage epidemic and the property selling in Antarctica.

"Everything okay?" she asked, sidling up next to me. Her hip brushed against my arm. She smelled like apricots.

"Yeah, perfect," I answered. "I was expecting worse."

I tried calling Larry but his communicator was off.

"Mr. Chao will be in Shanghai tomorrow," Rebecca said.

"For what?" I asked, still unable to get my head around the idea that he was alive.

"Attending a convention to show his latest movie."

"*Rodenticide?*"

"It's been huge a hit since the explosions. Everyone's been raving about it. Number-one hit all over the world."

I thought about how depressed he'd been over the lack of attention the film had initially received. Then reminded myself that I'd seen his corpse. I checked all the different links and pages. Reports, video, and photographs of Larry were everywhere. I was perplexed. Had I hallucinated his death?

"Dr. Asahi told me about the convention a week ago and said I should check it out as long as I was in Shanghai," Rebecca interjected. "A real-life big explosion is all he needed for fame."

I brooded on it, confused.

"How do you rank *Rodenticide?*" she asked.

"What do you mean?"

"I mean among the movies you worked on."

It took me a second to register what she was asking. "I'm not sure."

"What was your favorite movie to work on?" she asked, and I realized she was trying to get my mind off the situation.

"*58 Random Deaths and Unrequited Love.*"

"Why?"

"W-we wanted to make a movie showing how pointless everything was," I answered.

"You think everything is pointless?"

"I could have died out there and no one would have known. The overwhelming motivation for me to come back was to avenge Larry. If I'd known he were still alive, I probably would have just waited for him to come to the rescue."

Rebecca filled my cup with wine and took a long draught herself.

"Would you still make the same movie if you went back in time?"

"No one would ever make the same movie they did when they were younger," I replied and finished my cup. "What kind of movie would you make if you could make one?"

"I don't know if I'd ever want to make a movie."

"Why not?"

"I don't want to spend a year of my life suffering just so I can make other people happy, then wait to hear what critics say, hoping they'll like it enough so people can watch it. Why don't you make your own movies?"

"You already know the answer to that. I'm a 'follower'."

Rebecca chuckled. "My ex was a follower who wanted to be a leader. He never could accept that he didn't have what it took to be a leader. He eventually divorced me so he could meet other women."

"He cheated on you?" I wondered, surprised.

"He was honest enough to separate with me before sleeping with any other women. I respect him for that. Do men always want more?"

"I don't know very many that want less."

"What about content with what they have?"

"That takes a humility and a level of awareness that isn't much valued in our world," I said, knowing how hollow it sounded.

"Do you have that level of awareness?"

"I used to until I got married."

"She pushed you?"

I shook my head. "I wanted to give her the world for all she'd done for me."

"Why?"

"She gave me something no one else ever had."

"What?"

"Family. Even now, I'd give up the world for her."

Rebecca laughed. "I didn't know you were such a romantic."

"I like to pay my debts."

"So she's a debt to you?"

"At our wedding ceremony, her family had hundreds of people. You know how many my side had?"

She shook her head.

I made a big zero with my thumb and index fingers.

"It was humiliating," I admitted, thinking back to the day. "But she didn't care. Her family treated me like their own even though I had nobody. I'll never forget that."

"Why did you guys separate?"

"I was an insecure asshole who pushed her away," I answered, the drink making me more honest than I should have been. "I was pretty terrible to her near the end."

"Where is she now?"

"I don't know," I shrugged. "Unrequited love is my theme song."

"Doesn't have to be," she said. "Maybe you just like it that way."

"Everyone likes to make up movie versions of themselves in their mind."

"You have no other family?"

"Larry's the only other person I consider family."

"Did he come to the wedding?"

I shook my head. "He got entangled in a *menage a trois* with two sisters he'd been chasing for four years. I was pissed at him, but at the same time, I couldn't blame him. Still, he was supposed to stand in as my honorary brother. I was disappointed."

"Sorry."

"Don't be. Is there a way we can get hold of Larry now?"

"If he isn't picking up, I don't know any other way. But we can see him for sure at the convention tomorrow. Plus, I think the cast of *Star Force 22B* is going to be there and I've always wanted to meet them."

III.

It felt nice being able to use a real toilet. I'd taken these bowls for granted in the past. No longer. There was a noise muffler to mute my flatulence which was loud after exuberant usage. *Gastronomic bombs, you called them, Larry.* My stomach, unable to handle so much food, banished 80% of it out my ass. I cleaned meticulously, wiped my hands, and looked in the mirror. My cheeks had sunken in and I looked like half the man I'd been. I checked my weight and saw that I'd lost 60 pounds.

Rebecca was asleep on her bed. She'd set up a mattress on the ground and I lay down in her white sheets.

"Is it uncomfortable?" she asked which surprised me as I thought she was sleeping.

"Most comfortable bed I've slept on in ages," I answered her.

I lay on my side, rustled back and forth, scratched an itch.

She burst out laughing.

"What?" I asked.

"You fart really loud," she said.

I was embarrassed. "I had the muffler on," I offered weakly.

"Don't worry. I fart loud too."

"Sorry."

"Don't be," she said, laughing at me. "Do you like fruit juices?"

"Apple a day keeps the doctor away, right?"

"Organic apple a day," she corrected me.

"Why do you ask?"

"That's going to be our breakfast."

"Apples?"

"Fruit juice."

The window was open and I heard a woman singing a song in Mandarin. Cars honked and a couple drunks were causing a ruckus. Shanghai was always bustling, even in the middle of the night. L.A. had a different kind of noise. Linda and me used to hear people screaming, homeless people in vituperations against one another. There were constant gunshots, sirens blaring, and drones warning citizens to stay indoors while they searched for criminals.

"If you see a big roach running around, don't hurt it," she suddenly said. "That's my pet cockroach, Kafka."

"What?!" I exclaimed and got up. "Where?"

"He should be back in his cage, but he gets curious when strangers visit."

"How big?"

She appeared amused. "Don't tell me you're afraid of a tiny little roach."

"Where is it?"

"Check his cage on my shelf."

"If he's not there?"

"Check your bed."

The glass cage was damp and home to an ebony roach fuller than my thumb.

"He's been genetically modified to be smarter than your regular roach," Rebecca said.

"He's not tiny," I said.

Rebecca laughed. "You're like a hundred times bigger than him."

"I hate roaches."

"No matter how scared you are of him, he's a thousand times more scared of you."

"I'm not scared," I said.

"Uh huh."

"Can we shut his cage?" I asked.

"Makes him really grumpy. How about you just sleep on the bed?"

I turned to her.

"You afraid of me too?" she asked.

I got in the bed, turned away from her, and said, "Good night."

"Good night. And point your ass the other way. I heard what a deadly weapon it is."

IV.

I had a hard time sleeping, thinking about Larry and everything that had happened. In the morning, we took a cab to the convention center in Nanjing Road as parking was nearly impossible without paying a small fortune. Nanjing Road was the biggest shopping street in the world and got bigger every day. There were hundreds of thousands of pedestrians and all kinds of stores assembled as a honeycomb of merchandising. I saw massive 3D billboards of female actresses selling watches and hundreds of watch stores below, profiting from subjugating time into whimsical measures. The solar watch from the Han Dynasty was right next to the dictionary from a forgotten dialect as well as a series of multicolored video-game consoles from an age when you needed cartridges to play them. All the advertisements of beautiful Asians made sex blasé by their ubiquity even though they were designed to make women feel insecure and men lust after digitally enhanced women that didn't really exist. There was still haggling, vendors selling people things they didn't need.

The convention center blended in with the rest of the tall buildings, a structure meant to pay homage to the Summer Palace in Beijing with its classical Chinese architecture. Thousands of guests were waiting, many dressed in costumes from their favorite TV shows. Banners for the Global Entertainment Awards (GEAs) were everywhere, urging audiences to watch in two days. There were tables filled with vendors selling paraphernalia from the shows; posters, recordings, toys, artifacts from the filming, and green stand-ins for guns and props that were replaced digitally. Many walked around in the purple hoods of an old show, *Project Circumstance*, revolving around a sect of Chinese kung-fu fighting monks who also used laser beams. There was *Man-Boobs*, a reality show about obese men who fought hard to take part in bikini contests around the world, only to receive the scorn of those who wanted to see buxom women. *Star Force 22B* used to be one of the most popular shows in the world, creating a universe where humanity transcended its violent past to establish a society based on nobler virtues. They harnessed a black hole to propel a fleet of ships throughout the galaxy. I watched them growing up, inspired by their sense of honor to conduct myself in a manner that would make humanity proud. The crew of the original show was signing autographs and selling digital images of themselves for 100 SC. They looked so much older in person and even though it had been fifteen years since the show had been popular, it was depressing seeing them charge money for their images. They stopped attendees from taking their picture without paying via a digital scrambler and scowling assistants informed people to put their cameras away. The show used to represent the most egalitarian of futures, a universe where man was not inherently a brute bent on exploiting his neighbor. And yet, here they were, nickel and diming everyone. I knew they had to make a living. But seeing the thousands in line for an autograph made me realize what I'd always known; this was show business with an emphasis on the *business* part.

"You going to stand in line?" I asked Rebecca.

She laughed. "They're so old, I don't even recognize them anymore."

"You can pay 3000SC for a photo with the whole group."

"Is it that much?"

"Yeah."

"I think I'd rather pay my rent."

I felt worse for the extras, the actors who played aliens people had forgotten about. They sat in the corners, ignored, nary a visitor at their booth. They were trying to look busy scanning their holopads, assembling their goods on their table to make them tidier. Even if the main crew of *Star Force* came across as greedy, at least they didn't reek of desperation.

There was a huge image of *Rodenticide* playing on the big screen above. "The Number One Movie in the world!" the bombastic narrator declared. Rebecca tapped me on the shoulder. I turned and saw Larry thronged by fans, a fedora secure above his head.

Emotions overwhelmed me—I never thought I'd see him again. All the suffering I'd endured for the past few weeks withered.

"Larry!" I shouted. "Larry!"

Larry looked at me and grinned. "Where the hell have you been?"

I didn't understand how Larry could be living in front of me. I knew for a fact that I'd seen his lifeless body. And yet, here he was, breathing. "I thought you were dead."

Larry burst out laughing. "That's a nice way to greet me. You disappeared for almost two months."

"I-I was kidnapped by Shinjee's friends."

"Where did they take you?"

"I can tell you about it later," I said, noticing all the people staring at us. "Can we talk in private?"

"Absolutely. Can we make it later? I have a big crowd waiting for me."

"Yeah of course." I hesitated. "Larry, I hope you don't take offense at what I'm about to do."

"What do you—"

I grabbed his shirt and lifted it up to check his stomach. Sure enough, there was a tattoo of a frog and even the misspelled Mandarin. It was Larry alright. I couldn't believe it.

"There's a lot we need to talk about, man," I said to him.

"You can start with where you've been. But we'll talk more

later. Unless you want to join me? I'm sure they'd love to drill my DP about my films."

"I'll leave it to you."

He was whisked away by a big crowd. I felt happy for him, seeing how much acclaim the movie was getting from fans.

"You okay?" Rebecca asked.

"I feel like I've seen a ghost," I answered. "Except the ghost came back to life." I put my hand on her arm. "Thank you."

"For what?"

"F-for everything."

"You look like you need a drink."

"I could use one. In fact, I wouldn't mind getting drunk."

She smiled. "There's a million bars right outside the convention center."

We hit up one that was welcoming fans of Japanese gangster movies and they had all sorts of saké on sale. The waitresses were dressed up as white-masked geishas and the waiters had plastic guns strapped to their belts. We ordered a sampler of ten different sakés and guzzled them down.

"Am I crazy?" I asked her. "Did I even see anyone dead? Maybe I got it all mixed up."

I tried to recollect the specifics of that night, but it was blurry in my head, aggravated by the fact that my world was spinning from the drinks.

"Mistakes happen," she offered.

"You ever hear about a guy who mistook his best friend for a corpse?"

"No."

I looked at my empty glass and pointed at the bartender who filled it up. "Did you see all his fans? Larry was worried nobody would care about his movies. But looks like people do care."

"I love them," Rebecca said.

"We were making movies we believed in. I didn't care if anyone watched them or not."

"Is that just something all you artist types have to say? Because I don't believe you."

I chuckled. "I guess I did care a little."

"You guys can get back to making more movies."

"He was talking about making a big epic. Something to do with the Baldification."

"Can I get a walk-on role? It can be something small."

"Of course."

"So, connections do matter," she said.

"Anyone who thinks otherwise doesn't know what they're talking about," I replied. "Drink more. Everything's on me tonight."

V.

I had a hundred questions, none of them explicable. If Larry were alive, why had Shinjee kidnapped me, even if she did give me a way out? I owed her a visit. I owed a lot of people visits. Rebecca was singing and dancing and I wondered why she was spending so much time with me. Was I incapable of reading signals? Was she interested in me? She was beautiful. Not as beautiful as Beauvoir, but still very attractive.

"They're sending more colonists to Mars," Rebecca said, pointing at the news.

Trillions of dollars were being spent so a handful of astronauts could live on an enormous red rock when millions of people were starving in Europe.

"I heard Venus used to be like earth until pollution wiped it out and made it into a big poisonous ball of gas."

I used to love looking at stars with Linda. We'd make up our own constellations and draw imaginary patterns through the lights.

"I guess it'll be okay as long as we don't end up like that planet between Mars and Jupiter. Kaboom!" she yelled. "I think it'd be nice to live on Pluto."

"Why?"

"Wherever you go, it can only get brighter."

I stood up, then stumbled from the drink. She grabbed me before I fell. I was about to thank her when I saw her face right in front of mine. Her lips were just inches away. I could feel her breath on mine. I wanted to move my lips forward just a bit. We both hesitated. I wilted first. "I think I need to step out and get some fresh air," I said.

"Don't get lost," she answered.

I rubbed my eyes and walked out. It was pouring rain and I had no umbrella. The thunder boomed and the skies were painted black.

I still can't believe you're alive, Larry.

"Why did you come back here?" someone asked.

I turned around and saw a teen in a black trench coat. He had a translucent umbrella and white hair that reminded me of Tolstoy, the cricket champion. But this guy had a much leaner nose, smaller eyes, and bulkier frame. When I tried to examine him more carefully, he withdrew. I was too drunk to persist.

"This is my first time at the convention," I informed him, wondering if he'd mixed me up with someone else.

"They have such a nice arrangement now. You'll ruin it for them, Nick Guan."

How did he know my name? "Do I know you?"

"You're going to disrupt their plans if you stay."

"What plans? Who the hell are you?"

He laughed. "I know you're confused. Don't you get the joke?"

"No."

"You should be laughing."

"Why?"

"You're the punch line and you don't even know it."

"I don't know what you're talking about."

"Don't you?" he asked. "I'm a brewer of storms and I'm going to show you a storm unlike any you've seen before. Make sure you get out of the rain." He tossed me his umbrella, then ran off.

I went back inside and overheard Rebecca talking on a communicator to someone.

"—doing my best to keep him busy... What do you mean you gotta leave? You're the one who told me to keep him here... I'm not gonna sleep with him just to—no, no. I don't care how important it is. That's your problem. He doesn't know anything. At least not from what he's told me... You're just being paranoid." Who was she talking to?

She spotted me and ended the communication.

"Larry's manager called," she said.

"Where we gonna meet him?"

"Larry had to cancel because of an emergency press junket in America he had to fly out to. I think it's something related to presenting at the GEAs. He did ask if you'd be willing to go on a few press junkets in Europe."

I felt disappointed. There was so much I needed to talk with him about.

"Come back inside," Rebecca said. "I hate drinking alone."

VI.

The teen's words nagged me. Was everything going too smoothly? Maybe it was nothing, just all in my head. Rebecca had passed out and I carried her back to her place. Drunk and barely conscious, I helped her into bed, tucking her in. "It's so hot," she muttered, then wrestled off her shirt and bra to lay in bed. I saw her dark nipples clash against her skin.

"Larry," she called. "Larry, come to bed."

What the hell?

I forced myself to the bathroom and washed up; exited the apartment, flagged down a cab, and asked for the train station. I was taking the bullet train to Beijing. Maybe Rebecca's slipup meant nothing. But I owed Shinjee a visit. I also needed to see

George and see if I could procure some new gadgets.

As I boarded the train, I wondered if Rebecca was in love with Larry. Were they secretly lovers? It didn't make sense. I thought about what she'd said about the planets. I felt like that shattered planet and I'd just gotten back from Pluto. Only I didn't know if I was going to a brighter place or that oblivion beyond our solar system from which there was no return.

8. Machinations of a Prince

I.

I waited for George outside of his Beijing apartment in the morning. He smelled of bacon and beer. A group of people were practicing tai-chi outside despite the poisonous mist. Workers in gas masks were cleaning up the streets with traditional brooms. When George saw me, he quickened his pace and asked, "Vhat you doing here?"

"I came by to say hello."

"Hello. Goodbye."

He tried to walk past me. "George, what the hell, man?"

"I can't be seen talking to you."

"Why not?"

He looked up at the apartments, then down the street, a paranoid tension in his movements. "I can't compromise my family."

"It's just me, George," I said. "Do you not work for Larry anymore?"

He became extremely nervous, his eyes like tiny, scared slits. "Vhat you need?"

"I was hoping for light bombs and some other gadgets."

"Vhat for?"

"I'm investigating something."

George shook his head. "I can't help you."

He hurried forward, but as he did, he stumbled on the curb and fell. I immediately ran over to assist him. He whispered in my ear, "Go to Vudaokou Storage #301 and scan your finger-prints."

He rose to his feet and hurried away.

In all the years I'd known him, I'd never seen him so scared.

I took the subway to Wudaokou Station. Vendors sold used shoes, oxygen refills, and bottled water. It was always busy and the subway was jammed with people rushing to work, home, their lovers, and wherever else they needed to have been an hour ago. The subway TVs were covering the Mars launch, the first joint expedition between China and Brazil. Space was pitch black from the frontal cameras and I wondered what the astronauts talked about between the long hours adrift. I thought of the cells within my own body, venturing into different arteries, traveling along the river of my bloodstream. Every organ was a sprightly city, every neighboring cell a potential neighbor or rival. Were there blood scientists that studied the physics of my body, a history of a universe that would one day come to an end upon my death?

"*Dao le,*" the automated voice told us as we arrived at the Wudaokou Station.

A flood of people rushed out of the train. Another flood filled it back up. After Linda and I had gotten married, a part of me wished we would have stayed in Beijing. Despite its cancer-inducing atmosphere, it was still the city we met in. Could love conquer tumors? Most people here had gas masks hooked into their noses, plastic tubes sticking out of their mouths. It was the capital city and smog wasn't going to deter ambition. America's capital was relatively clean when it came to air pollution, but it was infested with crime. Washington D.C. had been declared a war zone eight times in the past decade, struggling with poverty from the neighboring areas. I still remembered a visit for a photo shoot outside the Thomas Jefferson Memorial. We were staying at a hotel and both Linda and I were starving after a late release. We asked the concierge what restaurants he'd recommend and he told us, "I would recommend not going outside."

"Why not?"

"You most likely will not be coming back, even with armor on."

We had to settle for junk food as delivery services ended after five p.m. throughout the city for safety purposes. Chips, cookies, and a soda salad tasted great when you were hungry.

Wudaokou Storage #301 was close to the station and there were Korean restaurants all over as this was Beijing's Koreatown. I'd have to save my craving for Korean BBQ. The storage warehouse was enormous but the front lobby was tiny, a red brick-affair with a young lady at the front desk playing some game through her goggles. She was flailing her fingers and hands in front of her as she controlled objects only visible to her.

I cleared my throat to get her attention.

"Scan in," she said.

Above her desk, there was a scanner. I put my palm against it and a retinal check followed. There was a confirming ring tone. To the right of me, a part of the brick wall slid open and an elevator awaited. I looked to the girl, but she was still playing her game. I entered the elevator. The door shut and I felt motion. When it opened back up, I was in a small room filled with weapons. It was dusty and the light had a motion sensor that triggered as I stepped in.

On the shelf, there were light bombs, an electric blade that could cut most metals, a small wooden gun that fired chemically coated paralysis darts, as well as a sleek flesh-toned skintight suit. If I wasn't mistaken, this was an adaptive armor suit that warded off most bullets and protected against knife thrusts. It was military-grade, something George must have salvaged from the African Wars. Even though it was designed to fit Larry, it was adaptive and shrunk to fit my body. I put it on under my clothes. Though it didn't provide protection for my head, there was also a black wig shaped like a crew cut that had titanium coating in-between without feeling too heavy on the scalp. I picked up a lens that would go over my eye like a contact lens and acted as a binocular, albeit with streaming data and thermal visuals that could be toggled. All the weapons were nonlethal. There was also a suitcase filled with cash, standard currency.

There wasn't any message or a note. But George had prepared

this, probably at Larry's behest. What was it all for and why include me on the entry codes? What was George so scared of? I had no answers and contented myself with the equipment. I could barely feel the armor under my clothes. I took a stack of cash just in case.

When I left the warehouse, the girl was still playing her game. She didn't even notice my departure.

II.

As soon as I stepped outside, a man in a black suit approached me. He was one of those "faceless"' men I'd heard about but only rarely seen. He'd had plastic surgery/image facilitation to make his face generic, plastic almost to resemble that of a mannequin, skin stretched like Botox gone awry. They were part of a special agency that provided guards that were indistinguishable from one another and could get away with anything since no one could differentiate between the thousands they hired. "My boss would like to see you," he said.

"Who's your boss?"

"Miss Rina Zhang-Gibson."

The Colonel? Chao Toufa's principal rival and the most dreaded military officer in the African Wars. "What does she want?"

"She wanted to welcome you back to Beijing. You can use the phone in the car."

"Do I have a choice?"

"Of course."

He led me to a red limo and I entered the backseat. There was a logo inside that was labeled *Zhang Zhang*, the brand name for her line of wigs. The projectors created a perfect 3D image of her in front of me. I'd never seen her up close. She didn't have a wig on, was older (60s maybe?), wrinkles as battle scars under her eyes. There was a tough duress imprinted in her face, a no-nonsense tautness in her lips. Even when she smiled, there was venom in her gaze. She'd seen things I couldn't begin to fathom. She wore a two-piece purple business suit with a white tie that resembled our old UN uniforms and I could read the tattoo from the insignia of her former African battalion on her scalp; a desert tiger. The King of Hell was there too, and I cringed when I saw the necklace of teeth around her neck.

"What brings you back to Beijing?" she asked.

I could either lie to her, or tell her the truth. Chances were, she was already steps ahead of me. Why did she want to speak to me, a nobody in the chain of things? I had to be careful, ready to jump out of the car and hurtle the light bomb at the guard.

"What do you want?" I asked back, not faltering from her eye line. It wasn't so hard knowing it was only a hologram.

"I want to know where you stand in all of this."

"In all of what?"

"This precarious situation we find ourselves in."

"What's precarious about it?"

"Larry was your close friend?"

"Still is."

"Commodities control the world," she stated. "In the past, the British fought a war for tea. Tulips were the rage for the Dutch. Oil drove most of the internecine Middle-East diplomacy in the early part of the century. Now, hair is the most precious of commodities. I suppose one day, that'll change. But now, we have to fight over who controls the production of hair. *Chao Toufa* has some secret recipe that allows them to make the most realistic hair anyone has ever seen."

"I'm not really involved in the business side of things. I just help Larry shoot his films."

"I've tried everything to find out that formula, but my spies have failed."

"I'm not trying to put you off, ma'am, but I really don't know anything about the formula."

"You know what I've found out in this business?" she asked. I shook my head. "Never underestimate the lengths people will go to quench their vanity. At any time, if you find yourself tired of this farce and want to make a deal, let me know. I can help you. We can do it over a phone call, or you can visit me in Bangkok."

"What kind of deal?"

"I don't want war with you."

"War with me?"

"I've been informed Chao Toufa is trying to make a move against my factories in Saigon and Detroit," she stated.

"Not that I know of."

"There's no need for a charade of innocence. Let's talk terms. What do you want?"

That's what I wanted to know from *her*.

"Respectfully, nothing," I informed her. "I don't have any information about the formula or a fight. I honestly doubt Larry does either, and I don't think the people who do are gonna tell me."

The Colonel regarded me coolly, not saying a word. The message ended abruptly. I stepped out. The messenger I'd seen earlier was smoking on the corner. I didn't care. Everyone was trying to push me around. So she was a psychopath. Could she be any worse than the religious nut I'd endured? I realized, probably. I suppressed a shudder and headed for the Korean restaurant where Shinjee worked.

III.

I couldn't get the deadly glower of the Colonel out of my head. Was I a target now? Was it her that George was so scared of? What made her think I'd know anything about the formula for the hair? Unfortunately, I'd have to deal with that later. Right now, my focus was Shinjee.

I knew she was trouble from the first moment I saw her. But I never thought Larry's relationship with her might nearly get me killed. As I went back to the restaurant, I thought about that first date when Larry told me Hyori looked like Linda to get me to go along. Why had he been so pig-headed about his desire for Shinjee? I felt pain in my teeth, smelled blood even though I knew there wasn't any. The more I thought about Shinjee, the more my gums hurt.

Was Larry getting into another mess with the Colonel? Would I have to rescue him again? Then my mind went to the convention center. He'd barely noticed I'd been gone. I had assumed if I had vanished, he would have scoured the planet to find me. Perhaps I wasn't as important to him as I had believed. The idea disappointed me. It was a wakeup call too. After Linda, I'd attached myself to Larry as he was the closest person to family I had. I'd been looking for family as long as I could remember, searching for it wherever I could, but never truly able to find it. I remembered my biological mother telling me that her birth dream for me was a cute puppy wagging its tail. Was my search for a new family as pathetic as a stray puppy trying desperately to find a home?

Larry always pursued lovers and while in the past, I'd forgiven him his vices, I realized, I was older now. We couldn't play the young man's game forever. I'd survived when I thought there was no way I was going to survive. We couldn't go back to the way things had been in the past.

I would confront Shinjee because I owed her for the suffering I'd undergone. I didn't know exactly what I was going to do to her. But I had to at least confront her. And then?

I felt myopic. The future was too distant. Pain was now.

IV.

The restaurant looked the same as before; a three-story building with BBQ grills and a courtyard. I had been expecting differences and was underwhelmed that there were none. I ordered a beer at the bar, walked through the restaurant but didn't see Shinjee. There were many drunk patrons gorging on kimchee, families enjoying grilled spicy squid, and foreigners who wanted to try something new. I spotted Hyori in a traditional Korean costume serving *soju* to a group of older businessmen, recognizing her by the tattoo of the mouse fighting the lion.

There was a back entrance that led to an alley they used to exit which was where we'd met them on our first date. I'd have to wait there for her later.

If anyone in the restaurant recognized me, they didn't indicate it. Maybe it was the crew-cut wig and the fact that I'd lost so much weight. I ordered a miso soup and rice, ate it slowly to give my body energy. Korean food could be heavy and I needed to keep nimble and spry which was why I held off on ordering any casseroles or meat. There was corn in my rice and my aluminum chopsticks felt heavy in my hands. The tofu in my soup was old, indicating this was from a bigger batch they'd kept boiling throughout the week.

After I finished my meal, I paid my bill and exited. The hostess and several waitresses bowed respectfully and wished me safe travels.

I walked around to the back alley and waited.

V.

It wasn't a long wait. Hyori was in a hurry somewhere and ran out by herself, focused on a phone call. She was blabbering in Korean about a guy she'd met and what a perfect body he had. With what Korean I knew, I translated what she was saying in my head. "It's too bad we gotta have him sent to a camp. We should just keep him around... I know we're behind on quota, but there's only so many we can send at one time... No, I missed that episode. She's such a drama queen... He deserves better. Much better. Like me." A squealing chortle followed.

I raised up my wooden gun and fired. A dart hit her in the neck. It must have felt like a mosquito bite to her. She took a few more steps before coming to a standstill, the chemicals paralyzing her body. I walked towards her and lifted her into my arms. "You've had too much to drink, honey," I said. "I'll carry you."

The best thing about the paralyzer was that it kept her fully conscious. There was a cheap love motel nearby masquerading as a KTV where I rented a room. The attendant gave me a lewd grin when he saw me carrying her in. "Needs somes protections?" he asked, his teeth colored piss yellow.

"I don't like rubbers," I told him.

"Have fun," he said.

VI.

The room had two display screens, a cheap green sofa, concrete floor, a fake plant, and a shelf full of beer. I put Hyori down on the sofa.

"Been a while," I said. I took the gun and fired an activator into her neck that would free the muscles in her mouth.

"W-who are you?"

I looked her straight in the face and from the confusion that stared back, I realized how different I must have appeared to her.

"I'm looking for Shinjee."

"Shinjee? Why?" She looked at me again. "Nick?"

"Where is she?"

"I heard you were killed trying to escape from the convoy."

"If I fire this one more time, your body will be paralyzed permanently. There is no way to reverse it, short of death. I'll ask only one more time. Where's Shinjee?"

"She's doing factory work."

"Where is it?"

Hyori gave me a Beijing address.

"What kind of security do they have there?" I asked.

"They don't need any."

"Why not?"

"No one would leave. They're serving the Great Leader."

I tried to look for the Linda in her, but couldn't see it no matter how hard I tried. I turned around and was about to exit when she shouted, "Wait, you can't just leave me here. Wait! What do you want with Shinjee?! She's a failure! Leave her alone! Hey! Nick! C'mon!"

I shut the door and rushed out the front. The toxin would wear off after a day. But I didn't bother telling her that.

"Done so fast?" the attendant asked.

"I'll be back."

VII.

The factory packed oxygen containers, recycling air and filtering out the toxins so that it was breathable. People could insert the cans into their gas masks. It was a popular item throughout the cities of the world as fresh air was more valuable than food in many places.

The filtering generators in this case were disgusting monstrosities that looked incapable of cleaning anything. Most likely, it was unpurified oxygen packed and sold to people at a slightly lower price by hawkers outside markets. People were breathing the same air they would have without a mask, only paying a premium for the pretty wrapping.

Just as Hyori had said, there was no security. On the outside, it looked like a normal business building with a fence around its periphery and signs written in both Mandarin and Korean. I spotted a conveyor belt that did most of the pumping and sealing of the oxygen. Eight vents spat out smog and the whole place was dusty, smelling of burning vinegar. None of the workers had on any protective gear, though they had to step out every fifteen minutes or so to clear their charred lungs. As bad as it was outside, it was worse inside.

I recognized one of those that stepped out as Shinjee. I had never thought her especially pretty, but I could recognize that she could be attractive to others. Something had happened to her since I'd last seen her. It was as though her skull had been reshaped and she'd taken a beating or two. She was skinny before, but now she was a twig, so frail, it looked like she'd snap upon contact. Her nose had been broken and patched back up, but not with any skill. She wore the white outfit of all the other factory workers and had a short purple wig on that had soot at its edges. There was no camaraderie among the workers, just forced civility.

There were a few ways to approach this. I had assumed I'd have to furtively paralyze her and take her away. But seeing the lethargic manner in which she moved, an instinct told me the direct approach would be most effective. She did not look like a woman afraid of death.

I waited for her shift to end. She scanned the bar on her card key to stamp out, bowed to some of her co-workers, then walked out with a limp. She chewed on a piece of bread as swarms of bicyclers passed her by. Exhaustion weighed down her legs and children outpaced her short walk home. She lived in a tiny apartment that appeared abandoned from outside because it was so old and decrepit. Graffiti painted the walls and the floors were dirty. She had to climb up six floors as there was no elevator and she shared a room with five others. They had a communal bathroom for the floor that stank of a year's worth of human feces where she washed her hands.

"I was expecting a lot of things, but not this," I said to her.

"D-do I know you, sir?" she asked.

"What did they do to you?"

"I'm sorry, sir?"

"It's me—Nick."

"Nick?"

"Larry's friend."

She examined my face. "You-you were killed trying to escape."

"So I've heard," I answered.

"H-how did you get away?"

"Does it matter? That night before you shipped me off. Who was that dead on the sofa?"

"W-what?"

"Whose body was on the sofa?" I asked again.

"It was Larry. Why?"

"Do I look stupid to you? Larry's alive. I just saw him."

"That's not Larry," she protested.

"Then who is it?"

"I don't know. But it's not Larry."

"I talked to him. It's Larry."

"Can't you tell the difference between a fake Larry and the real one?" she demanded.

"Why would there be a fake Larry?"

"I don't know."

"How can you be sure he's dead?" I asked.

"There were holes in his neck."

"That might not have been him."

Shinjee shook her head. "Larry is dead." And then I saw her well up with tears.

"Spare me," I said. "You didn't give a damn about him."

An indignant scowl brimmed at her eyes. "I loved him."

"Based on, what, the few days you knew him?"

"Love doesn't have a timeline."

"Life does. And he's alive."

"Someone's replaced him," she said.

"What happened to the body?"

"We weren't expecting to find him dead so we left him there."

"I'm supposed to believe that?"

"I had nothing to do with it," she said. "Why would I kill him? My job was to recruit him."

"For what?"

"To make films for the Great Leader."

"So you are a spy?"

"An ambassador, punished for my failure." She went back to washing her hands. "Why are you here?" she asked.

"I owed you a visit."

"For what?"

"You sent me to Hell."

"I gave you a way out and now you're back."

"I had to claw my way out," I said.

"I didn't want this for you or anyone else. What choice did I have?"

My mind was on other questions, like why would someone pretend to be Larry? The tattoo on his stomach was the same. Then again, that could have been faked. *Think, Nick. Put your brain to use. Your eyes deceived you once. Was it that first time when you saw Larry's corpse, or the second, when you saw him breathing in front of you at the convention?*

"I tried calling him when I first heard he was alive," she told me as she dried her hands. "He never picked up. He only appears in big public events and he's always attended by a big entourage. I tried going once, just to see him. He didn't recognize me. He was with four other women."

Her voice was earnest as were her expressions. She was still in love with him.

"It's so sad that the person Larry considered his closest friend can't even tell the difference between the real him and an impostor," she said. "You know how much he worried for you?"

"If he's dead and you loved him, who killed him?"

"I don't know."

"Why aren't you out there trying to find his killer?"

"Why aren't you?" she asked back.

"Because he's alive."

"And if he wasn't?"

"I would have killed his killer," I said, looking straight at her.

"You're not a killer," she said dismissively.

"You say it like that's a bad thing."

"In this world, it is. It's one thing to gain power, it's another to maintain it. Larry was a victim of a bigger game we weren't part of."

"And you?"

"I was naive enough to believe love conquers all. If you kill me, you'd only be doing me a favor. They'll make a martyr of me back home and give my family honors," she said.

"I'm not killing you."

"I know," she said. "And my family will continue to starve."

"You could leave."

"And doom my whole family?"

I had come here for revenge, and found the world had already taken it for me.

"That last film of his he was working on," she said. "It might be related to everything."

The one he'd been so cryptic about? "How?"

"I don't know. But it was the only thing he refused to talk about. And you know what a big mouth he had."

"Has."

"Had," she said. "Anytime you want my life, you know where I am. I won't fight it." She limped back to her apartment, daring me to follow.

I did not.

VIII.

Image facilitation could have been involved. Someone might have theoretically gotten enough surgery to look like Larry. But to sound like him, to have a similar height, and to be able to fool all those around him, especially with finger and eye scans at every corner of the Chao Toufa grounds? That was impossible. The more probable explanation was that Shinjee, beaten by her superiors, had lost her senses. It didn't explain the corpse that night. But it was more likely that when she was confronted by the fact she'd been just another fling for him, she'd rather accept he was dead than she was unimportant. No one else questioned his identity but her. I shouldn't either. Every logical thought in me urged me to go back to my apartment, pack up my belongings, sell everything I could, and spend a few years on the beaches of Cancun cavorting about. Yeah, drugs were every-where, but as the cartels officially controlled everything, it was one of the safest places in the world.

And yet, when it came time to input my next destination into the cab, I found myself hesitating to give my Beijing home address. What if Larry really had been killed? Could I just ignore that possibility? Could I ignore my own eyes? I thought about talking to Russ who'd been promoted to president of Chao Toufa. He might have more insight and give me the confirmation I needed to put the whole matter to rest. There was something else gnawing me. I put in the address for the Chao Toufa factory grounds, wondering if Russ would even see me. If he didn't, I'd pick up some of the equipment I'd left behind, especially my Pinlighter 1887, the pen camera that was so easy to carry. I called Larry to see if I could get hold of him. Even after five calls, he didn't pick up.

I watched the news on the ride there. It focused on the garbage negotiations going on in Antarctica. Reporters and military specialists speculated on naval skirmishes between Europe and America for dumping rights in what had once been a frozen continent. I flipped the station. A death-football game was on and crowds were booing that only five people had been killed so far even though the half-time show had just concluded (there were conspiracy theorists who speculated that the deaths were arranged beforehand and actors were swapped out in favor of surgery while they healed). There were the usual spattering of commercials for the upcoming GEAs, celebrating the best in cinema. I ordered a caffeine boost as I needed something to keep my mind sharp. An emergency news cast broke through. The actor who played Jesus Christ, James Leyton, had caught the flu and prayer vigils were being held around the world. Several older gentlemen being interviewed were crying as they said, "We pray that he gets better soon."

When I arrived at the factory, the guard at the security station asked for my identity. I gave him my information.

"It looks like you no longer have permission to enter, sir," he politely informed me.

"Call the president and tell him I'd like to see him."

"The president?"

"Russ Lambert. I need to speak with him."

"I can't just call the president and—"

"Get Larry on the phone then," I told him.

"Mr. Larry Chao?"

"Are you new to this job?"

"I-I started a week ago," he told me.

"Call his office and tell him Nick Guan wants to speak with him."

"Concerning what?"

"I need to get my camera equipment."

The guard went back into his post, made a few calls, and came back out. "Mr. Russ Lambert is out. But his assistant told me you could get your belongings."

"Thank you."

The cab drove in.

Demolition crews had finished the job on the destroyed warehouses, though no new construction had begun. I used to have an office close to Larry's, but someone else was in it now. A box with all my belongings had been put into storage and one of the assistants helped retrieve it for me. All I really wanted was the camera. I noticed a few pictures of Larry and me on set as well as several useless certificates from various festivals. I put the camera in my pocket along with the mini-boom that recorded audio better than any instrument I'd worked with. Told the assistant he could throw away the rest. The boom was an expensive prosumer version of a military product, designed to capture the voices of officers speaking in the middle of combat.

I swung by Russ's office but he wasn't there. His assistant, an elderly Chinese woman, asked, "Did you get your belongings?"

"I did. Larry asked me to check in with Russ. Is he at home right now?"

"He is," she answered, then hesitated, wondering if she should not have given that information.

"Great. Larry wanted me to see him ASAP. What was his address again?"

"I'm afraid I can't give that information out."

"I'll call Larry and ask him."

"Oh, no no, you shouldn't do that," she said quickly, and she was quivering.

"It's no problem. If I just make a call—"

"No need to bother him, I'll give you the address. Just please, don't tell either of them I told you."

"I won't."

"You have to promise me."

"I promise."

"Again."

"I promise." Her eyes were filled with terror and it reminded me of George's reaction earlier.

"Thank you," I told her after she gave me the address.

IX.

Russ owned a massive house that was four stories tall. There was good reason to envy the rich. I used to lie to people that I was really wealthy when I was a kid because I didn't want them to know I lived in a tiny apartment with my alcoholic cousin who was rarely home. Russ's home was the kind I dreamt about as a kid, so big, I wouldn't even know all the rooms in my house.

I programmed the taxi to wait outside and walked to the gate. I told security that Larry had sent me and they let me in without hassle. A butler met me at the front door. He had on thick black glasses that covered half his face and a green tuxedo. The house had an indoor swimming pool, antiquities from the Ming Dynasty, and a lot of deer heads on the wall. Russ was downstairs in a room shaped like a centrifuge. There were a hundred arcade booths with games from long ago forming four circular lines as though it were a hedge maze of electronics. I saw titles like *Double Dragon, Teenage Mutant Ninja Turtles, Moonwalker, Simpsons, Bubble Bobble,* and more. The floor was slowly spinning and with the bright lights and sounds, it reminded me of a roulette wheel. Russ was wearing what looked like a red dress and played a game called *Bad Dudes.* Chained next to him were a naked man and woman. The woman had white hair, a skinny frame, very pale skin, and looked similar to Beauvoir, the sister of Tolstoy, though nowhere near as beautiful. Her presence threw me off guard.

Russ screamed at the game. It looked like his character had died by a shuriken to the forehead from a ninja. Russ slapped the woman and kicked the man, releasing his rage. He had always seemed like such a nice person.

I had the feeling I should take a risk with Russ and expose all my cards. The boom was on and so was the Pinlighter up my sleeve to record our exchange. I should have been thinking about what to ask, but the cinematographer's instincts in me thought of dramatic angles, light reflecting off his face, the woman and the man chained to either side of him as contrast.

"You told security Larry sent you. But I know Larry didn't send you," Russ said.

"You're right. He couldn't have sent me because he's dead."

"What are you talking about?"

"Do you think that impostor could fool me? I was Larry's best friend."

Russ stopped playing his arcade game and turned to me, grim. "What was it that gave it away?"

Inside, a part of me collapsed. Larry really was dead. It took all my mental discipline not to break down.

"Everything," I answered.

"Who have you told?" he demanded.

"Tell me why and I'll tell you who I've told."

"It's obvious, isn't it? The whole company would fall apart without Larry. He used to disappear all the time so we hired someone to impersonate him whenever he was away."

"That's who's taken Larry's spot?"

"You're the only person who could tell the difference."

I fiddled with the camera in my sleeve, wanting to switch angles. "What about Larry's killer? Or was it you that killed him?"

Laughter bellowed out of him. "I'd have nothing to gain by killing him. Besides, this new Larry is turning out to be a monster."

"A monster?"

Russ turned back to his arcade machine. "What do you want?"

"I want to find out what happened to Larry."

"He had a lot of enemies."

"You have no interest in catching them?" I asked.

"If I tried to catch them, I'd have to acknowledge he was dead. Do you know what would happen to the company if word of that got out?"

"What?"

"We're in the middle of some very important negotiations," Russ said. "I'm securing the future of Chao Toufa. Maybe after we reach an agreement, we can look into what happened."

"Garbage rights?" I threw out there, remembering something Larry had said.

Russ stopped playing again. "How did you know?"

"Larry mentioned it."

"We have a lot of land out in Greenland and Antarctica that the US government is interested in."

"I don't see why they would care if Larry were alive or not."

"That's why you're not a businessman."

"You're right. I'm not. I don't get why garbage is more important than Larry's life. At least you could have given him a proper burial. Where's his body?"

I heard a loud boom, felt something punch me in my leg. I felt another blast to my shoulder that caused me to gyrate and stumble into one of the arcade booths. My leg became too weak to support me and I fell to the ground. It took a second to gather they were gunshots. I'd never been shot before. Shot at, yes, but even that was far off the mark. Fortunately, my armor had protected me, but it hurt like hell. There were probably deep contusions and I wondered what would have happened without the plating. I put it out of mind and stayed down, pretending it was worse than it seemed. I had no idea who had fired. Was it Russ? Or guards on the periphery? Or was there a security gun on the ceiling? If the latter, I had no way of getting out as I didn't have anything to take out a computer-controlled gun. Russ hovered above me with a gloating smile. Coming up next to him was his butler with his huge glasses holding a pistol.

"Should I kill him, sir?"

"No. I need him alive," Russ said.

The woman who resembled Beauvoir made a rustling sound and when the butler turned his head, I got out my gun and fired at him. The paralysis dart made contact, but bounced off his suit. He too had some armor underneath. I scrambled to hide behind another arcade stall and the bullet that was intended for my back blew the screen.

"Be careful where you fire!" Russ shouted. "Those things are worth a million SC each!"

"You should get out of here, sir," the butler told Russ.

"I need him alive," Russ reminded him, then bolted for the exit.

I thought of using a light bomb, but I'd seen his glasses and they would most likely protect him against that kind of measure. The room was slowly spinning. The music and sound effects from the arcade games made it difficult to extrapolate his location. My leg was throbbing and even kneeling against the booth made it sting. I peeked over to the side and did not see him. I knew he wouldn't aim for the head and this armor would hold against most shots which gave me a bit of an advantage. At the same time, my only option was to paralyze him in the face as that was the only area he had no protection, making things infinitely more challenging.

I swerved around a booth that read *Golden Axe* on the side, heard a gunshot, only to see it was from a game called *The Terminator*. For a moment, the screen turned black and I saw the reflection of the butler. I ducked quickly and a bullet blasted off the joystick. I turned around to fire, but he was gone. I sprinted for the outer circle and looked inwards. I saw Beauvoir and the other male, but the butler wasn't there. Was he hiding? Was he kneeling in wait? Was he getting closer or was he just stalking me until I fell right into his hands?

The arcade games looked like cartoons and were limited in motion, being stuck on a flat plane. I was stuck with only my two eyes and they weren't seeing anything. I had an idea. I placed my Pinlighter on top of one of the arcade machines and pointed it towards the middle. Then I took out the lens I'd gotten earlier, hooked the feed from the camera into the lens, and positioned it onto both my eyes. I'd gained another line of sight as a small visual screen popped up in the upper left corner of my view.

I dashed towards the middle of the room, hopeful that my motion would elicit a response. There was movement in the corner. Before I could respond, there were two loud blasts. One bullet barely missed my body and the other blew up the arcade booth next to me. I ducked under a stall, the woman and the guy cowering behind *Bad Dudes*.

I checked the Pinlighter feed. The butler was creeping up on me a row away. I got ready for him to get closer. When he was in proximity, I'd jump out and shoot him in his neck. I couldn't hear his steps as the games were making their bubbly sounds and their simulated MIDI tracks were too loud. I had to trust the camera. Half a minute later, the butler was right where I needed him and I rushed to the side, hoping to catch him off guard. But as I thrust forward, the pain in my legs caused me to buckle, and when I fired, the bullet was far left. The butler wasn't bothered by the shot and launched straight at me with a kick to my chest. It hit me right between the ribs and my breath heaved, my head feeling light. I couldn't tell if any ribs had cracked, but I didn't have time to dwell on it as he came with another roundhouse kick that hit my chin. I spun in the air and my gun flew out of my hand. He'd have an open shot if he took it right now. Even if it wouldn't penetrate the armor, the force of the blow would most likely leave me too debilitated to fight back. Fortunately, I channeled the cricket in me and scrambled away as quickly as I could.

I checked the camera feed again. He was standing a row away, his hand inside his pants. It looked like he was masturbating as there was a rapid back and forth motion near his zipper. Was he getting off on inflicting pain? The mockery of his actions infuriated me. I scoured the ground for my gun. I didn't know where it'd flown off to and I didn't have the time to look for it.

My combat training had been limited because I'd always intended to be a media guy. Even with all the survival lessons I'd taken, hand-to-hand combat had never been a focus of what I'd learned. As the saying went, desperate times called for desperate measures. If I could get his glasses off, then I could set off a light bomb and paralyze his motion. My lenses would protect me.

I charged straight at the butler. He grinned, took his hands out of his pants. I crashed into him, but before I could grab his glasses, he slapped me back and followed with a kick. I cringed, not so much at the pain, but the thought of where his fingers had just been.

The light bomb was in my right hand, ready to set off. I just needed those glasses to come off. I rushed him again, ready for him to kick me. He was flexible and more agile than I would ever be. But I was counting on that. Sure enough, the kick came to my cheeks. I let myself stumble and when he came for another kick, I ducked. This surprised him and left an opening for me to grab his body and pull him down. I ripped the glasses off and set off the light bomb.

The power of a star scintillated blindingly.

The butler screamed in agony.

I got up and searched the ground for my gun. It was lodged onto a booth called *Street Fighter II*. I picked it up, fired at the butler's neck, paralyzing him for at least a day.

I went to the two in chains and used my blade to cut through. The woman, who'd been blinded, leaped at me. I tried to pull her off, but as she had no clothes, I could only pull her hair. To my surprise, it stuck no matter how hard I pulled. Was this-was this real hair? In the bright light, she looked more like Beauvoir.

"Do you know Beauvoir?" I ventured, even though it was a far stretch. Her white hair reminded me of the package Larry had me retrieve from Dr. Asahi back in Los Angeles.

"That's the name of my sister," she said, eyes shut. "Unless you mean the author."

"We need to get out of here. Hold onto me."

I held the woman's hand and she held onto her companion's arm as we made our way out. I grabbed the Pinlighter and placed it back in my pocket. I streamed the recorded information into my lens and the network in case anything were to happen to me.

When we were back upstairs, I picked up two thin rugs and wrapped them around both to cover their naked bodies. "You should be able to see again in a day or so."

The woman tried opening her eyes but shut them again.

I asked her, "Do you have real hair?"

"No," she said. "There's no such thing as real hair."

I felt her hair again. There was no doubt. The man had a wig that clearly came off. He was coy, looking away, not saying anything. I looked back at the woman. Was she afraid of telling the truth? "What's your name?"

"Plath," she answered. "How do you know my sister?"

"She saved my life."

"Then you are our friend?"

I ignored her question and said, "We need to get out of here."

"Did she send you to get me out?"

"No one sent me."

"Then I can't leave."

"Why not?"

"I can't leave," she insisted.

"You're a slave here."

"I know what I am," she answered. "I can't leave until my task is done."

I looked at her hair and knew I had to talk with Rebecca and Dr. Asahi again. Larry's reaction to the package came back to me. *Skeletons*, he said after the explosion.

"Where are you from?" I asked.

"What do you mean?"

"I mean where did you grow up?"

"In Los Angeles."

"Where in Los Angeles?"

"At the Chao Research Facilities before they closed them down."

I didn't know they used to have their own research facilities in Los Angeles, especially with the Absalom Institute there.

"Can I take a sample of your hair?" I asked.

"Why?"

"I need it."

"For what?"

"Research for Chao."

She nodded.

I took out my Pinlighter, tugged on her hair, recording how strong it was and how the roots were embedded in her scalp.

"Ow," she said.

"Sorry."

I cut off a handful similar to the amount Larry had in the capsule and put it in my pocket.

"You want to stay too?" I asked the man.

He looked helpless. "Where would I go? Russ takes good care of me."

At that moment, Russ approached with a smile until he saw me.

"What's going on here?" he demanded. "Where's Manny?"

"Why does this girl have real hair?" I asked.

He turned around and ran away. I raised my gun and aimed. As I fired, Plath pulled on my arm. The shot was completely off.

"What are you doing?" I demanded.

"You can't hurt him," she said, her eyes partially opened even though it was causing her pain.

"You care about him that much?"

She didn't answer me. My legs hurt too much to give chase. Still, I limped after him. By the time I got out the front door, it was too late. He'd jumped into a car and driven out through the gate. I recorded the license plate, hoping I could track him later if I needed.

Plath and the man were still in the lobby. They didn't look like they were going anywhere. Should I try to force Plath to come with me? Honestly, I didn't know if I had the energy to even make it to the taxi and seeing how protective she had been of him, doubted she would be of much help.

I hobbled out the front and exerted all my strength to get to the cab. "Train station to Shanghai," I ordered. Where I really needed to be was the hospital again. I took off my pants and removed the armor. The skin where I'd been shot was black and purple, an island of dead cells floating in a violet death. How many funerals were taking place inside my body, how many loved ones lost? I lay back and slept for the drive to the train station.

X.

I dreamt about being a cricket again, only with much larger antennae. There were a few that were the size of small dogs and groups of them were whispering conspiratorially. I was furious that my apartment was infested with them and didn't know what I should do to get rid of them as I hated fumigations. Beauvoir actually carried two of the cricket corpses, fought one off and tossed it into the living room. I startled at the sight of crickets so big until I woke up.

I'd arrived at the train station and my cab was gently trying to wake me with a cooing ring tone. My hands went instinctively to my thigh and shoulder, rubbing the area where the wound had been. I could still feel the shock and jolt of the hit. I was lucky to be alive.

What next? I'd have to talk with Rebecca and find out how much more she knew than she'd let on. I noticed the news screen had the image of several factories on fire. The text below read, "Zhang Zhang Factories Under Attack." I turned the audio on and listened to the account of the explosions that had caused tremendous damage. "We still don't know what's going on," the reporter was saying. "But preliminary reports indicate explosives were used." This was the Colonel's company. Had Chao Toufa actually made a move to attack her? That was crazy, but this meant war.

I got out of the cab. My muscles felt sore. I was worried about the fighting that would ensue with the Colonel probably unleashing a full assault on Chao Toufa. Then it hit me again that Larry was really dead. It was hard to accept, especially as I knew there was a doppelganger out there. Should I confront him?

Should I expose the truth? I had my exchange with Russ recorded and I had enough friends in the media to ensure that the message would get out there. But my mind kept on going back to Plath's hair. It was real. She could grow hair. No one in the past 25 years could grow hair. How was this possible? How much did Larry know? Was this what had been haunting him? Was he trying to expose the truth? Or cover it up? Is that what got him killed?

No matter how I spun it, it depressed me to think that hair was the reason he had died. This should have been a cause for celebration among the people of the world. Someone could grow hair again! But I had the feeling there was something darker connected with this whole mess. Did Chao Toufa have the most realistic hair in the world because it was real? No wonder the Colonel couldn't figure out the formula. But if they did have real hair, why hide it? Why hadn't anyone else known about it? And why was Russ keeping Plath as a slave?

I bought a ticket and leaned against the wall, my thighs sore. My hands were shaking. I was exhausted. I needed a long, long rest. I hadn't slept since the day before the convention. But I didn't feel safe going back home. I had to find out what Dr. Asahi had learned from that hair sample, even though I had a pretty good idea what she'd found.

I thought about the Great Baldification. Everyone at that moment realized there was no God. I didn't mean a Creator or a spiritual being that brought cosmic order. I meant the genie we'd hoped would save mankind from itself. It was a wakeup call, but all these years later, most people still hadn't heard the alarm.

9. The Faceless

I.

I ordered a drink at the station bar after I arrived in Shanghai because I couldn't stop shaking. A hard shot of whiskey didn't help. If it hadn't been for the armor, I'd be a cripple or worse. I asked the bartender for an *er guo tou* that was almost 60% proof. That gave me a buzz and calmed my nerves momentarily.

I called Rebecca.

"What happened to you?" she asked.

I didn't know how much I could trust her or how to broach the topic of the conversation I'd overheard her having with—I didn't even know who she'd been talking to.

"There've been a lot of developments," I said, keeping vague.

"Developments?"

I've been shot at, I found out Larry is dead, and there are people who can still grow hair. "Can I see you, right now?"

"Of course," she replied.

"I'll be there in an hour."

The communication ended and I grabbed a taxi. As soon I got in, I passed out.

Honestly, I didn't remember how I got up to her unit. All I knew was when I got through the door, I headed for the bed and passed out again. I dreamt the whole time about running away from someone who was trying to shoot me.

II.

I woke up and found I only had my underpants on, bandages around where I'd been shot. I felt groggy and my head was a murky maelstrom. Two more days of sleep was what I needed. Rebecca was standing next to the bed, nudging me softly.

"How long have I been out?" I asked her.

"Four hours. Some guys came by and wanted to see you."

"What did they look like?"

"You can see for yourself. They look like they have masks on. I told them you weren't here but they've been persistent."

I looked through the door camera and saw four of the faceless men waiting at the door, goons that looked identical to the one I'd seen driving the Colonel's limousine in Beijing. Who were these men before they'd signed on to become anonymous brute force for strangers? Some of them might have been soldiers like me without family fighting their way for every inch. Did their lovers cringe when they saw their blank faces that barely moved? Seeing them talk was like seeing sock puppets.

"Is there another way out of the building?" I asked.

"No. Who are they?"

"Friends from *Zhang Zhang*."

"That's the hair company that just got attacked," she said.

"They think I'm involved in that," I told her, looking at the camera view again.

"Are you?"

"Of course not. The Colonel—that's their owner—thinks I have some say in what happens."

"According to the news, it's been bloody retribution out there," she said.

"What do you mean?"

"*Chao Toufa* had several of their facilities attacked. More than eighty people have been killed in explosions."

I looked at Rebecca and she appeared so vulnerable in her t-shirt and trainer pants. "I shouldn't have come here." My leg felt like a broken pylon. "Where's the armor?"

"Sorry. I took it off." She eyed the bruises on my body. "What happened?"

"I got shot."

"By who?" she asked, startled.

I stood up and started putting on my armor. "Can I ask you a kind of weird question?"

"Uh, sure," she replied.

"Do you love Larry?"

Her body took on a defensive slant. "Why do you ask that?"

"A yes or no would be great."

"It's a complicated situation."

Should I show all my cards or balk? "I know the real Larry is dead," I said. "I know the Larry you took me to see is an impostor." Even as the words came out, they sounded like a joke. I didn't believe them, or didn't want to. Was there really a difference? "I overheard you talking to him in the bar," I said, even though I hadn't been sure it was him.

"Nic—" she started, confirming my suspicion.

I cut her off. "What do you guys want from me?"

"Who says we want anything?"

I'd been a fool for thinking she had been kind to me out of the goodness of her heart. "Does it have something to do with the package Dr. Asahi sent?"

"I don't know what's in the package."

"You sure?"

"Yeah. What was in it?"

I slowly put my leg into the armor but had to do it carefully as fast motion was causing cramps. "You may not believe this, but there are still people who can grow hair. Chao Toufa is somehow connected to them, but I don't know how." If she wasn't trustworthy, if she was working for Chao Toufa, it would only be a matter of time before she betrayed me. Then again, it wasn't like I had much of a chance even if she wasn't a traitor. I needed information and revealing what I knew seemed the best way.

"That's impossible."

"That's what I thought too. But it's real," I said.

"Is that why Dr. Asahi was so desperate for me to find you?"

"Dr. Asahi?"

"After Larry's death, they couldn't find you so they asked me to look for you. But after they used the new Larry to replace the old one, they lost interest."

"Why?"

"I don't know."

"Do you love Larry?" I asked again.

"Not the real one," she answered. "His name used to be Harold Lew before all the surgery. He used to be an actor. We were friends until Larry—the real Larry—died. Then Harold and me became lovers."

"I know Harold," I answered, recognizing him as a minor actor in some of our films. He did have a resemblance to Larry, although he was a few inches taller. Image facilitation could have easily fixed physical differences.

"He's changed a lot. I don't think he can separate himself from Larry anymore."

"You knew it was a lie but you didn't say anything?" I demanded.

"They told me it was to maintain the future of the company and our facility. It would only be temporary until they set up a proper exchange of power."

The armor fit me snugly and I picked up my strap of light bombs. "What was the point of keeping me around your place earlier?"

"I wasn't trying to keep you. They just wanted me to keep tabs on you and make sure you didn't cause any problems. I'm sorry. I know you've been through hell. And Larry—Harold's a different guy now. He loses his temper all the time. I think he's sleeping with other women too."

"Do you know how *Zhang Zhang* is connected and why they care about me?"

"The only thing Larry and Dr. Asahi told me was to keep you distracted."

I sighed. "Can you call the police downstairs?"

"That's the weird part," she said. "I called them earlier and they told me everything was fine."

"What do you mean?"

"Those men have clearance to be here," she answered. "I told security that I wanted them out of here but they said there's nothing they can do."

That meant they had some arrangement with the police and wouldn't be killing us here as news of any deaths inside a prison-complex condominium would cause property values to drop drastically.

"If someone could grow real hair, why wouldn't they announce it to the whole world?" she asked.

I didn't tell her the business-driven answer that instinctively came to mind, but I think she saw it in my eyes.

"Profit?" she asked. If she had known about the existence of hair beforehand, she did a convincing job faking that she didn't.

"What are the chances of them breaking through that door?" I asked.

"Those doors have three layers of titanium. They'll withstand most explosives. Short of laser beams, and I mean the pure crystal kind, I don't think they're coming through."

"Are there security overrides?"

"There are, but those are just for emergencies," she answered, though a sliver of doubt had slipped in.

"Can I speak with them through here?" I asked as I strapped my paralysis gun into my belt. She nodded. "Hello, gentlemen," I said through the communicator. "What can I do for you?"

"My boss would like to see you," one of them said.

"Do I have a choice?"

"Of course," he answered in the same tone as the one from Beijing.

"Patch her through."

"She would like to see you in Bangkok."

"I bet she would, but I can't go to Bangkok right now."

"She has allowed you eight hours to arrange matters before

she insists you depart for Bangkok."

"That's generous of her."

"In eight hours, be at the Shanghai Pudong International Airport. We will escort you to Bangkok."

"What if I'm late?"

"We will assist in making sure you arrive on time," he answered in a voice bereft of menace that made it all the more menacing. Abruptly, they left.

"It looks like I have a date with four faceless thugs," I said to Rebecca.

I took out my Pinlighter and went to use her computer. There, I uploaded the footage of Russ Lambert confirming Larry was dead. I also had footage of the girl with hair. I had it on timed automail to several media friends in case something happened to me and those faceless thugs got me. I took out the locket of hair I'd gotten from Plath and felt it against my fingers.

Should I expose the fake Larry for being an impostor and reveal the possibility of people with real hair? I needed to head to Gamble Town, meet with Tolstoy and Beauvoir. Then track down Russ. I only had eight hours before the Colonel's thugs would be after me again.

While I was contemplating my course of action, Rebecca held out her hand. The fox necklace dangled from her fingers. "I don't think I should keep this," she said.

"You saved my life."

"I was keeping an eye on you."

"I don't care about your reasons. You still saved my life," I said. "Throw it away if you don't want it."

"What are you going to do about those guys?"

"I have no idea." I opened up the door. "Don't let anyone in," I told her. "And if I don't see you again." I stared at her. "Thank you. For everything."

She slapped me.

"W-what was that for?"

"Be strong," she said. "I hate weak men."

"You don't like short ones either."

"I'll make an exception for one, but not both."

The door shut. I hustled down.

III.

Hustle might have been an exaggeration. More like lumbering along. Walking was excruciatingly painful. The only place I could think of going was Gamble Town to visit Tolstoy and Beauvoir again. Maybe they could shed some light on what was going on as it was clear they were connected to Plath.

I got into the cab and asked the computerized driver to head to the airport. On the television, the incidents at all the different hair factories were being highlighted. I called a journalist friend, Lena, who served in Africa with me. She was giddy as she always was whenever there was lots of news to cover. Scenes of violence and death were interspersed with sexually explicit ads reminding people about the upcoming Global Entertainment Awards in Los Angeles. Both Jesus the General and Rhonda would be there, sharing a dance duet, although the prayer vigil was still ongoing and millions throughout the world were praying for his recovery from his flu.

"I've got something big," I told Lena.

"Bigger than the attacks?"

"The real reason behind them," I replied. "Where are you?"

"I'm in Seoul right now, but I'm heading over to Hong Kong," she said.

"Send me your HK address. Or can you make a quick detour to Shanghai?"

"I can. But you need to give me a hint what this is all about."

"Hair," I replied, and would offer no more.

She didn't seem convinced, but we had a lot of history together. "I can be there in 25, maybe 35 minutes if customs is tough."

"I'll pick you up from the airport."

The communication ended and I called the hotel in Gamble Town where Beauvoir was staying. Surprisingly, the operator patched me through after saying, "She's been expecting your call."

"Hi, Nick. Nice wig," she said.

"You look very nice yourself," I answered, marveling at how beautiful she was. "I met your sister, Plath. I know what's going on. At least part of it."

"She told me."

"Can we talk?"

"I think my brother wants to see you anyways."

"Your br—"

Something crashed into my taxi and I heard Beauvoir scream, "Nick!"

Almost immediately, the whole compartment was filled with green gel, freezing me in place. It was designed to protect me from collisions as the car spun out of control. I could still see, though my visibility was filtered by the green gel that made me feel like a fishing bob in the ocean. Had I been in a car accident? That was impossible. There hadn't been car accidents outside of America for decades, unless someone had taken manual control? Or had there been an automated failure? The gel was good for me and had medical palliatives to sooth my muscles. My shoulder and leg were grateful.

"Nick! Nick!" Beauvoir called.

I heard sirens and an ambulance arrived almost immediately. I tried talking through the gel, but my voice came back as a muted echo. Four EMTs pulled my cube out using medical shovels and carried me to the ambulance. Smoke was rising from my car and I saw a jeep had hit me from the front. Each of the EMTs had hats covering their faces. Crowds were watching me from the sidewalk, curious as they'd probably never seen a collision in real life. One of them opened the back door of the vehicle and I saw his face, or lack of. He was one of the Colonel's men. Another faceless EMT grabbed a syringe and injected it into the gel. I became drowsy.

IV.

I was strapped to a bed. My clothes were still on. There were eight faceless guards I could see. We were in a basement, or was it an abandoned hospital room? There were stretchers in front of me, medical signs covered with dust that looked like they hadn't been washed in years. The main faceless guard was dressed in a doctor's blue surgical garb. He played with a scalpel, twirling it between his fingers like it was a pencil-sized baton.

"I thought I was going to see the Colonel," I said.

"You will," Dr. Faceless told me. "But we have a few hours to get acquainted."

"Hooray."

"Did you ever wonder how we became the way we are?"

"I actually did."

"Good, because you're going to find out directly."

"What do you mean? I don't wanna be part of this. Hey, man—"

"One more word without permission, and I will cut out your tongue. The only reason I haven't done so already is the Colonel would prefer your tongue intact. But she's open to having you type out your answers when she interrogates you later," he said. "Anything more you want to say?" I kept my mouth shut. "Good. All of us were like you at first, uninitiated to the pleasures of pain. I promise you, by the end of your trials, pain will cause you bliss."

I'd never thought I had a handsome face. But I still liked my mug the way it was and I had no interest in becoming "faceless."

"None of us wanted it either," the doctor continued. "I know what's going through your mind. All of us experienced it the first time. You wonder what lovers, what family, what friends will think? The good news is, they won't recognize you. Not unless you try to expose yourself. But if you do, you'll find out how superficial all relationships are. Only when you lose your physical identity can you find your real self."

Was he trying to convince me what he was doing was going to be good for me? I was eager to retort with some smart-ass remark, but I didn't want to risk losing my tongue. It was cowardly to threaten my tongue which ranked second only to my manhood in terms of organ priority. Not that I looked with diminishment at any other part. I liked my body intact. Was there some way I could pull a Sampson, blow up my body and take all of these thugs with me? Just on principle, if I was going to die, I wanted to take as many of my enemies with me as I could. Unbelievable. He was still talking. Would he ever shut up? Many of these bad guys had to put on such a tough exterior for their followers, the only chance they had to relieve stress was with their opponents. In this case, I was more victim than opponent. Well, as long as he was talking, it meant he wasn't going to cut my face up. Did I have any options? My hands were sealed too tightly for me to grab anything. Could there be a self-destruct button on my armor I didn't know about? If I ever got out of here, I had to make a request to George to add it. I knew in Africa, they sometimes gave the infantry poison-capsule teeth so they could kill themselves rather than suffer torture. The only problem was a few of them set it off accidentally during visits with prostitutes that caused a huge scandal and resulted in the banning of poison teeth throughout the world. Why was it that idiots always got laws changed to accommodate their dumb proclivities?

"When this is done, you will be as obedient as a dog, more ferocious than a bear, and more deadly than a viper," he said. *Great examples, asshole.* "But first, we have to change your face. I will tell you, we will not be using anesthetics. You will have to endure it directly." He waved the knife in front of me. "You two will become intimate. You must learn to control and channel pain. Pain is pleasure. Repeat it for me. Pain is pleasure."

"Pain is pleasure," I repeated.

"You say it without conviction because you haven't experienced it yet. But soon, it will be your mantra, your creed of faith."

The sock-puppet motion of his mouth disturbed me. Usually, thugs like this had deep crevasses in their faces, a grave look about them that was all business. But this guy appeared as though he were talking out of a mask made from flesh. And he wanted to make me like him? Why couldn't people suffer in misery by themselves? I'd complained about friends in the past that hoped friends could be a sponge for their interminable negativity. This faceless doctor took that to another level.

The knife came down along my neck. I didn't feel anything at first, just warmth along my neck. The pain followed a few seconds later as my sensors cried havoc and let loose the Chihuahuas of war. Blood slithered down the side of my neck.

"What do you want to know?" I asked. "I'll tell you anything. Larry is dead. The Larry out there is an impostor. I don't know who set off those explosives, but I wasn't involved. I just came back after I was nearly taken a slave by—"

The doctor laughed. "We don't care about your secrets," he said. "All we care about is carving away your face and making you one of us."

The knife landed in front of my ear and slowly slid its way towards my nose. Again, the same delayed pain response.

This guy was serious and there was nothing I could do. Or was there? Did I have to give up on my face?

Next time I saw Beauvoir, would she even recognize me? Or would she be horrified by me, thinking I was a thug there to take her away? The pain was intensifying. He wasn't cutting deep. Just the surface. But my skin ruptured along its surface and all my cells were panicking that their ozone was being penetrated by a foreign object. Cell broadcasters projected potential

Armageddon and many unbelievers became proselytes in these dismal times. No matter how old I got, my mind felt young, but my body was there to remind me that I was getting older by the second. I couldn't believe this doctor had endured the same thing I had at some point. The cycle repeated. So many cycles I'd been part of, jet streams of violence I rode, trying to escape, finally reaching a current I couldn't get out of, stuck in a whirlpool that meant I would drown. Fighting for oxygen, seeing the shore just at a distance, blood tattoos for my face ripped in strident lines. I wanted to close my eyes, but the doctor used his fingers to pry them apart. His hands had bulbous veins. He flashed the knife next to my eyes, wanting me to see the blood dripping at the edge. I could have sworn he was smiling, though his lip corners couldn't stretch that far.

I refused to give him the satisfaction of knowing he was breaking me. With his next cut, I screamed out loud and laughed.

He said, "You think this is humorous?"

"Not at all. You don't need to convince me pleasure is pain. I already know it. It's what everyone's been trying to tell me my whole life."

"That was just the warm up," he said. "Prepare yourself for the Colonel."

A visual projection of the Colonel appeared. Her arms were behind her back as she approached me. "I gave you a chance, didn't I?"

"I had no idea they would attack you. I was just chasing down Larry. I—"

"Don't play the fool! You think I don't know about your power play?"

Power play? "I don't know what you're talking about. But as long as you don't have faceless guy here cut up my face, I'll do anything you want."

"It's too late for negotiation. You've destroyed several key factories. What did you think that would achieve?"

She was blaming me? "Name your compensation," I said.

"Your eternal servitude," she replied. "Your undying gratitude."

The projection ended. Negotiations had failed. If I couldn't talk my way out of this, there had to be another way. My light bombs had been removed. Even with my armor on, there wasn't anything I could do about a blade to my face. As Dr. Faceless waved his knife around, I tried to shake my way off the bed. The restraints were too secure and I prayed for a miracle.

It came with a dropping sound and one of the faceless falling over. The doctor turned around and I saw a man with white hair rushing at another guard. He moved gracefully as though he were performing a swan dance. When he lunged his hands, the ferocity of his plunge was feral, his mouth crunching into his nose, his nostrils flaring with savagery. He used a metallic chopstick to perforate their necks. One violent thrust in the pipe works of their esophagus resulted in a spray of blood splattering out. It was all in slow motion, the faceless men unable to scream as their throats were choked with blood. Flashes of white lit amid a wavelength of death. I could see the blood cut off, the guards crumbling to their knees, their pants becoming a wrinkled mess. Even in agony, they could make no expression. Only their eyes betrayed them, the slit of their pupils grasping. They were victims of this reaper who sowed with his chopsticks and divested with his fingers.

When he'd finished killing the guards, he came to the doctor. The doctor had his knives but the killer was too quick. From behind, I saw a chopstick cut through where the doctor's right eye should have been. Then another through the left side. The doctor crumbled to the floor.

My savior approached me. There was blood on his white hair. He was the man who'd given me an umbrella outside the convention center. I realized he was also the man that had killed Larry Chao using those sharp and pointed chopsticks.

"I'm Voltaire," he said as he unloosed my straps. "We have a lot to discuss."

V.

A woman named Austen who must have been a sister to Beauvoir and Plath stitched up my face. There were a few others who appeared to be brothers to Voltaire and carried guns. They all had white hair.

"You're related to Tolstoy?" I asked Voltaire.

"He is my brother. He spoke highly of you."

"What'd he say?"

"That you have guts."

"He saved my life. And now *you've* saved my life. Thank you." He shrugged.

"You've dealt with a lot of them?" I asked, referring to the faceless.

"Even if they move and breathe, they're not really living."

While I was grateful to him for saving my life, I was positive he was Larry's murderer. I wasn't sure what my proper reaction should be. "How did you find me?"

"My sister, Beauvoir, insisted. Fortunately, I have sources among the faceless. Brothers who have sacrificed themselves for the cause," he said.

I didn't want to imagine what he meant by those words. "Why did you come?"

"We are more alike than you can imagine," he said. "We both could not protect the ones we loved."

"What are you talking about?"

"Larry told me about you," he answered. Before I could ask more, he asked Austen, "How long before you're finished?"

"Another ten minutes," she answered as she patched me up.

"We need to hurry or we'll be late."

One of the others brought me my armor and weapons.

"Is this all of it?" Voltaire asked me.

"I think so."

"Put it on."

If he was worried about me turning on him, he didn't show it. I was tempted to paralyze him and set off a light bomb. As though he knew what I was thinking, he asked, "Do you want to know what Larry died for?"

"Of course," I answered.

He put his hand on my shoulder. "I'll show you."

VI.

His group was small—seven white-haired men and five women. They walked like a clergy in a ceremonial procession, dressed in white robes. There was an ephemeral quality to all of them, asexual in appearance. It was a result of their unblemished skin and their perfect hair.

They escorted me out of the grounds that turned out to be an abandoned hospital. A convoy of four black cars awaited us.

"Where are we going?" I asked.

"Airport."

"Are we going to Bangkok?"

"No. America," he answered as we both got into the car.

"Why?"

"Do you know why the Colonel is after you?"

"She thinks I have the formula for the secret hair."

"Do you?" He laughed.

"You all have real hair," I replied as the car began driving.

"Which was harvested to make the best wigs," Voltaire said. "You lived a tough childhood?"

"Tough childhood is relative. You?"

"I will show you my childhood. Soon. When we arrive in America. Let's get back to the Colonel and Russ and why he wanted an impostor Larry."

"Because he wanted to move into garbage?"

"You really have no clue?"

"No," I answered.

Voltaire laughed and shook his chopstick at me. "I'm almost tempted not to tell you."

"Tell me what?"

He tapped his chopsticks on his knees, musing on a thought. "Larry had no family," he said.

"Yeah, I know."

"That's why he willed his entire fortune to you."

"He doesn't control his will," I replied, knowing that super computer of his, set up by his father, controlled everything.

"He did control it."

"It's some computer that his father created."

"It's a lie," Voltaire said with wide eyes. "He seemed like an idiot, and he always told that lie, but no such machine existed. He was in charge all along. And he willed control of his entire business and all of his fortunes to you. You are one of the richest men in the world. There, there, close your mouth. That's why the Colonel blames you. She thinks you're in control. And that's why Russ wanted a fake Larry installed until he could figure out a way to change the will in his favor. Unfortunately, the will is locked by law and can't be changed without express approval from you."

I couldn't register what Voltaire had said. It felt so surreal. "Is this what this is about? This is why you saved my life?" I asked. "You can have all his money. I don't want any of it."

Voltaire nodded as though he approved of my words.

And then it came back to me, how Larry invited me along to the business meeting before his death, the mysterious pieces of advice he alluded to. Was he trying to prepare me to take his place? But me? I was the worst possible candidate to leave all of this to. I was always a follower, always a person who supported those in charge. I never aspired to more. Voltaire's revelation was so crazy, I couldn't believe it. The only thing I ever wanted in life was a family.

"A lot to mull over?" he wondered.

"I don't get it."

"Neither did anyone else. I didn't expect it."

"I don't want any of it. I just want out."

"That's what Larry said when he found out about us."

"About you?"

"The crimes his father committed," Voltaire said. "But when it came down to it, he couldn't leave it behind."

"What kind of crimes?"

"You'll see. But for now, we have other matters to discuss."

"Other matters?"

"Do you like the GEAs?"

Why was he asking me about the Global Entertainment Awards? "I've never watched them."

"Why not?"

"Not interested."

"My whole life, I grew up watching them. We were forced to. You see, we were told our hair was being shorn off to make hair for the rich and famous. We were told our lives were worthless apart from making the wealthy look more beautiful and handsome than they were. So every year, we had to watch these celebrities show up with hair cut from our own heads. I was envious of them. So envious."

We watched footage from the GEA opening ceremony, the stars arriving on the red carpet. We arrived at the airport shortly afterwards, driving around the side to Larry's private airplane in his private landing strip.

Voltaire went off to talk with his brothers and sisters. Another member of his family let me into the airplane, a huge jumbo jet with two floors. Larry often used this plane to ship his film crews. Multiple compartments had been installed for his private parties. It was a slick silvery color, a hybrid between a commercial plane and a military space jet. I was given one of the bedrooms and lay down to rest.

I wished I could have talked to Larry, asked him what was going through his mind. It was strange to think of myself as one of the richest men in the world. Memories from my childhood flooded me. I thought of my biological father beating my sister and me. My mother would scream, "Shut up! Shut up! You both deserve to die for crying so much! You idiots! You'll be killed and no one will care. Do you think anyone will miss you? No one will care!" More blows, blood spilling everywhere. We'd both be punished by having our meals taken away for days at a time. I remembered competing with my sister to see whose stomach could make louder grumbles. It was always a happy event when my biological parents went traveling for business. Cousin Baochai would bring cans of Spam and we'd cook them, pretending they were a grand feast. Spam pizza, Spam steak, Spam burgers; we imagined what the food would be. We paraded around the house and made all sorts of noise, not having to be afraid of waking anyone. I used to be jealous of other kids who'd get nice lunches packed for them. I'd be even more jealous of the students who could afford to buy whatever they wanted at the school cafeteria. There were so many things I wanted when I was younger. I pretended like I didn't care about anyone or anything, hiding behind the camera, recording all the things I'd never been able to enjoy. It was my only comfort.

Gene Liang was the name I was born with, the name I cursed. That name came to represent everything I hated and despised in my life. I wanted to shed it. When I joined the army and they gave me a chance to input any name I wanted, I picked Nick Guan, mainly because Guan Yu, a hero of Chinese literature, was one of my favorite characters. According to history, Guan Yu formed a new family with Liu Bei and Zhang Fei and swore a blood oath in the Peach Garden to become brothers. He was a warrior who valued loyalty and honor above all.

I swore to myself that I would start over, make my own way in the world and never look back on the past. That was the beginning of the end of my relationship with my sister, Kelly. But the onus of shedding the past became an albatross in all my relationships. I'd gotten so used to family members treating each other horribly, I had no idea how to do it properly myself. Even when it came to eating, I'd greedily eat as fast as I could, afraid someone else might eat it. Little kindnesses could be seen as vulnerabilities. As for hugs and warm embraces, they were absent and I had a hard time showing affection to women, even Linda. She basically had to retrain me in the art of family, what it meant for people to love each other rather than be at each other's throats.

I struggled so hard to make it in the world. Working on Larry's movies took up too many hours. But when I turned to a company job, I found out climbing up the corporate ladder and becoming a good automaton was beyond me. I couldn't get used to the instability of it all and hated the miniscule cubicles with managers who'd yell at us for every infraction. "You think you deserve a job. There are a million people out there who would kill for your job!"

I failed at being a husband and a worker. I was laid off like all the other employees, hired and fired at the whimsies of corporations that didn't care. Rather than opening up to Linda, I hid in a shell, got petty and cruel, argued with her over nothing instead of being grateful for what I had. Linda was a saint. I was so thoughtless, so unnecessarily mean in my verbal attacks. It was what I'd grown up with and I latched onto it as a defense mechanism. Poverty brought out the worst in me. Where Spam had been a welcome boon in my childhood, when we resorted to artificial meat under different brands, I got sulky. How could it be that after all these years, Linda and I couldn't eat whatever we wanted? The travesty of it made me angry and I refused to eat anything she cooked. She couldn't understand, thinking she'd done something wrong. I felt too petty to tell her what I was feeling. The misunderstandings compounded.

On TV, everyone paid lip service to the American Dream; the affordable suburban house with a decent job and the ability to raise a family in a safe environment. There were even some who complained that middle-class life caused disillusionment because it was too easy and boring. I had to wake up at five every morning, strap on armor, hope I didn't get shot, and seal up our apartment so we didn't get robbed while I was out working at a minimum-wage job which I'd gotten solely because I was a war veteran. Meanwhile, celebrities were worshipped and sports stars were treated like Olympians while the poor were hidden away so the media could project an image of invincibility to the world. Us, the indentured servants of the world, in plain sight, paraded when spectators came by, then told to get into place and play our notes in an insane harpsichord of broken chords. No one minded that the symphony sounded like a tune from hell as long as they were getting fat.

And now, an unexpected twist in things.

An irony of life.

Larry willed me everything.

I was rich. Richer than anyone I'd known or envied. And the odd thing was, I'd never aspired to it. Never even imagined it.

I kept on wishing Larry was there so I could talk to him, ask him what he was thinking. I tossed in bed, unable to fathom what he'd done for me. I couldn't believe it. No one ever did kind things for me. No one. I mean, I used to dream that someone would come along when I was young, tell me I'd accidentally been abandoned by a great family who had now come to claim me. But that never happened. The only people who had ever shown me true kindness were Linda and her family. They treated me like I was one of their own and I'd betrayed them with my insecurities, pushing Linda away when I should have held her in my arms. I was an idiot and accepted a life of solitude as payment for my idiocy. I didn't deserve a family. But for Larry to have done this. I-I just couldn't believe it.

This inheritance would have conditions like Voltaire and the Colonel. This was not bloodless money. But Larry's act was more than I deserved. There was so much more I needed to find out.

VII.

Voltaire and his white-haired army were raptly watching the GEAs on a holoscreen in the middle of the plane. They'd removed many of the chairs and about fifteen of them were present. The screen was state-of-the-art technology that made it seem like the celebrities were right there in front of us, even though we were on deck and they were in Los Angeles. The ceremony had just begun and audiences could swap through one of the 30 live hosts, each with a distinct style. The same applied to type of music, type of scenery, as well as camera angles that could be customized by all for their viewing pleasure. "In the category of best naked body, we have—" the broadcaster was saying.

"Get a nice nap?" Voltaire greeted me.

"No. Can I speak with you? Privately?"

"You may speak freely. This is my family and I have nothing to hide from them."

They were watching me, curious to hear what I'd say. All of them had a venomous vitality about them that I knew could be triggered to tear me to pieces. I had to be careful how I responded. "I have a journalist friend who I was going to tell about the hair and Larry's death. I can still do it. If you help me to reveal this to the world, we can tell everyone your story."

Voltaire and company snickered. "You think we seek justice?" he asked.

"Don't you?"

"You think we seek the pity of a public who never cared whether we lived or died? No one will care about our story. *No one*," he emphasized. "It'll just be news for a day to them that they wonder over, then forget."

I approached closer. "I think it'll be more than that. You have real hair. That's one of the most significant discoveries in history. They can figure out what went wrong, and at the least, make sure any wrongs they've committed get righted."

"Oh, the governments of the world have known for a long time what's gone wrong."

"They have?"

"Of course they have."

"What was it?"

"Everything," and they all laughed again like they were watching a comedy and their laughter cues were lit up.

I didn't understand. Didn't they want things to get rectified? This was their chance. They could spread the word about any wrongs done to them.

Voltaire gazed directly at me. "What do you think about the Mars expedition?"

"I don't know. It seems really expensive, especially right now."

"But it's captivated the world, no?"

"I guess so."

Voltaire laughed. "It's all fake, a charade to amuse people."

"What?"

"A few of my spies found the media and visual effects departments creating the show. Did you know they're located in Vancouver, not Mars?"

Suddenly, I heard screaming. Behind me, several of the men brought forward an actor that I recognized all too well. It was Jesus Christ played by James Leyton. At least the beard and the hair matched.

"Is that—?"

"Indeed. I promised you a storm. And now I will deliver it. I'm going to kill everyone wearing a wig at the Global Entertainment Awards. Then, I'm going to take over the broadcast of the Global Entertainment Awards and kill Jesus on live TV."

"You can't be serious."

"Last time someone did it, they changed the world. Pontius Pilate created Christianity by crucifying Christ and revolutionized the course of mankind for over two millennia. Will it be any different this time around?"

10. Cycles

I.

All eyes were on the Global Entertainment Awards. At first, I'd hoped Voltaire had been exaggerating or posturing. But then, the murders began on live television. There were gunshots and bombs going off. Scalps were being sliced and tattoos were torn apart by guards with huge machetes. The strangest part was that the networks weren't cutting away from the carnage even though people were gushing blood, limbs were sliced off, and famous celebrities were being mowed down. Whoever was in charge of the media kept the feed live, audiences still able to alter the camera angle, zooming in and out of angles they wanted to see. Some of the corpses received particular attention with ratings in a side column indicating which visual spheres were garnering the most views. The editing was so precise, it felt like I was watching a movie rather than real-life footage.

"You can't do this," I protested.

"Why not? Is their life more precious than ours?"

"They didn't hurt you."

"They fueled the trade that killed countless of my brothers and sisters. And now it's our turn."

"What will this achieve?"

"In our world, entertainment is the only reality. Even wars are filtered by men like you. Did you ever stop to think about the ramifications of your edits?" he asked me.

I'd edited out a lot of dead bodies and explosions. "No."

He handed me my Pinlighter. "Record us."

"What?"

"Don't play the hypocrite," Voltaire warned.

"He's not God. He's just an actor," I protested.

"The public can't tell the difference," Voltaire answered. "Turn it on."

When I hesitated, he lifted up his chopstick. I felt foolish being held up by a chopstick, but I knew what they could do and complied.

His brethren put on masks of the faceless goons. They held James Leyton securely in front of me. He'd been struggling at first. But as soon as my camera was on him, he composed himself. My signal got picked up by one of the computers on board, syncing them together.

James Leyton became Jesus on camera and had a solemn gesture on his face as he pronounced, "Father, forgive them, for they do not know what they are doing."

"Oh we know alright," one of them declared, prominently showing off the brand logo of *Zhang Zhang* on his arm.

They took off Leyton's wig and started cutting off his scalp. Even though I didn't like the show and had never bothered watching an episode, I couldn't help but shudder at the sacrilege and the mockery of it all. The actor remained tranquil, or at least clung to it until the pain became overbearing. At first, it was a discomfiting gesture, followed by clenched brows. Within a few seconds, he was howling, unable to control himself. Blood had splattered everywhere and as the screaming intensified, he shouted, "Father! Into your hands I commit my spirit." A knife was thrust through his mouth to silence him for eternity.

I shut off the camera, wanting to delete the memory from my head.

Voltaire put his arm on my shoulder.

"Now we take care of another impostor."

They brought the fake Larry in. I dropped the camera and refused to film, rushing back to my room. I couldn't watch Larry be killed twice, even if this one wasn't real. A minute later, there was a chime on my door. I ignored it, but it rang multiple times.

"What do you want?!" I asked.

The door slid open and it was Beauvoir. "You shouldn't let it bother you so much," she said.

"It's a massacre!" I answered.

"It's a political statement," she replied. "Voltaire is the oldest of us and has seen the worst of it. He knows what he's doing."

"Murdering people on live television?"

"That's what we've been driven to. It's the only way to get people to take notice. Do you know what happened to that man who tried to enslave you at the cricket races?"

"No."

"He's in a coma because he suffered too much brain trauma during your match. He might as well be dead. Do you regret what you did?" she asked.

"Different situation."

"How?"

"That was for my survival. What did Jesus ever do to you?"

She smiled and said to me, "I wondered after you. You were so beat up when I first met you. Cricket matches don't suit you."

I took a deep breath and kept my eyes away from her. "How is Tolstoy?"

"Good. Busy. He has lots to do in Gamble Town."

"This is twice you saved my life."

"What do you mean?"

"They were going to cut me up if you hadn't sent Voltaire."

"I couldn't just let them kill you."

"Thank you." I stared at my Pinlighter. "The only thing I've ever been good at is taking pictures and shooting movies. I can't believe I just shot a murder."

"I like your movies."

"You've seen them?"

She nodded. "After you left, Voltaire asked me to learn as much about you as I could."

"Why?" I asked, surprised by the revelation.

Right when she was about to answer, Voltaire came up from behind her. "Beauvoir, Tolstoy needs to talk to you. Call him."

Beauvoir nodded and slipped away.

"How many dead?" I asked.

"The death of every celebrity is worth 10,000 corpses," Voltaire replied and it was sad to admit that people felt closer to the stars than their own family and friends. "We've almost arrived. Get yourself ready."

"For what?"

"You have a choice to make. But I need to present all the parameters for you to be able to make an informed decision."

What was he talking about?

"You want an extra suit of armor? Never know when stray bullets might come your way in Los Angeles," Voltaire said.

II.

I felt like I was in the middle of a funeral procession. Five black limousines took us to the Institute. All the billboards, advertisements, and personal TVs were focused on the pogrom on television. There'd never been anything like it, not live, not without editing the way I used to do for everything broadcasted from the African Wars. People got to see brains and guts spilling without FX artists to filter everything with dramatic poise.

All the channels had multiple layers of commentary. Everyone wanted to know, *who* was doing this? All fingers seemed to point at the Colonel and *Zhang Zhang*.

Freeway traffic was at a surprising minimum and I soon recognized the hills to the side of me as those near the Absalom Hair Institute. I didn't know what Voltaire had in store for me, but I would find out soon enough. He had on crimson armor that resembled a space suit, hexagons and octagonal plates turning him into a blocky warrior. It seemed an eternity ago when Larry first asked me to come to the Institute so I could pick up that hair sample and meet Rebecca. Those seemed like bloody simple times in comparison.

III.

When we arrived, dozens of his white-haired brothers and sisters were already there, attired in battle suits. There were similar facial features between all of them, highlighted by the hair, though there was enough variance to emphasize their differences. They warmly greeted Voltaire as he arrived, pumping their fists, thrilled by the arrival of their brother and leader.

"Any casualties here?" Voltaire asked.

"None," one of his brothers replied. "The Institute members offered little resistance."

"Their drones?"

"We infected their systems with the help of the traitor."

Traitor? Who were they talking about?

"The bombs?" Voltaire queried.

"We'll have them ready within the hour."

"Excellent work, Hawthorne," Voltaire said. "Gather your group and dissipate. We will meet at Destination Zero in three days."

I had no idea what Destination Zero was, but Hawthorne and his buddies sprinted into place.

"They all know what this place represents," Voltaire said to me. "Even Larry to a certain extent had an idea of what they did here. But you. You'll get to see with virgin eyes."

I remembered Plath telling me she'd been raised in Los Angeles. "You lived here?"

"This used to be Chao Research Facility Number 07," he answered. "This is a homecoming for many of us."

We walked through the lobby where I'd first seen Rebecca. Dead bodies were splayed against the walls. Many researchers had their necks slit open.

"Why do you have to kill all of them?" I asked.

"The name on the outside has changed, but the people inside haven't. There are others who must still be hunted down, those who were lucky to be absent." I was reminded of Rebecca. "Do you know how many they've killed?"

"Can you explain what the hell is going on?"

"Wait five minutes and I will show you," Voltaire said.

We arrived at a huge elevator. Twelve others came aboard including Beauvoir who was staring at her feet, curling her hair behind her ear several times. She wore thin black armor that cleaved to her body and reminded me of a Kevlar corset. The elevator descended. Voltaire spoke to them in a foreign language I didn't understand. They laughed heartily. Some made odd gesticulations my way. There was more laughter.

When we reached the bottom floor, Dr. Asahi approached, saw me, and demanded, "What's he doing here? He can't see me!"

She was the traitor. But why had she betrayed her fellow researchers? What could Voltaire have offered her?

"Dr. Asahi. I assure you, you have nothing to be afraid of. Nick here will not expose your involvement."

"How can I be sure of that?"

Voltaire eyed two of his brothers. They grabbed her and dragged her away.

"What are you doing? Where are you taking me?!" she shrieked. "You can't do this to me! I played it straight with you! I always did my best to help you!"

"When it was convenient," Voltaire murmured. "Just like you conveniently betrayed your colleagues when it was inconvenient to be on their side."

"What are you doing to her?" I asked, knowing full well that her fate was sealed. I thought about the package she'd analyzed for Larry and wondered why she'd been stumped by it as she worked here.

The hallways, aside from the bodies, were like something from the gallery of a rich taxidermist. There was the severed head of a panda on the wall as well as a horse suspended in liquid, hair flowing in swirling fractals. There were creatures I didn't recognize, ones that had gone extinct like the chimpanzee, buffalo, and yeti. Voltaire's hands were folded behind his back, his armor giving him the bearing of a general surveying the battle scene. Eight researchers were hung in a hallway. Fifteen corpses were piled on top of one another. Everywhere, his family greeted him with a reverence that verged on worship. His authority was unquestioned.

"Why are you keeping me alive?" I asked.

"I told you, we have a lot in common." He turned to me. "If I was going to kill you, I wouldn't have gone through the trouble of saving your life."

One hallway led into another and another. The corridors went on seemingly forever. There were computer terminals at every corner, glass walls with laboratories where they presumably studied hair. Several of the machines resembled the telescopes they pointed at space, only in reverse, examining strands of hair. We came to a very dark hall filled with tiny compartments that could have been lockers. There were approximately a hundred on either side. The doors had latches and slits as windows. It looked like a space where they kept monkeys and bigger rodents.

"This is where I grew up," Voltaire stated. "I spent the first eight years of my life in locker number 15."

He opened it. If I rolled up into a ball, it would barely fit me. I couldn't imagine being inside there for ten minutes, much less eight years.

"They stuck you in there?"

"With masks," he added, smiling. "To make sure we breathed pure air. They fed us intravenously, cleaned us with a spray inside the unit." He reached his hand inside and felt for a module that had tube ports and a sprinkler on it.

"Why'd they do this?" I asked.

"To track down the cause of the Great Baldification. They had to know the culprit. Was it solar spikes, pollution, or junk food?" Voltaire posed, a caustic edge to his questioning. "They had to study it and more importantly, recreate it. Twenty years ago, Larry's father, the senior Dr. Chao found out our father grew hair when no one else did. He wanted to know why. So he had my father impregnate hundreds of women who gave birth and had their babies taken away so they could be raised in this blind hell. I would have preferred brimstone and fire to being stuck in a black void. Our deceased father had a skin condition that prevented him from going out in the sun. He'd spent all of his life away from it. But whenever he went outside, his hair would start falling out."

"The sun?"

"There were others who had never been in the sun. How come they were bald? The senior Dr. Chao tried everything on us. Many died. So many. And for what?"

I could not imagine what their lives had been like.

"When I turned five, every month or so, they'd take us out, cut our hair until we were bald, then send us back in. That's how I came to know there were others like me. Any who disobeyed or were troublesome disappeared in the next hair cycle and we'd never see them again."

We had both grown up prisoners in our own homes, subjected to cruelties others could not possibly understand. In degrees, his was by far the more extreme, but it was a fury I empathized with.

"How did you get out?" I asked.

"We were eventually released," Voltaire said.

"Someone had a change of heart?"

"You could say that."

Voltaire led me out of the hall, down the corridor, up a flight of stairs, until we arrived at a huge space that could have been a warehouse. There were thousands of glass cages set up in rows as though it were an aquarium. But there weren't fish within. There were scalps of heads, hair growing from them and swaying like plants underwater. Mechanical arms with clippers and harvesters covered the ceiling, wires and tracks giving the arms full mobility. I stepped closer to make sure I was seeing right.

"Dr. Chao never found out what exactly caused the Great Baldification. But he found a way to recreate hair in perpetuity. These are the heads of my brothers and sisters who sacrificed their lives so that Chao Toufa could produce the best wigs in the world," Voltaire declared. "The doctor kept the skin producing hair even without the rest of the body attached by releasing timed doses of synthetic hormones into the preserving solution at freezing temperatures."

"What happened to the bodi—?"

"Terminated," Voltaire said to me. "After he discovered this new method, he had no need for us. So he sent us out into the world five years ago like sheep to be devoured by the wolves."

"But that would risk exposing your secret."

"He assumed our hair would fall out when we were back in the sun. But it didn't. Still, it wasn't a big preoccupation for him. He was dying of stomach cancer."

"So what happened?"

"We slipped off his radar. As we had been sent out with nothing to fend for ourselves, we had to carve out our own paths," Voltaire said. He furrowed his brows and stared at one of the heads in the tank. "Beauvoir, take him upstairs and wait for us."

They were going to do something here. Destroy it? Obliterate it? Salvage the heads? Commemorate all those they'd lost? There were so many heads and so much hair. I tried to get it out of my mind that those scalps once belonged to people.

I followed Beauvoir out of the chamber.

"You grew up in one of these too?" I asked.

"Yes."

I grimaced, thinking of her being stuffed into a compartment, tubes sticking out of her body, used for experimentation so they could provide wigs for strangers.

"You will help our cause?" she asked.

"I doubt there's anything I can do."

"You're the owner of Chao Toufa."

"In name only."

"Names are important," she said.

"Why are all of you named after authors?"

"I don't know. One of the researchers gave us all our names. Maybe she loved literature. Do you like literature?"

"I usually watch the movie versions of famous books," I admitted.

"Me too. Too bad there won't be any new movies for a while."

We entered the corridor with all the animal heads. Above, I saw the fresh body of Dr. Asahi hanging from a rope. Her feet were twitching and her eyes were crossed with blood. Had she been confused by the package because she had not known the group of them had been sent out to fend for themselves? Not that it mattered with her corpse hanging from above. I felt terribly sorry. Then I thought about those scalps underground and my pity dissipated into conflicted aversion.

"There's something I want you to know about me," Beauvoir said.

"What?"

"I did things. Things a proper man might not appreciate about a lady. I did it so we could survive," she said.

"I understand."

"Do you?"

It pained me to think of it. I knew she was much tougher than I was. Anyone who survived down here had to be. I was in no place to judge her for anything. "You forget what I endured during the cricket matches? You do what you have to do."

"That's what you did?"

"That's what everyone does."

She nodded. "You were married before."

"Yeah."

"Larry told Voltaire you hadn't made love to a woman since your ex-wife."

"He told him that?!" I exclaimed, embarrassed and incredulous.

She laughed. "It's okay."

I missed Larry, even his big mouth. *Did you know about all of this?* How had a wig factory become involved in these kind of horrors? *What was your response when you found out? I really wish you were here, old buddy.*

We entered the elevator and went upstairs.

I remembered Larry talking about making the Chao Toufa documentary, exposing everything. Was this what he had in mind? Was he going to reveal all the atrocities committed here?

Why did you leave everything to me? I still couldn't understand him. What could I do? I'd seen how quickly Voltaire dispatched of those faceless guards. He had his army here. If I tried to resist and escape, they'd have me hanging from a rope. I was not only out of my league. I was in a world of pain that was beyond my orbital comprehension.

"If you were in our position, what would you do?" she asked.

It was tough to answer because I wasn't in their position. I told her so.

"You don't have to tell me the answer that won't get you in trouble. You can tell me what you're really thinking," she said.

That was the problem though, wasn't it? I had no idea what to think about any of this.

"Have you been to Kauai before?" she asked.

"The island republic?"

"Yeah."

"I haven't."

"It's beautiful there," Beauvoir said. "The whole island seceded from America and they have an artificial barrier around the island that keeps the water fresh. You can swim there and snorkel without having to worry about radiation. The luaus are so much fun and those fire dancers are the most talented I've ever seen. There's chickens everywhere and the waterfalls are amazing. It's like being transported to another world."

"I've heard. I never had the chance to go though. Too expensive."

"We have a place there. Kauai has no extradition laws and Larry helped us buy a huge ranch in Poipu."

"Really?"

"You could come and stay with us."

As I was about to answer, Voltaire came up.

"We're moving into the next phase of our operation," he said.

"The next phase?"

"This is where you need to make your decision."

"What's the decision?" I asked.

"When Larry found out the truth, he was devastated. He swore he would correct it. And in a sense, he tried. But we weren't interested in corrections. I gave him three options. Be part of our campaign, give up the entire company, or die in retribution for his father's crimes."

"Which did he choose?"

"He couldn't. He dallied."

"Is that why you killed him?" I asked Voltaire.

He did not flinch from my gaze. "Yes," he replied. "He could not give up the factory, nor could he join us as he couldn't bear having so much blood on his hands. In the end, he was his father's son. Are you your brother's keeper?"

"I don't know what you mean by that."

"You're the owner of Chao Toufa. You understand what we were subjected to. Join our cause."

"How?"

"Do you like my sister, Beauvoir?"

Beauvoir looked at me. "Of course," I answered. "I owe her my life."

"Marry her then. Join my family. Run Chao Toufa with her by

your side," Voltaire said.

"What? D-does she agree? I mean, she's much younger than me. Shouldn't she marry someone she loves?"

"She's taken a liking to you," Voltaire said.

I looked to Beauvoir who said, "Come stay with us in Kauai. You're going to love it there."

"Do you object?" Voltaire asked.

"Of course I don't object," I answered.

"Then it's settled."

"Wait a second," I stopped him. "I married once. And I failed. I think too highly of her to subject her to me."

Voltaire laughed. "If she can deal with any of us, I'm sure she can deal with you. You two will live a life of comfort. Make no mistake as I want to be transparent in this. I will run the day-to-day business of Chao Toufa. But as long as that is amenable to you—"

"I don't fear death, but you mentioned the middle option of giving up the company," I said.

"Sell all the assets and give it to a charity of my designation."

"Just to be clear, that charity will fund your future operations?"

"Exactly."

Larry was given these exact same options, but he couldn't choose. Voltaire was right. Larry could not abandon his father's legacy, but he couldn't accept it either. Who could in their right mind? But if he were to join Voltaire, he would have been part of more murder which would have been against who he was.

"When you came for Larry, did he fight you?" I asked Voltaire.

"No," he said. "He accepted it." I could see it in my head, a million thoughts warring inside him. All this time, I thought I knew Larry, but I hadn't really known anything. "I warned him earlier."

"With the bombings?"

Voltaire stared grimly at me. "It's a cycle. Nobody ever leaves except through death."

"The cycle can be broken," I said.

"Nobody breaks it. No one can let go."

I thought of Linda, our whole marriage poisoned by my past. Then I looked at Beauvoir. Living a life of decadent luxury seemed beyond a fantasy.

"Voltaire!" one of his brothers shouted. "Voltaire! The news!"

"What about it?"

"Turn it on."

There was a television in the lobby. A woman in a bikini was saying, "—am one of the producers for the show and our network was hijacked by a cyber terrorist group during our broadcast of the GEAs that simulated the murders. We're here to assure our fans that what you saw was just a fake. All the actors and actresses are still alive, though there were some explosives that went off. Fortunately, no one was harmed and the police were able to capture several of the perpetrators. In fact, we have Mr. James Leyton here with us to assure his fans."

An exact duplicate of James Leyton came on screen and I could not tell him apart from the real one with his beard and robe. "As you can see, I am fine. I appreciate all the letters and messages of concern. The cyber terrorists who thought they could fake my death are in for a surprise. We will not be scared. We will not be terrorized by threats. We will find you and shower Godly vengeance down on your heads."

As Leyton went on, commentators speculated that this had all been part of a publicity stunt to promote Leyton's new book, *Resurrected*. Voltaire pursed his lips. "They just don't get it."

"H-how?"

"Image facilitation," Voltaire replied. "People won't even be able to tell the difference."

"But—"

He lifted his hand to me. "This is my concern to take care of. Is your decision settled?"

I looked back at Beauvoir and the memory of the lust that consumed me during my cricket attack came back to me. I would have loved to have held her in my arms and lose myself in her. At the same time, I thought about Larry.

"I'll sell all the assets and donate them to your charity," I said.

Voltaire, who was about to leave, stopped. "You can't be serious."

"I am. Though I have two conditions."

"What conditions?"

"I want Larry to have a proper funeral."

"The dead don't care about funeral rites," Voltaire said.

"I do."

He glowered at me. "What's the second?"

"Rebecca Lian used to work here. Leave her alone."

"You care about this Rebecca enough to refuse me?"

"I've never seen a more beautiful woman than your sister in my life," I said truthfully and looked to her, then back at Voltaire. "But you killed Larry. Larry was the only family I had. And to put it bluntly, I would rather die than join you."

Voltaire grunted, clearly irritated. He assessed me with his eyes, his fingers rolling his chopsticks between them. He was deciding whether he should kill me or let me go. I was ready for anything. I would have accepted anything. "I can't fault you for that. I'll have Russ Brand draw up the papers. We'll need your signature."

"Of course."

We got into the limousine while Voltaire made some calls. We headed down through the hills. On the freeway, traffic was in full force and everything was at a standstill. It might as well have been a car lot as there were thousands of cars going nowhere. The projectors turned on and formed a visual image of Russ. Next to him was Plath.

"All the papers are ready," Russ said as the screen flashed with a digital contract that I could confirm with my fingerprints. There were bruises all over his face. "You sure about this?" he asked.

I nodded. It started raining outside. I saw the naked joggers again, protesting the madness of L.A. gun fire, risking death and worse. For what? I didn't know.

"Nick. Think about this again," Russ pleaded. "If you join Voltaire, you can live a wealthy life. You'll have a beautiful wife and live a life of luxury, never wanting for anything. Kauai is beautiful year-round. Believe me, you'll experience things you've never even—""

I took off my shoes and my pants.

"What are you doing?" Russ asked, terrified that if I sold everything off, he'd have no company to run anymore.

I slipped my shirt off, unloosened the chest plate of my armor, and removed the helmet.

"Have you lost your mind?" Russ asked.

I went to Beauvoir, kissed her hand. I was about to say something to Voltaire, but stopped, realizing there was no point as he was engrossed in planning his retaliation.

I dropped my underpants. Put my finger on the bell, approving the complete liquidation of the company. Opened the door. The rain was coming down heavy and traffic was an automobile quagmire. The herd of naked Americans was halfway by, banging cars as they passed. I got out and ran next to them, completely nude. It was the first time in my life I felt free.

Author Acknowledgments

Bald New World would not be possible without some amazing folks. I would like to thank James Chiang, Jason Jordan, Kristine Ong Muslim, Kyle Muntz, Ofer E., Richard Thomas, and God. Craig Wallwork is not just an amazing writer, but one of the most gracious people I know and I'm indebted for his support. A big thanks to *pacificREVIEW* and editor Shannon Snyder at San Diego State University who published the short story, "Rennaili," which was the inspiration for the first chapter in the book. Thank you to editor John Berbrich of the Barbaric Yawp who published the first ever Larry Chao story, "58 Random Deaths and Unrequited Love," back in 2005. I also would like to thank all the amazing writers and filmmakers who created the crazy dystopias that fired the imagination of my youth—there are too many to list here. Thank you to my incredible editor, Phil Jourdan, at Perfect Edge Books for giving my baldies a home, as well as Dominic James for his wonderful copy editing. And thank you to my wife, Angela Binxin Xu, my caring and generous in-laws, and my uncle and aunt-in-laws—my family.

PERFECT
EDGE
BOOKS

"There are many who dare not kill themselves for fear of what
the neighbours will say," Cyril Connolly wrote, and we believe
he was right.
Perfect Edge seeks books that take on the crippling fear of other
people, the question of what's correct and normal, of how life
works, of what art is.
Our authors disagree with each other; their styles vary as widely as
their concerns. What matters is the will to create books that won't be
easy to assimilate. We take risks, not for the sake of risk-taking, but for
the things that might come out of it.